The Rainbow
Has No Pink

This novel is a work of fiction,
as are the names and charcaters portrayed herein.
Any resemblance to persons living or dead
is purely coincidental.

Published in 2008 by 30° South Publishers (Pty) Ltd.
28, Ninth Street, Newlands, 2092
Johannesburg, South Africa
www.30degreessouth.co.za
info@30degreessouth.co.za

Copyright © Hamish Hoosen Pillay, 2008

Design and origination by 30° South Publishers (Pty) Ltd.

Printed and bound by Pinetown Printers, Durban

ISBN 978-1-920143-29-9

The Rainbow Has No Pink

Hamish Hoosen Pillay

30° South Publishers

About the author

Hamish Pillay was born in 1978 in East London in the Eastern Cape of South Africa. He studied at Rhodes University before pursuing a career as a marketing consultant, specializing in events and talent management. He worked for the ICC 2003 Cricket World Cup, prior to which he was employed by Justin Nurse's satirical, controversial Laugh-It-Off Promotions. In writing *The Rainbow Has No Pink*, his first book, he seeks to publicize some of the more bizarre aspects of the former apartheid regime and highlight how "the reality is that apartheid is not over". He lives and works in East London, where he enjoys gardening, reading and blogging.

"We have looked the beast in the eye. Our past will no longer keep us hostage. We who are the rainbow people of God will hold hands and say, 'Never again! Nooit weer! Ngeke futhi! Ga reno tlola!'"

Archbishop Desmond Tutu
The Truth and Reconciliation Hearings
April 15, 1996–July 31, 1998

To my mother, Jameela and brothers, Suleiman, Yaseen and Mohamad Saliem

Prologue

The cold wind scratched the bruised and beaten skin on his face. His left eye had closed completely. He realized now that he had seen the old car at various places during the day. He should have known better than to think it mere coincidence. The men had tied his hands behind his back and tied his feet—as if he could run away in such a condition. They'd told him to kneel down and wait. The gravel tore into his knees.

They were discussing something so quietly that he couldn't make out the words. Just faint, ominous murmurs.

The men in black hadn't said a word to him since they'd dragged him into the car, not even when they beat him. People usually verbalize their hatred while they beat you. Not these three—they were either professionals or were afraid of getting caught. He no longer felt cold. You eventually stopped feeling cold if it went on for long enough.

They had brought him to this isolated beach for a reason. He was used to it. Some guy noticed you, noticed that you were different, that you weren't the same and would build up a slow, blistering, boiling hatred. It would start with loud comments, embarrassing comments and a pathetic attempt at provocation. He knew this behaviour. He had learned over the years to deal with this kind of unwanted attention. He knew he was different. They knew he was different too.

Usually some jerk would attack you in the parking lot, beating you, threatening you. It had happened more than once. You couldn't go to the police. The police in these parts didn't want to do anything. They didn't care. Besides, who would believe you?

Kneeling on the gravel near the abandoned building on the beach, he waited for them. He could smell the familiar scent of the saltpans. They had stripped him down to his underwear. His scars were bared for them to see. But it was not his scars they were interested in. He could barely see out of one eye; the other had swollen shut. Three guys. He heard the gravel crunch as their footsteps approached behind him.

"Hey, I give discounts for group tours. If you would line up in …"

He didn't hear the two shots hit the back of his skull; one exiting through his forehead, the other blowing the top of his head clean off in a bloody mess. His body and what remained of his head lurched forward into the gravel.

The three men got into their pale-blue Datsun and left, leaving their victim, lying in a pool of blood and skull fragments.

One of them dialled a number and spoke into his cell phone, "It's done."

One more and they would have fulfilled their mission.

*****

Ellen Fischer, although friendly, was a very private person. She had been working as a corporate manager for the last couple of years but few of the staff knew her well. No one from the consultancy had ever been invited to her house. She only socialized with her colleagues when it was absolutely necessary. She said very little and she liked it that way. People asked too many questions and expected you to reciprocate when they shared details of their own lives. She valued her privacy too much to share her life story with all and sundry.

She reached over to her desk drawer. The meds were almost finished. She needed to see her doctor tomorrow. She could go a few days without them, but her condition was sensitive and keeping it under control was vital. Best not to take any chances. She had a standing arrangement with the doctor whenever she needed him. People in her condition didn't make appointments.

Louise, Ellen's PA, was the heart and soul of the office. She was bubbly, with an infectious good humour that made you feel as if you were old friends even if you had only just met.

Louise had long ago given up trying to fix Ellen up with guys she knew. Ellen was a bit bigger than most other women her age, but she was a fantastic person to work for. Maybe she was too broad shouldered. Her neck was certainly thicker than that of most women. Perhaps she'd played a lot of sport in her youth. But it wasn't Ellen's physical appearance that had discouraged Louise's matchmaking attempts; it was Ellen's reaction. She didn't want to meet anyone; she was quite content on her own. No, she didn't need to have sex. Louise could not understand. But then maybe it was just a case of different strokes for different folks.

Ellen looked at her watch. She was feeling rather weary today. Exhaustion was a symptom of the regular injections. The weight gain was a given with Ellen careful not to make it any worse. Water retention, her doctor said. Maybe it was time to go home. Ellen called Louise to her office.

"I'm off home. You should do the same."

Louise peered in through the door, "When I'm done with …"

Ellen cut her short. "The work will still be there tomorrow, I promise."

"Thanks!" She bounded back to her desk.

Louise sometimes seemed ridiculously energetic. Ellen felt tired just watching her. She looked through the glass separating her office from Louise's desk, watching her bend over her workstation, click close the windows, tidying her desk before she left. She was a shapely woman. A pity about her boyfriend. A fridge repairman with all the presence of a pimple. That body wasted on an unappreciative man like that. Her full, rounded breasts and firm buttocks complemented her curvaceous figure. It was obvious she worked out at the gym. She often gave guys the wrong idea. Unintentionally, of course. It was easy to understand how this happened, a woman of her earthy sexuality talking to you as if you were old acquaintances. Men fell over themselves for her. Who knows, maybe in another life. She must be amazing in bed.

Louise finished packing up and gave Ellen a cheerful wave goodbye.

Ellen tidied her desk and started packing her things. She locked up and made her way to her car outside.

The parking lot was already deserted. People were always in a rush to get home. Ellen couldn't even begin to understand what that was like. She had a flat in Hatfield, neighbouring the diplomatic suburbs. She was single so she could afford it. It was a luxurious flat. She was lonely but that was her life—she had accepted it. The drive home was quiet. Most people were already home by now.

She parked her car in the basement and made her way up to her flat, carrying her briefcase. She felt like she had been toiling building pyramids all day. Her body was sore. She was exhausted. Her brain ached. The doors were double-locked but the security gate in front was always tricky. You had to perform some magic act with the key to open it. Luxury apartments, my arse, she thought. The body corporate management was useless and seemed bent on intentionally ignoring her. She had mostly given up.

She checked her messages. Nothing on her answering machine. Not that she'd expected any messages. She checked her cell phone. She had the habit of switching it to silent and forgetting to switch it back. One missed call. Louise. She dialled her number.

The phone rang again before she could activate the call.

"Hi, did you get my message?"

Ellen was performing a mental shutdown. "No. Was it important?"

"No, not really, Reggie from legal, well, we're having a farewell for him tonight. I know this is short notice but I was thinking that if you weren't doing anything …"

"Louise, I hope you're not trying to fix me up again?"

"No, not at all Ellen, I was just trying to see if you would like to join us."

Ellen had disappointed them enough. She declined every invitation her colleagues extended to her. Maybe she should go. She didn't want them to feel that she thought she was better than them.

"What time?"

"Around eight at Uncle Joe's in Hatfield." Louise returned to her normal exuberance.

"Okay, give me a few minutes to shower and change and get myself together. See you at eight then."

"Thanks Ellen. I'm telling you, you won't regret it. See you at eight. Bye."

"Bye."

Ellen put the phone down. She knew that she was going because it was just another excuse to see Louise, and it wasn't like she didn't stare enough at work. The attraction was purely physical. That boundless energy was off-putting after a while, though.

There was no parking outside Uncle Joe's. The nearest was a parking area behind the complex. Well, she wouldn't stay too long. Just a quick drink, a chat to Reggie, wish him well, maybe a drink with Louise and her boyfriend and then home.

One drink led to another. Reggie and his girlfriend were leaving to work in the UK for a couple of years. He was still young and had a ton of student loans to pay off and this was the only way he could afford to marry his sweetheart. She was cute but an obvious social climber. It had been her idea to work overseas because she couldn't wait to get married and her parents were pressuring her. Ellen looked at them. They would break up soon enough. There was only so much a man could take. If they did get married, they would divorce. How long could you stay married to someone who constantly deferred to daddy? Ellen looked at Reggie, the poor bastard. He was the proverbial rabbit caught in the headlights.

The liquor was going straight to her head. People were very xcited to see their manager out on the town with them that everyone insisted on buying the boss a drink. Eventually Ellen found a quiet spot on her own. It was all too much. She was out of her comfort zone. She needed to sit somewhere where she wouldn't be noticed. Louise came over and chatted for a few minutes but the substance of her conversation was lost on Ellen who was trying to think how to slip away.

She eventually left with Louise and her fridge repairman. The air outside was frosty. The kind of air where you gasp and take deep breaths until your skin becomes numb to it and your lungs start to chill from the inside out. She pulled her jacket tighter around her.

"You okay to drive home?" Louise asked, the committed personal assistant.

"Yes, I'll be fine. I've driven home drunker than this. Besides, I'm just tired. I need to get some sleep if I'm going to make work tomorrow."

"Oh, okay. Where did you park?"

"Across the road. I'll be fine. Now go home; it's cold out here."

Louise was holding the fridge repairman tightly.

"Okay, goodnight, see you tomorrow."

"Yeah, see you."

The mixture of alcohol, exhaustion and the biting cold air caused Ellen to walk awkwardly. Carefully calculated steps.

She made it to her car and let out a sigh. It was freezing. She put the key in the ignition and switched the heater on. She waited a few seconds before starting up. The doors locked automatically.

The roads were usually deserted during winter evenings, so the drive home didn't take her long. She approached her apartment block and reached for her remote control. There was no one in the vicinity of the electric gates. She made her way in. The usual cars were inside—the Mercedes SLK, the Z4M Roadster and the Opel GPC. A playground for young professionals, people who earned big and weren't afraid to show it. Their cars were not extensions of but rather substitutes for their personalities. Next to the Roadster was a beat-up old Datsun which looked incongruous in the showroom-type garage. Someone either had visitors or had spent their entire savings on purchasing their flat. The sectional title allowed for owners only to occupy their flats, no letting out. They maintained strict standards. Ellen liked it for the location and the privacy. People with all this security were usually too paranoid to snoop on their neighbours.

She exited the elevator on the ninth floor and hurried towards her flat, rummaging through her bag for the keys. Oh, the thought of fiddling with keys and gates made her blood boil. She would have a word with the superintendent in the morning; they paid his salary and if he couldn't do his job they would have to find someone else. He always pretended not to understand English when she spoke to him but strangely understood it just fine when other tenants asked him to do things for them. Son of a bitch!

She found the key and rammed it into the lock. The gate opened without the slightest resistance. She unlocked the door and keyed in the alarm code on the pad to disarm the system. She was about to close the door and put the lights on when a large fist crashed into her face, out of nowhere. Her vision flickered at impact. A brief, second-long blackout. Her brain trying to make sense of it. She thought she had heard something crack in her face. Two other men rushed in and slammed the door. She didn't have time to say anything, let alone gather her wits.

The three men started beating her as she tried to shield her face with her arms. She dropped to the ground. They said nothing to her or to each other, just punch after kick after punch. She felt like her brain was bruising with the number of smashing intrusions it absorbed. She retreated into her mind, disengaging herself from her body. What the hell was going on? She hadn't experienced this kind of repugnance since her youth. She didn't bother trying to stand up. If she passed out, maybe they would take what they wanted and leave. God, why had she drunk so much? Why had she gone out? Please God, let this be over soon.

They were talking to each other now. The voices were faint and echoed. Her eardrum was probably damaged. The voices sounded like distant poundings, rhythmically beaten out. Two firm grips on her arms and she was being dragged. Her shoes came off as her feet bumped along the carpet. She wanted to move her body, resist the force dragging her, but her body no longer belonged to her. They had control and there was nothing she could do, except try to hide inside her mind. Was she being punished? Why hadn't she heard them coming up from behind? How drunk was she? Why couldn't anyone hear the commotion? She was on the bedroom floor. She saw two men rummaging through her belongings, looking for something. The third was ripping her clothes off. She wanted to put an arm up. She needed to do something to stop him. But her body had long since stopped obeying her will. She was an observer.

Naked on the floor, blood was streaming from somewhere on her head. She could feel it, warm, running off her now-matted hair. She lay helpless.

One of the two men went into the kitchen and came back with her blue toolbox. The one she kept under the sink. He mumbled something and she heard laughter. Her blood ran cold. The one who had ripped off her clothes forced open her legs and ran his hands up her thighs. He pointed to something and the others laughed.

"Ons moet hier goed maak." *We'll make this good.*

The other two laughed.

"Dit lyk amper genuine." *It almost looks real.*

Each man proceeded to enter her forcefully, sodomizing her repeatedly, taking turns while the others scratched around the flat, looking for something. Then it was over. They dressed, leaving her bloody and naked on the floor. Ellen wanted to die. This is what it felt like to be raped. Her body wouldn't move. She expected them to finish her off. Anytime now.

One of them opened the toolbox. They dragged her limp body onto the bed and then forced tools into every damaged orifice in her lower body. She wanted to scream. She tried to force her body to react. Nothing. She lay there, still, both eyes swollen shut, covered in blood. Her body torn, ripped apart, housing the contents of her toolbox. Finally they stopped—they had achieved their objective, for the moment. She could feel the cold metal inside her, cold and rough. She felt shattered. Broken. Why did death take this long? Why were they still here? One of her assailants then picked out a yellow box-cutter. He held it up for the others to see.

A deep voice said, "Maak klaar." *Finish up.*

"Nou sal jy leer." *Now you are going to learn.*

The sharp tear she felt was the box-cutter ripping through her abdomen. She felt her insides filling up. Warm. Liquid. The sudden sharp pain was replaced with nothing. She could feel them cutting, but she no longer felt pain. She felt cold.

Ellen's mind was far away when they finished. They had her body. But she wouldn't let them have her mind. It was detached. They can't win unless they have your mind. Lessons from another lifetime were coming back to haunt her as a final sick joke.

The truth is they had won a long time ago. Her body ached and it felt like death was living inside her, waiting to explode. A slow, vengeful pain clawing at her, reminding her how close she was to oblivion. She rolled over. She couldn't hear anything. Nothing. No hands holding her. No punches or boots to the face. Oh God, please don't let me die like this. What if someone found her like this? Naked. Torn. Ripped apart.

She called out. Her voice came out like a whimper, unrecognizable, a choking plea for help. She crawled towards the bedside table and reached over to the wall. The light from the outside caused her body to glisten. She found the button. She pressed it. No sound. She hoped it still worked. She collapsed to the floor. Death wasn't supposed to feel like this.

Several kilometres away a response unit was dispatched to the flat. The two young security men readied themselves. They could be faced with anything. Silently they both prayed that it was a false alarm. Neither had plans to die that night. Please let them not have guns.

All the training in the world couldn't have prepared them for what they found when they reached the ninth-floor flat.

Part I

Chapter 1

Ayesha sat at her coffee table. She dragged on the last of her cigarette before stubbing it out forcefully. She had tried turning down another dinner invitation that morning when her mother phoned and woke her up to read her the Fajr morning prayers. She had stopped praying over a year ago. A year is a long time to be miserable. Every new day felt like yesterday. And the more her mother pushed her to get on with her life, the more she felt the need to abandon her life in order to try and recreate herself. Creating a new life at thirty was easier said than done. Dinner was always some awkward affair where some concerned relative tried to stick some 'nice boy' on her, some accountant or doctor or pharmacist or even a lawyer. All were well-off, tall, light-skinned men from respectable families. And the fact that she was as responsive as an amoeba was cause for concern with said relatives.

"What's wrong with Ayesha? She got a problem with all these boys. What's wrong with them? They nice and fair and they all got money. She won't have to work again. They come from good families."

Ayesha's mother knew better than to try and impose strange men on her daughter. But bowing to the duress of family and outdated custom she disguised each potential match with the excuse of eating dinner.

"You sleeping?" Her mother always found a way of sounding surprised when she phoned at six a.m. and found her daughter asleep.

"No, I was just playing tennis. You want to join me?" Even at that early hour Ayesha's sharp tongue did not desert her.

"You forget who you talking to, hey? I'm not one of those people you work with. Your father said you must come to supper tonight."

"No ma, no supper, no men, okay? I just have too much work and I don't have the time …"

Her mother cut her short. "You don't have the time for anything, I see. Every time I phone you, you sleeping but you have to work. You getting up to no good if you ask me. You got time to loaf but no time for namaaz. Ya-Allah, I give up with you, child."

"That's why I said you should have had more kids. If I had some brothers and sisters you could harass *them* in the early hours of the morning."

"You think I'm harassing you? What kind of life is that for a young girl …"

"A young divorcee," Ayesha interrupted.

"You can't live like that on your own. Just now you will be too old for children and then no man will want you. You need a man. A good man."

"Who says I want another man? Can we have this conversation later? I have to get up for work. I'll speak to you later, okay?"

"Well, you come after Maghrib. Your father and I want to talk to you. Okay? Salamalaikum."

Ayesha was about to say that she had already said no and that was her final answer, but she couldn't win with her parents. They demanded and she obeyed, whether she liked it or not. At least they weren't forcing her to re-marry. She was lucky. They were disappointed that her marriage with Iqbal had collapsed. Her mother had slapped an aunt who'd made a snide remark about love marriages. This was the same aunt who had wanted Ayesha to marry her son.

Just over a year ago, Ayesha was on assignment with a team tracking hi-jacked luxury cars for 'export' out of South Africa. It was a delicate situation—the head of an overseas car manufacturer had been shot, along with his driver. There was pressure to solve the case and Ayesha's unit had been appointed to get the wheels of justice moving. Ayesha, a law graduate, was a member of the Special Crimes Unit, a division with far-reaching powers to investigate special crimes, both commercial and criminal, that were beyond the resources of the ordinary police. She'd come after two weeks in the field and found a note from Iqbal saying that he had found someone else and had decided to move in with her. He wanted a divorce because he was tired of hurting her. He was sorry but the loneliness had driven him to it. He had packed his clothes and left. The keys were on the kitchen counter. She could keep the flat and the one car. She wanted to tell him that she was pregnant. She didn't get the chance. The miscarriage was unfortunate, said some family members, but it was meant to be. Fate. How that annoyed her.

That was a year ago. She had prayed so hard but he never came back. Everyone said the same thing—*taqdeer*, fate, if he was meant to come back he would. How could God allow such humiliation? She had prayed before she got married and asked for God's blessing, but here she was, four years later, alone. Was God playing with her? She'd stopped praying and it had helped. The divorce was quick. Neither side bothered quibbling about anything. None wanted anything and Ayesha eventually moved out of the flat into her own apartment. The thought of living in the space where she had been betrayed sickened her.

She got up from the table. She would start switching off her phone at night, although that would be difficult with work obligations. She went to her room. On the dresser was the magnetic-strip ID card with her photo and the name Special Investigator Detective Ayesha Mansoor. Next to the ID card was a standard-issue handgun and pair of agency-issue handcuffs.

She picked them up and walked to the bedroom door. She lifted a dark plastic jacket off the hook and slipped it on. On the back of the jacket were the bright-yellow letters 'SCU'—Special Crimes Unit.

On the front pocket was a white cobra in between two swords. She looked at herself in the mirror. She was putting on weight. She had not spent much time out in the field lately, having been stuck behind a desk since the miscarriage. But she still looked good for a thirty-year-old divorcee. She had mid-length hair and skin of a medium hue, darkened by the sun. Her mother complained when she saw her daughter after her stint in training, "My poor daughter, you gone so black." Men still turned their heads when they saw her, though. She looked slight compared to her male colleagues, most of whom had tried to proposition her without success.

She was determined to get her life back. Today was that day. No more desk job. My life belongs to me, she kept telling herself, as if the repetition would convince her that she was in complete control.

She hadn't left the parking lot of her apartment building when her phone started ringing. It was the controller. There was a crime scene in Hatfield, Pretoria. A callout from the director. The SCU director was a short man with a shaved head. He'd probably started going bald and had decided to rid himself of the inconvenience of the remaining patches of hair. He had been nagging her to get back into the field and to stop swimming in self-pity. People had affairs and broke others' hearts all the time. It was nothing new. She'd had a miscarriage, so what? Did she think she could have looked after a child in her condition? She'd wanted to cry when he said that. But he was one of those people. Hard, but well intentioned. Get back out there and do what you're trained to do. He said this almost every time they bumped into each other. The director deliberately maintained a cold exterior—flippant, insensitive. Most people would have quit after comments like that. But she knew he meant well.

Her work now was mostly liaison with DoSS—the Department of State Security, DoJ—the Department of Justice and the Prosecuting Authority. Government had taken a tough stance on crime and the SCU now led the fight against crime, from investigations to preparations for prosecutions. Their main focus though was high-profile cases. Major names implicated. The public impact stuff. The rule was simple—go after the big guns but make sure you get a conviction. They had a seventy per cent conviction rate and cracked about eighty per cent of their cases. This was attributed to the number of specially trained officers in the unit and their knowledge of how to effect proper arrests and secure convictions.

The controller didn't say what the crime was, however, and Ayesha was taken aback by the request. It was unusual for an SCU agent to be summoned to a crime scene. Not unknown, but unusual. The standard procedure was for the police to refer the case to SCU. At times there were references from the DoSS, DoJ and the Commissioner of Police.

Traffic annoyed her; sometimes she wished she had taken up a job at a law firm and worked in one of those nice offices out in the quieter suburbs. Long before she pulled up to the scene she could see the flashing red and blue lights of medical and police vehicles. There was a small Opel Corsa with a yellow flashing light parked outside. With regular South African Police Service patrols, security in the area was tighter than the normal due to the number of government ministers and foreign diplomats living in the neighbourhood. The jacaranda trees were bare. In spring the pavement would be blanketed with purple flowers.

She parked her car across the road from the taped-off building and walked up to the guarded entrance. She pulled out her ID card and flashed it at the police officer doing candy-tape duty outside. He nodded her through. As she walked past she could feel a few of the officers giving her the once-over. She stopped and glared, causing one to turn away and stare at his shoes. She opened the door and let herself in. She took the elevator to the ninth floor. The doors opened and a police officer asked her for ID. Annoyed, she pulled out her tag and clipped it to her jacket. The policeman waved her through.

She found the flat easily enough. It was the one with the hive of activity outside. People in dark jackets with official lettering were scurrying about, taking pictures, measuring, dusting, scraping and inspecting.

Director Ben de Villiers was reading the riot act to an officer. Ayesha walked in and was immediately shocked back into the reality of fieldwork. Across the spacious white walls of Ellen Fischer's apartment hung the evidence of an invasion. The assailants' hatred was crudely blatant, with obscenities scrawled in what she assumed was the victim's blood. She didn't feel sick at the sight of blood, but she was nevertheless stunned. She had almost forgotten the hard reality of fieldwork. This was the reason for the mandatory bi-annual psychiatric testing for all SCU field operatives. As much as you felt you were in control, nothing ever prepared you for the next crime scene, nothing.

She stood in the doorway, trying to come to terms with her surroundings. Director de Villiers saw her gazing at the walls of the lounge. He dismissed the officer whom he had been chastising and called Ayesha over.

"Ayesha." He was a true Afrikaner and proud of it. He made every effort to speak English even though his accent was thick. Eyebrows had been raised that an Afrikaner had been chosen to lead the government's elite new squad of crime-fighters. But he had a no-nonsense reputation. He had been accused of racism when he suspended one of his senior officers. The officer concerned had been implicated in a shakedown of pimps, prostitutes and small-time drug dealers. The media went to town trying to convict the newly appointed director on the grounds of his previous relationship with certain known apartheid assassins and his previous position in covert SADF— South African Defence Force—operations when he had been involved in operations in Angola and Mozambique. At the trial a black judge upheld de Villiers' decision and found the suspended officer guilty, calling him a disgrace to the new dispensation. The director had maintained his composure throughout and the media frenzy died as quickly as it had started.

He was a good man, a man with many contacts in very high places. He had lost his wife about eight years ago in a home robbery gone wrong. His only other family was a daughter who was about to graduate from medical school. He was a hard man to get along with but he was fair and protected his unit as though his own life depended on it. He knew there were forces that would like to wrest control from him. He answered directly to the minister and parliament.

Ayesha walked over to the director. He was wearing a tracksuit and a woollen cap, looking like he'd recently woken up.

"What happened here?" Ayesha asked quietly.

"Nice way to start your day? Welcome back to the field," the director grinned wryly.

"I take it the victim was important. Murder is it?"

"No, she wasn't important and no, she was not murdered. How did you know it was a she?"

Ayesha pointed to the blood-printed words of lesbian and whore and bitch on the wall. "So what are we doing here? Unless she was sleeping with someone important then I don't know …" Ayesha was confused.

The director took Ayesha over to the window. "Look where we are. Half our bosses live around here. The minister phoned me this morning at around four to tell me that he wants our unit to investigate. The victim is forty-year-old Ellen Fischer; she works at one of those consultancies near Hatfield. She was attacked some time this morning, probably around one. What we have been able to establish is that the cameras in the garage were knocked out last night. The caretaker says that they were faulty and he'd asked management to do something about them. So when they went out he didn't think it was serious. The victim was raped and brutally assaulted. She has been taken to a private clinic. You can pick up the details from the hospital later on. But the armed response people are still here. You might want to ask them a few questions." The director summoned a police officer and mumbled something in his ear, pointed at Ayesha and then left.

Ayesha looked around. She took out a pair of rubber gloves from her police-issue jacket. She went to the bedroom. The walls were also covered in bloody graffiti. Hatred manifested through words printed in the victim's own blood. The bedroom looked like a butcher's floor. The bed was crimson and the carpet stained almost black. There were smudges on the wall near the panic button. A large puddle had formed by the side of the bed, obviously where she must have collapsed when she had pressed the button.

A half-empty toolbox lay open on the bedroom floor. She would need to see the victim's injuries report, but in the meantime she could question the armed response guy. She approached the youngster sitting at the kitchen counter. He was smoking nervously. She looked at him. He couldn't have been more than twenty. Poor kid. He must be a mess. They didn't train security personnel for this sort of thing. They didn't pay them enough for that.

The security man stuttered and stammered his way through Ayesha's questions. He'd found the victim a mutilated mess on the floor. He thought she was dead because of all the blood and the hammer sticking out from between her legs. She'd moved and he'd radioed for emergency services. No, the door was open when he'd arrived. He hadn't seen anything else. Who does things like this? The young man stared vacantly. Ayesha decided she would ask the unit's shrink to offer him some counselling.

Next she spoke to the SAPS officer on site. There were no signs of forced entry, the alarm was not armed, the door was open, she obviously knew the perpetrators and she had been rushed to a private clinic. It was touch and go. Whoever did this had to be some sort of Satanist. Surely! Ayesha raised a cynical eyebrow. No, it wasn't Satanism. But it was ritualistic. A purging of hatred. People did things like this because it was in their nature. She asked the officer to send her a preliminary report when they were done. The fingerprint guys were still busy. Two sets of prints had been found. Possibly perpetrator and victim. It would take some time; there was always a backlog. Ayesha told him to send the prints over to the unit. They would do match-ups with the victim and hopefully have some identification within a day or two.

If this were the case that had brought Ayesha back into the field she hoped it wasn't a sign of things to come. The crime was obviously a crime of hate but who were the perpetrators? Why? How? She would have to profile the victim. Only two sets of prints. That was going to be a problem; there was no way one person did this. Violence was always exacerbated when a crime was committed by a group. She had in the past seen some vicious serial-killer crimes, ritualistic acts performed on the victim but the intensity of the bloody graffiti and the assault ... this was personal. The victim knew her assailants or they knew her.

Chapter 2

Marissa Vermeulen was happy. She'd felt like smiling—from the time she had woken up and made love to her husband, until the phone call from her parents, asking her to pick up a bottle of wine on her way to their weekly luncheon. Gauteng wasn't the most beautiful place in the world but there were days when you woke up and couldn't imagine being in any other place. Marissa sat contentedly in her garden. The maid was watching her child. Her two-year-old son, Cobus Jr, was the image of her husband. Blond hair as opposed to her own dark features. They had tried to get pregnant for such a long time. Seven years of rumours at the family get-togethers about something being wrong with her or with Cobus Sr; some even going so far as to suggest adoption. Relatives showing more concern than good upbringing demanded. Then one day she went in to see her doctor and she was told she was pregnant. She carried little Cobus to full term and it was in every way a normal birth. They had given up trying for more. They had been blessed with one child and that was enough.

The maid put Cobus Jr into the car seat and buckled him in, making sure he was secure. Marissa came outside wearing her white suit. Even though she was going to her now-retired parents' house for lunch, it was important to dress well, to show that you had a good life, to look the part in case any of her father's important friends came by. Even though he was retired, many of his former colleagues still popped in, always addressing him with the utmost respect.

Hyde Park's shopping mall was an exclusive affair, mostly designed for the expensive tastes of bored housewives who had time and money to spare. It was on the way to her parents' home so she could easily stop and pick up a bottle of wine.

The only problem with shopping on a day like this was manoeuvring young Cobus Jr in and out of the car. Marissa bought a lovely apple pie and a bottle of wine for the lunch and packed the parcels in beside Cobus. She should have brought Lena with her so she could have waited with the baby in the car. But then what would she do with her when she got to her parents' house? They didn't keep a maid so who would Lena talk to? She couldn't sit in the car the whole day; Marissa's day would be spoiled because she would have to rush back home. She needed to think of a future solution.

The Jo'burg sun was warming the car. She should have brought her swimming costume, she thought. She pulled up to the gate at the nine-foot white wall, the top lined with razor wire. The solitary double gate served as the only access into what was one of the typical fortresses that posed as homes these days.

Marissa did not notice the tan Ford Cortina which had followed her from her house to Hyde Park and which was now parked in the road across from the driveway. She pulled up next to the intercom and reached out the window but she was too far away. She considered reversing and bringing the car closer. Too much effort. She opened her door to lean over and reach for the intercom. This was annoying. Why didn't they just give her a remote? She had been asking for one for ages.

Leaning out of the car she thought she heard footsteps but by the time she'd processed the thought, she'd already received a kick to the head. The door slammed and she was struck again—jarring in the head—spinning. Her first thoughts instinctively were for her baby in the backseat. Cobus would kill her if anything happened to the baby. A man reached into the car and fiddled with something. She heard the sound of the central locking as the door behind her opened. She tried to grab the man standing at her door. The futile clutch of a mother desperate to protect her child. She felt something hard and cold strike her head. Darkness and then warmth running down her face and neck. Please God, don't let them take my baby. Please God … the rest of her pleas faded into the blackness.

The Ford Cortina that had pulled up to the house with three occupants was now speeding away with a fourth in the backseat. Young Cobus Jr was unaware of what had just happened or that his mother lay bleeding in the driveway of his grandparents' house.

Chapter 3

It had been two days. Marissa was sedated almost permanently and every time she emerged from her near-comatose state she was wracked with guilt, thinking about her lost child. She would break out into fits of guilt-induced hysteria. Her husband wasn't making things any easier. He wouldn't communicate; he'd just asked if she needed anything. This was part of the reason she had asked her parents if she could stay with them rather than going home to Cobus. Cobus was a criminal lawyer and, for a brief second, Marissa thought that maybe it was one of his clients or someone from that part of his life who was trying to punish them for something he had done. No, this wasn't her husband's fault. It was random. But, please, dear God, don't let anything happen to the child. She knew she should never have opened the car door; she should have checked. This was her fault. She was a terrible mother.

Dr André Blignaut, Marissa's father and grandfather of the kidnapped Cobus, paced his lounge. The rather ample room was now occupied by SAPS officers, some fiddling with wires and phone cables, others typing into laptops, while others stood around, guns holstered, chatting as if this were an everyday occurrence. He wanted to tell them all to fuck off out of his house. He wanted to tell his son-in-law to fuck off with that stupid angry look on his face because that wasn't helping his daughter. Ten years ago he would have found the kidnappers and personally supervised their removal from society. Ten years is a long time. The kidnappers obviously didn't know what they had got themselves into. He might be retired but he still had contacts. Well, those that hadn't run off to live in places like Angola or Mozambique, pretending to be farmers. A good number of the doctor's former colleagues had gone underground but the ones you really wanted were still around if you knew where to look. If this didn't work out by tonight he'd make a few calls.

Dr Blignaut was a secretive man. He was a psychiatrist and had spent many years in the employ of the South African Defence Force. Unlike his colleagues who travelled a lot, the doctor had maintained several projects and was lucky enough to have had a nine-to-five job. His wife, Annette, had never asked what he'd actually done in the military. With the number of boys sent to the border to fight the communists, God only knew the things they had experienced. It was a bloody war but it was God's work. When they came back they needed to be reintegrated into society. They had their whole lives ahead of them. Hence the need for a psychiatrist, she assumed.

After he'd left the SADF he spent eight years in the small university town of Grahamstown, where he headed up the provincial psychiatric hospital. When he retired the couple moved to Johannesburg.

The phone rang. Talking stopped and men rushed to the beeping sounds and flashing LEDs on black boards, while men at laptops stopped typing and motioned to the detective to answer. The detective signalled Dr Blignaut.

"Hello?" The doctor wasn't sure how he should sound. What if he sounded too confident and they did something to show him where the power really lay?

"This isn't the mother, unless you've been on hormone therapy for two days." The words were clear, confident.

"This is Dr Blignaut, Cobus Junior's grandfather. My daughter has had to be sedated."

"That's a terrible thing. Well, Dr Blignaut, I hope you are ready. I want one million rand by tomorrow. I will phone in due course with directions."

Dr Blignaut tried to think of a way to stall but the caller had already hung up. The officer on the laptop shook his head.

The detective looked at the doctor. "Do you have access to that kind of money?"

"Yes. But I can't get it now. What if he phones at six in the morning and wants to make the drop, surely …" The doctor was growing ever more anxious.

The detective reassured him, "Even the kidnappers know that you need time. It's not going to do their cause any good to rush you and they don't get their money. We'll be at the bank first thing in the morning. I'll call ahead so long. Maybe we can formulate a plan and get the manager to open up early for us."

Detective Arthur Turner reached into his pocket and retrieved his mobile phone. He dialled his commanding officer. He would know whom to phone and whose arm to twist. The victim was only two years old. What kind of a sick fuck did this? As his commanding officer answered, Cobus Sr came outside to light up a cigarette. The SAPS knew him well. He was paid generously to help free the very people the SAPS tried to put away. The people that he was now praying the SAPS would find. In a way, Arthur Turner thought he deserved this, but not the child.

Chapter 4

Marissa sat in the lounge ... waiting like everyone else. She sat staring into space. The sedatives gave her a zombie-like appearance. Glazed eyes, skin that hadn't seen sunlight in days, hair that hadn't seen a brush. She had insisted on being present when the kidnapper called. Conversation had dried up today. Detective Turner and Dr Blignaut had been to the bank and right now two officers were packing the money into two black sports bags. The rest of the team fiddled with gadgets and plans as if preparing to go into battle.

The expected early call never materialized. Hours crawled by with anxiety levels rising with every second that ticked away.

By lunchtime Marissa was sliding into hysteria. "Why haven't they phoned yet?" She was pacing the room, on the verge of a panic attack.

Her husband tried to calm her down. "Honey, please just relax. Everything is going to be fine. Honey?" Cobus Sr searched for the magical word that would make his wife sit down and be calm.

"No, I won't just relax, I won't be fine. You bastard. This is your fault. When I said we should leave this fucking country because things were getting out of hand, because we had no future in this country, because I didn't want to be a victim, you said you couldn't because of your job. Now look what's happened! This is your fault!"

Marissa flopped to the floor and sobbed. Annette Blignaut rushed over to her daughter. She turned to Cobus Sr, giving him a look that said her daughter didn't mean any of it. The look told him to go outside for some air. Everything was going to be fine.

Cobus left the room. The lounge was silent; the officers pretended not to have heard the outburst. He went outside and lit a cigarette. He tried to stop tears from welling up. It was part temper—part broken heart. He knew that if he didn't get his son back he would lose his family. Please God, he prayed, bring back my son.

Time ticked by with even the policemen starting to get anxious. They had all expected an early call. But it was almost four o'clock and the phone hadn't rung once. The lines were in working order. Detective Turner had had the lines tested repeatedly. But still no call. He hoped that nothing had gone wrong overnight and that the kidnappers hadn't simply cut their losses and dumped the child's body in the veld. It had been known to happen. Detective Turner was not about to bring up this possibility, however.

When the phone rang just before four o'clock, everyone stopped breathing for a few seconds.

Dr Blignaut picked up the receiver, "Hello."

"I'll make this short. Firstly, put the money in two black refuse bags. You're going to drop the money off. We'll pick it up with no interference. If it's all there and we have no problems with the police, you'll get your grandson back before the eight o'clock news. Okay? Get into your car and take the N1 to Pretoria. Keep your cell phone on. You have one hour." The caller hung up.

Dr Blignaut slowly put the phone down.

Detective Turner had heard the details of the kidnappers' request. He got up and told the two policemen who had packed the money neatly into the sports bags to transfer it into black bags. "Double the bags. I don't want them breaking when we take the money out."

Dr Blignaut left the room and went to his study. The detective followed him. The doctor was scratching in his safe.

"Are you or Cobus going to drop off the money?" asked Detective Turner, watching from the doorway. He stood there long enough to see the doctor pull out a small-calibre handgun and put it in his jacket pocket.

"I hope you're not planning on taking that with you?" The detective assumed that the doctor would be making the drop-off. Dr Blignaut did not respond.

"We can keep you under police protection the whole way. Give me the gun."

"Detective," the doctor's voice was authoritative, "I am not sending my son-in-law out to handle something that is his fault in the first place. If he knew how to look after his family we wouldn't be in this shit. And as for the police, you can all stay here. I don't want to risk my grandson's life. The money means nothing and they can have it. I will pay anything to get my grandson back."

The detective felt like a small child being chastised by a parent. "Please, even a helicopter … just let us …"

The doctor cut him off. "I said no. If I smell a hint of police involvement, I will make sure that you don't even get a job watching the crowds at the rugby. Now, if you will excuse me ..."

The doctor packed the money into the boot of his car. Detective Turner put a hand on the doctor's arm. "Give me your gun."

"What?"

"You heard me, give me your gun. I cannot allow you to take a gun with you. You don't want us to go with you and we cannot guarantee your safety or that of the child. So, if you don't mind, I would like your firearm."

"You can't stop me! Do you know who I am?"

"I don't care if you are the president. I *will* arrest you and send Cobus in your place. You are endangering your grandson's life."

Something must have registered with the doctor. He pulled out the handgun and handed it to the detective. He got into his car and drove off with barely a glance at the detective in his rear-view mirror. He'd deal with him when his grandson was safely back home.

Regular text messages came through telling the doctor where to turn, reminding him of his route to Pretoria. What was starting to nag at the doctor was the volume of traffic. It was moving at a snail's pace. His anxiety gnawed away at him. He toyed with the idea of calling the text-message number. No, what if he upset the kidnappers? To hell with it, if he didn't let them know he was stuck in traffic they would get impatient. He tried calling the number but received the message: "The subscriber you have dialled is not available. Please try again later".

The doctor tossed the phone onto the passenger seat. A message-alert beeped. He snatched up the phone. "Don't call us, we'll call you."

The traffic inched forward. After half an hour he found himself under a bridge nowhere near Pretoria. The messages had stopped. As far as he could see there was traffic; you couldn't weave a bicycle through it. How the hell would he make it to Pretoria? He didn't even know the address. What were they thinking? Everyone knew that Jo'burg traffic was horrendous, day or night.

Two homeless black men approached his car. He'd heard stories of vagrants coming up to cars stuck in traffic and breaking the windows with a spark plug and snatching whatever they found on the seats. They walked straight up to the car and tapped on the window. He tried to ignore them. They knocked persistently. He continued to ignore them. Why wouldn't this damned traffic just get a move on? He had no time for beggars. Yes, life was hard for everyone. Then one of them said something that caused the hairs on the back of his neck to stand up.

"Give us the money or you won't get Cobus Junior back."

The doctor looked up, stunned.

They were not black people. They were white. Dressed to look like black beggars. They wore long, musty overcoats, tattered gloves and woollen headgear.

"Where is the money?"

The second man pretended to be washing the rear windscreen.

He had a bottle of water and some newspaper but the water was oily and made the glass murky. He walked round the car to the front windscreen and did the same there. The doctor popped the boot. The first man lifted it open and grabbed the bags. The window washer mumbled something about pulling over before they both suddenly disappeared.

The doctor tried to follow them in his rearview mirror but he couldn't see—it had also been oiled up. He picked up his phone and contemplated calling the detective. But they might be watching. How had they known where he was? They had clearly planned everything down to the last detail. He tried to look through his windshield but it too was a greasy, blurry mess. He leaned forward but still couldn't see a thing. The wipers only made it worse. It was some kind of oil and no matter how much he tried to wash it off using the car's window-cleaning system, it wouldn't budge. He pulled over into the emergency lane. Drivers behind him showed impatience with a mixture of gestures and abuse. He was stuck. He couldn't move. He phoned Detective Turner. They had not planned for this. He should have had the police with him.

What if they were not the kidnappers? What if they had been hired by someone working on the case? Johannesburg was riddled with corruption. Someone with inside information who would confide in someone with the requisite skills, splitting the proceeds and who gave a fuck about the two-year-old whose life depended on it. The detective said he would send someone out immediately. The doctor put his head in his hands, slumped against the steering wheel and did something he hadn't done in a long time. He cried.

It was only when he got home just before eight that he realized he was the key to the kidnapping. It was just before eight when he realized that the past always caught up with you... eventually. It was just before eight when he saw the grey faces of the police officials and the detective who wanted to be anywhere but there. It was just before eight when he realized he would never see his grandson again.

It was six the next morning when a parcel was dropped off. Inside the parcel was a small polystyrene box. Detective Turner opened the package after it had been checked for explosives. Inside he found two things. Wrapped in plastic on top of the ice was a VHS tape and under the ice, in a translucent, plastic container that might not look out of place in a refrigerator, was something the detective was not prepared for. From the outside he could see the red gel-like substance tinting the inside. He imagined it was something like a finger or an ear. He had seen such things before but it wasn't an ear or a finger. The severed scrotum with bloodied testicles was that of a young boy.

Chapter 5

Ayesha Mansoor was feeling extremely irritated with her mother and was trying just as desperately not to show it. Mrs Mansoor was being her pathologically blunt self about her intentions. Mr Mansoor, on the other hand, knew his daughter. It didn't matter how wonderful other people thought a potential suitor was; if his daughter wasn't interested, then he wasn't. He looked at his thirty-year-old divorced daughter sitting across from him at the dinner table with that feigned look of happiness. That was the look she wore permanently and was the cause of much concern for her parents, mainly her mother. The truth was that his daughter hadn't been the same since she'd learned of her husband's adultery and had endured the stress of the subsequent divorce and miscarriage. Her ex-husband was from a wealthy, popular family. It was expected that men from his neck of the woods would cheat on their wives. What was not expected was for husbands to divorce their wives. It was generally agreed in the community that he was wrong for divorcing her and embarrassing her in such a manner. And yet, Ayesha came out of it all smelling as if she had just crawled through a sewer pipe, permanently tarnished in the eyes of the community. What kind of woman divorces her husband so another woman can marry him? There must be something wrong with her. It was less than a year later that her ex-husband's new wife was pregnant. Mr Mansoor had heard the rumours that his daughter was barren, or worse, a cold fish who'd forced her husband to go elsewhere, that anyone who wanted to work as a policewoman had to have something wrong with her, that she might even be a lesbian. Mr Mansoor ignored the vicious rumours with dignity, but was angered by the denigration of his daughter. What right did they have?

Ayesha sat opposite Dr Aadil Munshi, a wealthy, forty-something ear, nose and throat specialist. Aadil, as he insisted on being called, had been married twice and yet was still in favour with potential mothers-in-law, possibly attributed to his lengthy beard (piety) or his family and profession (status) but the most likely reason was that he had money, having amassed a small fortune. It was well documented that he had business interests in China and Dubai.

Ayesha made polite conversation, once or twice making her lack of interest blatantly clear by ignoring his questions. How were you supposed to get to know a person with your mother glaring at you from across the table and constantly inquiring if you had eaten enough or did you want another drink?

Ayesha knew the pressure her mother was under living among the clans of Indian suburbia. She realized that the other mothers would gossip about her having a divorced daughter who was thirty, single and childless. Her life was meaningless in their eyes, but you could see the expectation on her mother's face. A match with the good doctor would be a trophy—a gag to stick in the mouths of the rest of the community. It was a repetitive game of one-upmanship, where mothers and indeed families used their daughters in some universal competition. Ayesha wished she could be one of those daughters who put up with a husband's shit to please her family and save her parents the embarrassment of having a divorcee for a daughter. But she had learned her lesson the first time around. It was no one's fault except her ex-husband's for being a cheating bastard, but she should never have been in a rush to get married. She should not have put such pressure on herself.

Aadil babbled on, making polite conversation with Mrs Mansoor, Mr Mansoor having long since started counting down to when his guest would leave and he could read his paper.

It wasn't until after tea and *esha salaah* that Aadil said that he had to be off. He offered Ayesha a lift. She politely declined. She had come in her own car. He insisted on driving behind her to make sure she reached her flat safely. It wasn't safe to travel from Laudium at that time of night.

Ayesha pulled up outside her eight-storey pink apartment block with its remote-controlled gate and security cameras. Aadil pulled up alongside her as she turned into the driveway. She gave him a brief wave. In the rearview mirror she could see him pull off. She would have to have a serious chat with her mother about her choice of dinner company. That she would do in the morning. Right now she was too tired—too exhausted to bother phoning. She got out of car and gave her father two missed calls on her cell. That was their signal that she was home safely.

Chapter 6

Dr André Blignaut was up unusually early. There was purpose to his early rising. His own wife had been sedated, along with his daughter, the mother of his only grandson. His son-in-law was being useless as usual. The videotape. That's what had actually woken him. The voice, the way the kidnapping played out, the money—there was a sense of familiarity that tugged at his memory. He struggled to put his finger on it. He hadn't really slept; he'd re-lived the whole experience over and over. His grandson was dead and it was his fault. It didn't matter that he had delivered the money. His grandson had probably had a death sentence on his head even before he was born.

André Blignaut stood in front of the washbasin mirror. At sixty-five, he looked every bit his age. He found it difficult to look at himself. The video played over and over again in his head. The voice was cold and calculating, organized, meticulous in the words that were chosen. But this was not some random act. It was vengeance exacted on a young child, revenge for what Dr André Blignaut had done in his past.

The lead detective was in a state of shock—the family was in a state of shock. The hostage was no more except for a pair of severed testicles—and then there was the videotape.

The voice on the tape was clear and precise as the footage showed visuals of Marissa and young Cobus Jr leaving their house, being followed to Hyde Park, inside the mall, then driving to her parents' house and then the violent kidnapping in all its graphic detail, with the one kidnapper kicking aggressively at Marissa's head. It was sick, like a snuff movie.

"So how does it feel, Dr André Blignaut? Surely you must have known that this day would eventually come? You didn't think you would die before we came to collect? We wish it could have been sooner, but you know how these things work out. We thought we would send you the part you didn't send home to our parents, to see if you noticed any difference? Have you?" The voice became more intense, almost a slight loss of control. "At least he won't have to live to deal with it like we did. You should have killed us. You *did* kill us. You jailed us. Now you share our loss. I know you will come after us. Remember that there is nothing that you can do to us that will make us afraid. You cannot hurt us anymore. You killed us a long time ago."

The tape went snowy and the detective stopped it. Everyone sat in silence. Marissa turned to her father and was about to say something when she started gagging. Before anyone could react, she passed out. The older man sat there, dumbstruck, lost. Cobus Sr stood up from attending to his wife and stared at the doctor. The doctor didn't look back as he went to the bedroom.

That was yesterday. Now he looked at his face in the mirror. The lines etched on his face offered proof of the things he'd seen and done. Each line a record of his life. Of the price he'd paid, something none could imagine. He was a soldier, a man who'd made sacrifices, sacrifices for the greater good. He'd made decisions that ordinary people didn't have the stomach for. He could feel his gut tensing, anger growing inside. He had only been doing his job, trying to help people and yet this, this was the result. He shook his head as if to settle his thoughts. He got dressed and left the house. There was a way to solve such problems, to show that he wasn't some toothless old man, to make up for his grandson's life.

Chapter 7

Private hospitals in South Africa were how you pictured a private hospital should look in the twenty-first century. Lendt Park Hospital was no different. Friendly staff, clean and none of the unsavoury smells associated with some of the government hospitals. Ayesha made her way through the front door and flashed her credentials. She didn't wear her police-issue jacket except at a crime scene. She kept it in the car should she be called out to one. It seldom happened, but now and again it did. The security officer at the door directed her to the hospital receptionist.

The receptionist took Ayesha's ID card and suspiciously scrutinized it, before handing it back and pressing a button on the intercom. "Dr Johnson, Dr Johnson, please report to reception."

The intercom was silent for a few moments.

"Dr Johnson will be with you shortly," she said to Ayesha.

Ayesha sat down and picked up a magazine. The collection on the coffee table contained the usual outdated *Time*, *You* and *Huis Genoot* magazines. There was the standard batch of articles in the collection of *You* and *Huis Genoot*—the famous cricketer who refused to see his love-child, the kleptomaniac from the northern suburbs and, Ayesha's favourite, the woman who was left for dead by an ex-husband after a particularly savage beating but was now re-married and about to have her first child with her new, caring and understanding husband. *Time* magazine had a terrible picture of Obama on the cover and an article about what to expect if he became president of the USA.

A tall man with auburn hair approached Ayesha as she was flipping through the magazine. He was in his forties, his hair greying slightly at the temples. He slouched slightly. "Hello, I'm Doctor Johnson. I believe you want to see me."

Ayesha looked up to see an unfriendly man in a white coat standing over her.

"Hi, my name is Ayesha, and I'm with the Special Crimes Unit. I was hoping I could speak to you about a patient who was transferred into your care this morning." She took out her card and showed it to the doctor.

The doctor took the card and gave it a cursory glance before handing it back. "I think we'd better go to my office. We're going to need some privacy. Please follow me."

Dr Johnson's office was a typical, impersonal hospital room. He shared the desk with a doctor who was on duty when he was not. There was a bland desk-and-chair combo with the obligatory chart showing what the human body looked like under all those layers of skin. A white metal bed stood against one wall. There was a door behind the desk, probably into bathroom. The walls were the standard white, proof that this office was a transit zone and owned by no one in particular.

Ayesha took a seat. There was an orange manila folder on the desk. Dr Johnson made his way to his side of the desk and sat down in front of Ellen Fischer's folder, which he handed to Ayesha. "The patient is stable but unconscious. We are keeping her under close observation as she only stabilized this morning. She has several broken ribs and a broken eye socket and cheekbone. She suffered massive internal injuries. I frankly don't know how she survived."

In the folder was a generic diagram of the human body sprawled across the opening page. Some sections had been coloured red to show where the body was damaged. It was the kind of diagram that looked like it belonged in an insurance report for a car accident. Next to the coloured-in bits were the scrawled annotations that only doctors can decipher.

"When we did the tests, that is the swabs and the rape exam to check for lacerations and wounds associated with a sexual assault, we noticed some scarring.

"And this is the part where I ask what kind of scarring?" Ayesha leaned forward slightly, her lips pouting, a common expression when her attention was being held and she was trying to focus.

The doctor looked pensive, as if searching for words that Ayesha would understand. "Well, apart from the lacerations and bruising associated with the assault we noticed some old scar tissue." He paused. "Surgical scarring associated with transgender surgery."

Ayesha pursed her lips as she tried arranging the information into some type of order in her head. "I … I don't get it? What do you mean by transgender?"

"The patient had a sex-change operation at some point.:

"What!"

"She used to be a man."

Chapter 8

Dr André Blignaut parked his luxury blue German sedan in a rundown part of Johannesburg. The car looked out of place amid the hustle and bustle of the area. Women sat on plastic milk crates selling sweets and loose cigarettes off cardboard-box counter tops on the pavement. Loud Congolese music blasted its way onto the street and a man with a microphone lured passers-by into his shop with announcements of special offers. It was a typical African street scene with lanky, dark-skinned Africans trading everything from sheeps' heads to cellular phone accessories. This, though, was not some typical African city with garbage-strewn streets. No, this was South Africa, completely different from rest of the continent; even if geologically still a part of it. Although the area was adjacent to the Johannesburg CBD, it was mostly home to illegal immigrants, refugees and the ever-widening stream of people coming to the city of gold with dreams of a better life. They generally ended up as tenants in some rundown building that had long since been abandoned by its owners. Such buildings had been taken over by slum-lords, rent was collected and people continued to live in them, dozens to a room, despite the derelict condition or the hazards, health and structural. Local government knew what was going on but generally turned a blind eye. They didn't have the resources to close them down or relocate people to more suitable accomodation. Chances were that you moved one batch of people only to have another batch move in the next day. People died—mainly in fires—but that was life.

Dr Blignaut set his car alarm. A futile gesture—this was Hillbrow and his car had become a target from the moment he took that off-ramp. It wasn't because he was white and Hillbrow was now a predominantly black neighbourhood. There were still white people here, some too poor to have moved when the immigrants moved in. Some still operated their businesses here, paying protection to this group or that—Senegalese, Nigerian, Congolese, whatever, the contents of Pandora's Box when Mandela was released from jail. The thought of walking in Hillbrow made the doctor feel sick. The smell of raw sewage mixed with the odours of too many people living in too small an area reached down into your stomach and belted your insides until, even if you didn't want to look at the decay, it managed to infect your every sense.

The doctor walked briskly down the pavement, his head lowered to avoid attention. All the while he had to dodge the hustlers thrusting at him this pamphlet and that flyer. Apparently Dr Hoosein, from Mali, could solve any problem ranging from erectile dysfunction to bringing back a lost love or winning the lottery.

White and black prostitutes walked the street. They strutted past the doctor, trying to make eye contact, that show of interest which might lead to a liaison. A police van drove by, the occupants momentarily looking at the doctor before putting his presence down to a transaction with one of Hillbrow's delights.

He walked briskly. He would have a tough time explaining his presence here if something happened. The walk from his car to the seedy little nightclub was short enough though. The problem was if he returned empty-handed. He could feel desperate eyes looking at him, his jacket, his hat, his watch, his shoes and the slight bulge in his pocket. Mixed with the smell of rotting garbage and sewage was the stench of desperation. This had better work out.

The bouncer at the door of the nightclub patted him down before returning to his bar stool at the front door. The doctor wanted to ask him a question, but his interest was on the show inside.

A blond woman in a red thong gyrated to Isaac Hayes' 'Chocolate

Salty Balls', made famous by the animated TV show, *Southpark.*

The bouncer was used to seeing all sorts here. Rich, poor, fat, thin, old and young. He didn't mind. Sometimes they got a bit rough in the back rooms or they didn't want to pay or argued about not having enough cash on them or sometimes the old white guys got attached to the young nubile imports from the north and became jealously over-protective. Some even caused a scene during the shows. Whatever the case, he did what he was told when he was told to do it. No questions. So what if she had led him on and he had spent his entire salary buying her time or lavish gifts? Not his problem.

It was smoky inside and smelt of stale wine, sweat and lust. The lighting was bad but that helped when some of your performers looked liked they had escaped from Dr Moureau's lab. Dr Blignaut looked at the gawking men around the stage. A big man, wearing one of those shirts that looked like it belonged on the beach, held out a wad of what looked like R50 notes. He looked Nigerian but in these parts it was getting increasingly difficult to tell. A young redhead—about nineteen and probably Eastern European—began a lap dance. The doctor turned away. There was still something not right with a black man touching a white girl in that way. It sickened him. He glanced back briefly, his own curiosity getting the better of him. She was sitting or rather grinding on the client's lap. One hand grabbed at a breast, squeezing it, while the other made its way down the front of her red thong. The bouncer at the door got up and walked over to the pair. He said something in the big man's ear. The man got up from his seat and, taking the entertainer with him, made for what the doctor assumed were rooms for the clients.

"What'll you have?" asked a young white man of around twenty behind the bar. He was wearing an over-washed grey T-shirt and faded black jeans.

The doctor shook his head. He leaned over and the barman met him halfway, his head cocked.

"I'm looking for Slang. I hear he works here."

The barman glanced at the older man. No one asked for Slang. In fact, no one ever came around looking for Slang. The barman turned, looked at the security camera above him and gave a hand signal.

A door opened next to the bar and a man came out, another black man with a foreign look about him. He leaned over the bar as the barman pointed out the doctor who was trying to pretend that he was enjoying the entertainment. A black stripper was caressing a beer bottle, being cheered on by group of men of various races. The club smelled of decay, human decay, the decay of dignity, people who had resigned themselves to selling what was left of themselves in order to live. The doctor despised the fact that he had to be here. His hatred for the kidnappers grew inside him. Every second inside the club was another cinder fuelling the hatred. It sickened him. The testicles in the box. The tape. Son of a bitch! He would find them. It was only be a matter of time. It wasn't about the money. But they wouldn't live long enough to spend it, of that he was sure.

The man that who had come through the door approached Dr Blignaut. "You looking for Mr Wessels?" His English was good but with a strong Portuguese accent, probably Mozambican.

"Yes, I want to see Slang. Where is he?" The doctor didn't turn around. He had seen the man come out.

The man looked towards the security camera behind the bar and signalled. The door buzzed open. "Follow me."

Hannes 'Slang' Wessels was the owner of the Magic Snake, a strip club and whorehouse licensed as a nightclub in downtown Hillbrow. His employees called him Mr Wessels, even the ones who despised him. Slang was not a man to be messed with. Despite his age, he was still quick in a fight; he had once broken the arm of one particularly disagreeable patron who was more than twice his size. The patron threatened to sue but he never did. But that was before he got Oscar to work security. He couldn't afford to be in the public eye too much. Not these days.

Slang was ex-security. Not the type that paraded around in a fancy uniform with a torch at the local shopping mall. Slang was ex-security for the old government. He had worked military operations in Angola and Mozambique with occasional stints into Zambia and Tanzania. He later joined the Security Police where his special skills were used on local South Africans 'in country'. While in the army he would lead small squads into foreign territory to neutralize African National Congress, ANC, operatives, tipped off by some intelligence organization or other, often the CIA. Sometimes it was just a case of destroy; you simply destroyed what was in front of you—it didn't matter. Not to his bosses. It sewed panic and discord—the desired objective. Once, on his own, he had to cross into Zambia to assassinate an MK leader—MK, or Umkhonto we Sizwe, the ANC's armed wing. Zambia allowed the ANC to train their military operatives inside their country, operatives who would sabotage the apartheid government's attempts at creating a peaceful—yet divided—dispensation. That could not be allowed. That was his job, therefore.

It became more interesting when he moved to the Security Branch where he got to fight his own South Africans. Slang also spent time training young misfits, the drug addicts who found life on the front line too taxing. He weeded out the potential psychotic killers from the cannon fodder and 'programmed' them to see things in perspective, his perspective of course. The Truth and Reconciliation Commission had labelled him a psychopathic death-squad leader, a gratuitous killer who was being given a second chance by the grace of God. He was granted amnesty, unlike most of his colleagues who'd run for it or ended up in jail. He'd told the TRC that it wasn't death-squad work and he didn't kill people for pleasure. He was protecting innocent, hard-working South Africans from anarchy, from terrorists who wanted to create chaos and prevent people from living peacefully. He was only doing his job and following orders.

His job ... a lawyer shot and killed in his bedroom after he had been forced to watch a masked man rape his wife and slit her throat. A young man electrocuted by his testicles because he refused to give up his comrades' whereabouts. Slang was an expert on torture. He was generally called for when a confession was needed; such was the strength of some of the MK comrades that aggressive persuasion was sometimes a requirement. His favourite technique was holding a man, or a woman for that matter, down on the floor, naked, with their hands and feet tied behind their backs. He would put a wet pillowcase over their heads and pull it tightly over their faces as he drove his knee into their spines. Sometimes they would give in immediately and confess. Sometimes they would soil themselves. Sometimes the pillowcase would fill up with vomit and the bastards would choke to death. You had to be careful with that. Other times they suffocated or had a heart attack. There was no telling.

The doctor was led to a dark room with multiple monitors glowing in black and white, illuminating the room. An office chair with a high back faced the monitors, smoke curling up from behind it. The door closed and the doctor approached the desk in front of the chair. There was an old filing cabinet to one side and a couch on the other. It was a strictly functional office.

Slang stood up as if still in the army and a senior officer had just entered the room. The two men shook hands and sat down. The doctor tried to make chitchat before describing the events that had brought him here. Slang offered unconvincing condolences.

The doctor looked away dolefully. "Dis hoekom ek hier is." *That's why I am here.*

"Ek verstaan nie ..." *I don't understand.*

"The police are terrible at best and we both know that they will never catch these people and if they do, they'll get off or escape or whatever." The doctor sounded like he had more to say. He was trying to avoid stating the obvious.

"Look, doctor, I'm not a private investigator. I run a nightclub. As much as I want to help you, this is not what I do. I think you have the wrong man." Slang knew there was more. The doctor wouldn't come all the way down into the inner city to ask him to help in a police investigation.

"I know that. And I, more than anyone, know the reality of trying to start again in this ... *new* South Africa, but it's not that simple." The older man pulled out the VHS cassette and slid it across the table. "Our pasts have come back to haunt us."

Slang picked up the cassette and looked at it. "What's on here?"

The doctor stood up. "Our pasts." He threw a business card on the table and walked out.

Slang sat at his desk. This was serious, there was no doubt. Every former apartheid operative was on his toes. And even if you hadn't spoken to anyone for more than a decade, it wasn't a surprise to receive a phone call. Usually it was some sort of plea for help or a warning to say that the authorities were onto them. You had two choices: stay and answer the inevitable questions about what you did during apartheid or flee and do 'security' work in some Third World country. He had seen the hearings that mentioned Dr Blignaut's name as a perpetrator of war crimes. The charges never materialized because of lack of evidence. News reports had been minimal. Maybe it was due to the fact that reporters didn't know how to classify, let alone verify, his victims. And yes, he did have victims. The doctor's name was 'out there', uncomfortably so for a man of his standing and reputation. The smell of it all simply wouldn't disappear.

Slang swivelled his chair around and wheeled himself to the video player. He slipped in the cassette and watched as one of the monitor screens turned blue and came to life. The cold voiceover began with visuals of Marissa Vermeulen and a small baby. It was a man's voice.

No, it was a woman's. It was definitely female. For a second his blood ran cold. He knew exactly what had happened and why. Now was just the case of the who. The tape came to an end as Slang reached across the desk and picked up the business card and his cell phone.

Chapter 9

Ayesha Mansoor was whirling her chair in front of her PC. The case was becoming more and more complex. She was trying to break it down into smaller components. Director de Villiers was nowhere in the office and she needed someone to talk to about her thoughts on the current developments. The desk phone startled her back to reality, shaking her from her carefully constructed mental crime scene. In her mind she'd arranged the victim with neat labels according to the evidence she'd found. Photos of the crime scene strewn across her desk were slowly being uploaded into her memory.

A hand on her shoulder shook her further from her thought process. It was Director de Villiers. "Any news on that case? I'm meeting with the minister this evening."

"The victim is recovering okay, I guess, especially considering what happened to her. But I think we have a problem."

De Villiers cocked his head. "What do you mean, a problem?"

"Well, it's not really a problem, but …" Ayesha was stalling. She felt a little awkward talking about it. "Well, the attending doctor took me aside. It appears our victim is or was the recipient of a transgender operation." She felt more comfortable describing her latest discovery in clinical terms.

"I don't understand." The director shook his head as if to process the information.

"The victim had a sex-change operation. The victim was a man and had an operation to become a woman." Ayesha waited for a reaction.

The director stood there, looking at her blankly for a moment.

"Get hold of the case officer in our PE office. They had a transgender assassination two weeks ago. It was handed to us for some reason. Get everything you can out of the people down there and update me on the progress." The director kept abreast of everything that happened throughout the country. He was usually the best port of call for latest information.

"What do you mean, assassination?" Ayesha looked up at her boss who had already turned to leave.

"The victim was found on some deserted beach, all valuables in his possession, hands tied behind his back. He was in the kneeling position with two bullet holes in the back of his head. He had been beaten up, but apparently during the capture process. Phone the case officer and he'll tell you everything you need to know. I have to go—call me with any new developments."

With that the director strode off to his office. He was not really an office kind of guy—he met with people. He was the crime-fighting unit's public image. That was *his* job—to make sure people saw the unit doing *its* job. How he managed to keep up to date with every case across the country was anyone's guess. It was a standing joke that he only slept for an hour a day.

If Ayesha thought the phone call to the Port Elizabeth office was going to get her anywhere she was greatly mistaken. In fact it opened up more questions than answers. The victim in Port Elizabeth was a forty-something male, shot twice in the back of the head, execution style. The cause of death was massive trauma to the skull as a result of the two bullet wounds. The victim had been beaten up beforehand, possibly to subdue him prior to the killing.

It was the medical examiner who'd picked up a problem with the identification. The ME had noticed that although the victim looked male for the most part, he was missing the most important parts. Upon further inspection it was established that the victim had been the recipient of a transgender surgical procedure. All the transgender clinics were subsequently checked for records but nothing was found. The identity document was fake as the number did not exist—nor the person. Eventually identity was confirmed through fingerprint cross-referencing with old SADF records. Ayesha phoned the fingerprint unit. They were still sifting through various records. She told them about the success they'd had with identifying the PE prints from SADF records and suggested they do the same for her case.

She replaced the receiver and contemplated phoning her boss. She was sure that he would know exactly what to do with this information. If only her victim would gain consciousness then maybe something would fall into place.

She went over the evidence again. Who was Ellen Fischer? Why had she been so brutally raped and left for dead? It was not a simple case of an attempted murder or a gratuitous rape; the perpetrators were somehow sending a message. But what? The graffiti on the wall showed that they knew their victim. It wasn't random. The assault with the hand tools—that was designed to make her suffer and done by someone with a pathological hatred. The rape? Someone else knew she was actually a he. Blackmail? Maybe she'd refused to pay? She needed more information. There were too many questions.

Chapter 10

The Transgender Clinic situated in Sunninghill was a modern building more closely resembling a mansion than a medical facility. It boasted two tennis courts and a swimming pool. Men wearing blue overalls and toting gardening equipment walked the pristine lawns among stone horse carvings. Ayesha made her way to reception. She had phoned ahead and asked for an appointment with the director. She was told he was out but his assistant, Dr Lategan, would assist with any queries. She announced herself at reception and took a seat. The clinic had been a government facility during apartheid but in 1994 had been bought out by a private consortium. It handled all transgender referrals in the region.

A tall, blond woman who looked nothing like a stereotypical doctor walked up to the receptionist, who pointed in Ayesha's direction. She approached Ayesha sitting on the waiting-room couch, flipping through a magazine.

"Hello Ms Mansoor? I'm Dr Lategan, the director's assistant. How can I help you?" The doctor's hand was outstretched as if choreographed.

Ayesha put the magazine aside and stood up. "Hi, thank you for seeing me at such short notice. Is there somewhere we can talk, privately?"

The doctor looked around and motioned for Ayesha to follow her. The two women walked outside into the gardens. Nurses with clipboards strode the pathways, while on the manicured lawns patients sat in garden chairs absorbing the sunshine.

"There are some questions that I was hoping you could answer."

Ayesha wasn't sure how to handle the conversation. She struggled with the concept of how someone could be a man one day and a woman the next. She didn't even know what the right term was for referring to her victim—he or she? A victim who was still unconscious in hospital. A victim who could not offer the slightest bit of assistance. She didn't even know if she had the victim's real name.

"I'll try to help as much as I can." The doctor's tone was pleasant but unassured.

"As I mentioned on the phone, we have a victim who was brutally attacked a few days ago. She is still unconscious but, since it was a rape and assault, we proceeded with tests … the attending found signs that the victim might have had a sex-change operation. I was hoping that perhaps you could look through your records, maybe check if our victim came through this hospital or any of the other provincial facilities."

Dr Lategan stopped and looked at Ayesha in askance. "I'm not sure … you are aware that I cannot discuss a patient's record with you? They do have the right to privacy."

Ayesha had been hoping it wouldn't come to this. For once, couldn't people just take her word for it and co-operate? "Look, doctor, there is a woman in a hospital bed who was brutally raped and assaulted. Now if anyone wants a transgender op in this country they have to apply to one of the provincial facilities and then you and your team determines if they are genuinely transgender or just wasting your time. You offer treatment, surgery and post-surgery support. That much I know but what I need from you is to check your records or let me do it. Otherwise, I can get a court order and come back here with a whole team of officers and rummage through everything. So far I have got nothing. You can help me or I can help myself." Ayesha was irritated and wanted to get on with things.

The doctor looked taken aback, her shoulders slumping. Ayesha's temper had got the better of her, but she made it appear as if she had every intention of carrying out her threat if she wasn't extended the assistance she needed. She knew she could get a court order but the resultant press coverage would create unwanted exposure which would likely mean a roasting for her.

"I would like to help you. But you must understand that there are issues here that could land the Minister of Health in the Constitutional Court." The doctor was visibly shaken.

Ayesha tried a softer approach. "Look, chances are she has no criminal record and the fingerprint report when it eventually arrives on my desk will be of no use. Her identity documents are probably fake and, more importantly, I don't have the time to wait for Home Affairs to verify the ID number, or not. You see, time is of the essence because my boss wants results because *his* boss, the Minister of Safety and Security, wants those results. All I'm asking is for you to see what you can do and help me find the people who did this to her. Can you understand that?"

The doctor nodded. "We have extensive databases but you will have to come back tomorrow. The data clerks are half day today. You can come back early tomorrow and I'll tell them to be prepared for you. You can have access to the fingerprint files and other patient identification records. The psychological profiles, though, I must insist on allowing only limited access to. Those are sensitive and are still protected by privilege."

Ayesha understood. She thanked the doctor and agreed to come back the next morning, She took her leave and made her way to her car. As she opened the door her phone buzzed.

"Hello?"

A lab technician from the office responded. "Hey, Ayesha, you told me to call when I got that info you wanted. The ID number turned out to be a dead end. We don't know who our victim is. The copy is good, probably got it from one of our downtown Home Affairs but the number doesn't exist. Interesting though, the other fingerprints are flagged by SANDF. Former 231 Battalion members. The rest is sealed. You're gonna need the boss on this one. I only have have limited access to South African National Defence Force files. I'll keep checking on the victim but she isn't turning up on any criminal databases and there is no record of her in any system. All bank cards are in the fake name."

"Do me a favour, cross-reference her prints with the SANDF if you can. Tomorrow we'll have access to a medical database. I'll fill you in later."

"Okay, ta."

"Thanks."

Ayesha put the phone back into the hip holster. She got into her car and drove back to her flat. She needed to phone her boss but not from the office.

Chapter 11

Hannes 'Slang' Wessels approached the edge of the pond. An elderly man sat on the bench tossing breadcrumbs into the water, which large fish were fighting over. He looked like any other ordinary old man—woollen cap, scarf and thick winter coat. One of many who passed the time by sitting in the park, feeding the fish or the ducks or just sitting.

Slang sat down on the bench. The older man opened his shopping bag and slipped out a brown file. It was an SAPS manila folder. He placed it neatly on the bench between them and carried on tearing off small bits of bread and throwing them into the pond. A few ducks had gathered in front of the bench.

"I'm glad you called. The police aren't helping."

Slang made to pick up the folder.

"No. Pick it up after I leave. I want you to find who killed my grandson, find out where his body is buried, if it is, and bring the remains home to me."

"Doctor, you know this is going to cost money?"

"I know."

"I was just trying to warn you."

"My daughter needs closure."

"I understand."

The ducks were squabbling over scraps of bread. The noise was jarring.

"You're no longer a colonel and your men are no longer loyal," the doctor stated.

"Ek weet." *I know.*

"There is a key in there for a post office box. Tell me how much money you need and in twenty-four hours you can pick it up. No one will be any the wiser."

Dr Blignaut stopped feeding the fish and the ducks. He was leaning back, staring at the sky. His voice, however, was clear and precise in describing what he wanted done. "Slang, I want to know who is responsible. You can finish off whoever the hands are, I don't care, but I want to know who the brains are. And then you can do whatever you want with him ... or them. I don't want them going to jail. Am I clear?"

"Ek hoor." *I hear you.*

Slang reached into his pocket and pulled out a thick padded A5 envelope. "A cell phone and charger with a new sim card. There is one number on it. If you need anything, leave a message on voicemail. I'll check it and phone you back. It's prepaid so buy your airtime the old-fashioned way from one of those spaza shops. When we're done, throw it away—sim, phone, everything."

Dr Blignaut picked up the envelope and slipped it into his shopping bag. He got up without looking at his bench companion. He walked away, secure in the knowledge that whoever was responsible for this appalling crime would soon receive what he, or they, deserved.

Slang sat a while longer. He picked up the folder, opened it and glanced over the pages. There were copies of all the reports, from the phone number used to call the doctor to the pathologist's report on the testicles that had been delivered to the house.

He felt something twist deep inside. Not because he hadn't come across such atrocities before, not because it offended any sense of morality. No, it was because, as he sat on that bench scanning through the reports and statements, he saw a mirror of his own techniques in the handiwork. He had trained these people. At the very least they had been trained by his people; of that much he was sure. The videotape had been evidence enough but seeing the reports confirmed everything. Anger bubbled up inside him. If they could get to the doctor, it was only a matter of time before ...

He closed the folder, tucked it inside his belt and drew his coat closed. He walked to his car, clear about what he had to do next.

Chapter 12

The warehouse was just one of many former homeland businesses that had closed post apartheid. It had been the apartheid government's idea to have white South African businesses open up near the homeland borders to benefit from the endless source of cheap labour and, furthermore, the blacks would not need to travel into the South African hinterland, the white hinterland, the white homeland. Various tax incentives were offered. It was a way of showing that apartheid worked. The warehouse was just one of the many abandoned along the former Bophuthatswanan border after the demise of apartheid, as companies moved back to the cities with their established infrastructures and markets. They'd lost their tax incentives; they didn't need to be out in the sticks anymore.

The window frames, along with the panes, had long been removed. Even some of the brickwork was gone. There was very little left. Doors, windows, fittings and anthing else that could be carried off had all long since disappeared. Today though, the warehouse was being used as a torture chamber. In what used to be an ablution block four men stood over a beaten and bloodied man who was tied to a chair with a black cloth bag over his head.

"I don't know what you're talking about!" The man was screaming through the black bag. Three black men were punching him. The dull thuds of fists striking flesh filled the air.

"Open his shirt. Keep the bag on." Slang stood to one side smoking a cigarette. He had smoked a lot since they'd arrived with their charge, saying little. Just the occasional cursory nod when he needed to confirm a further beating.

"I just need a name, one name or better still, all the names, because I checked, you're too stupid to do this on your own. I mean, you bag a million bucks and you're still around—you're pretty fucking stupid." Slang was hoping to get this over with sooner rather than later.

The man in the chair was in his late twenties. A small-time criminal, his involvement in the kidnapping was a job promotion. Slang knew he didn't have the brains. He had the balls but no brains which was probably why he had been chosen.

"Look here, numb nut, I can stop my friends from hurting you. Just tell me who employed you. You're too fucking stupid to have done it on your own. You want to know how I found you? You changed your sim card but you didn't change your phone. You see, when you make a call there's a signal your phone gives off. I take that number and see which other number it has been linked to and your number came up. You really are fucking stupid. Dof!" Slang let out a long sigh. "I'm tired. Leave him in the chair, wet him down and tip over the barrels. You see, fuck knuckle, I got time and until you tell me what I want, I'm going to torture you. I don't care if you piss yourself or shit yourself, you're fucked. If your employers are so bad ass, why the fuck did they hire you? You, a fucking moron. Huh?" He flicked the man's forehead with his finger.

The man winced.

Slang turned to his crew. "Fuck him. Let's go."

The man shivered. They hadn't left. He couldn't see them but he hadn't heard them leave. He sensed their presence. They were testing him. They had told him that he might be tested. But he had to hold strong. He could make it in the outfit if he proved himself.

"Do it," Slang barked.

They sounded like black men. The one doing all the talking was white but the rest were black. Do what, he wondered to himself. He could deal with this. He had to prove himself, make a name for himself. Then he'd move up the ladder.

Two of the men kicked over several twenty-litre drums. The contents slowly oozed out. It was viscous, spreading inexorably over the floor. It crept between the toes and eventually over the feet of the man in the chair.

"You smell that? That's industrial glue. Soon your eyes will start to burn, your throat will start itching and the glue will slowly burn the skin off your feet. You'll get headaches and you'll vomit all over yourself until you have nothing left to vomit. You'll want to sleep but you won't be able to. You will start to hallucinate. And just when you think you've had enough, you will beg me to make it all stop. You can scream as much as you want. No one will hear you. I'll be back when you're ready to talk. Enjoy yourself, bru."

Slang smiled, turned and motioned his men to follow. The man in the chair screamed something like, "You won't break me", but Slang ignored him and carried on walking towards the car. He knew that the ablution block had poor ventilation and it was cold which would simply add to the victim's pain and discomfort. There would be an unholy mess when they came back in a few hours.

Fortunately the glue was flammable. Getting rid of the evidence would be simple enough.

Chapter 13

Ayesha sat opposite Dr Aadil Munshi in Queen of the Nile, one of Johannesburg's top restaurants, wondering how she had let herself be talked into a follow-up 'let's-see-if-there-is-potential' date. Her mother had badgered her in the days following the dinner where she'd met Dr Munshi for the first time. But her mind was on the case. Director de Villiers had stressed the importance of solving it quickly so that the wealthy and powerful could sleep easy in the knowledge that they would not be the next victim. Dr Munshi was blabbering on about his community work which he did every Saturday and Sunday at Baragwanath Hospital and how nothing shocked him anymore. One patient had come in with a gangrenous arm after being stabbed in a shebeen brawl a few weeks earlier and now he was blaming the doctor because they'd told him that his arm was going to have to be amputated. Ayesha sat politely, studying him, trying to picture him as a boy. Had he been short and stocky? When had he started wearing the beard? He now looked like a garden gnome, minus the pointed hat of course. She smiled to herself, trying not to giggle. Anything to pass the time, keep her mother happy. A woman in a glittery red outfit approached the table. The tables were the low kind that you sat around on comfy cushions. Waiters in white uniforms with black waistcoats and, occasionally, hostesses approached the couple.

"Would you like a belly dance?" The woman looked like she was Eastern European. Her accent was foreign but Ayesha couldn't pinpoint it. She didn't look Egyptian or Turkish or from any other Middle Eastern country traditionally linked to belly dancing.

Aadil Munshi looked at Ayesha. The uncertainty on his face was obvious. Ayesha was amused. She tried not to appear so as it would have embarrassed him further.

The doctor looked up at the woman, "We will call you when we are ready, thanks." His voice was thick with discomfort.

Ayesha glanced at her watch. Aadil noticed. He continued his meal. He tried to make more conversation. Questions about the case she was working on were met with a bland, "It's sensitive and I wouldn't feel comfortable discussing it over dinner right now. You do understand?" Aadil nodded and smiled weakly. He could feel his frustration building. He hated the pressures from his ageing parents. He had to find a wife, yet at his age he wouldn't find one who hadn't been married before, let alone one without children. In the eyes of his parents, Ayesha was going to be as good as it got without him having to shop around for a woman half his age. So what if she had been married before? At least she didn't have any children. For a while his parents had taken him to meet the daughters of family friends whom he'd never met. The girls were nice enough but they were just that, girls. He wanted a woman, not a girl. He had been through too much and wasn't prepared to wait until a woman matured. Children didn't interest him. He simply wanted a companion. If this didn't work out his parents had a whole string of widows and divorcees waiting to be tested over dinner. Some with children, some without. Ayesha was the preferred choice. She was still young enough to have children and she was educated. He had money and if they did get married he hoped she would stop working. Maybe then she could have some children, if she still could, especially after what had happened the last time around.

He smiled politely, blabbering on, trying to kill the awkward silence with light anecdotes but he could see that she was somewhere else. She was probably only here to keep her parents happy, probably had a boyfriend that no one knew about, probably a white one. This was more awkward than he could have imagined. Both here under duress from their parents. Aadil wondered what excuse he could use to break the news to them. Maybe he should just come clean. Tell them to stop.

Tea arrived and the waiter poured it into the tiny glasses in ceremonial style, holding the glass low while slowly elevating the teapot until the glass was below his waist and the teapot at shoulder height. He set the glasses down and waited in the wings until Aadil asked him to bring the bill. Aadil's conversational attempts had been reduced to pleasantries about the décor and how he had an early morning the following day. Ayesha smiled politely, glancing at her watch.

"Ayesha."

Ayesha focused. Something about his voice shook her back to the present. The light tone was gone from it. His face had changed, not cold, just serious.

"Look, I'm sorry you had to come here. I mean, I know …"

Ayesha interrupted, "No, I really enjoyed myself tonight." But she didn't believe the words coming from her mouth. She noticed his expression change, from pleasant to disappointed.

He held out his hand to stop her. "I think we're both adult enough to say what we mean. You're only here because of your parents and I'm only here because of my parents. This whole evening has been awkward. Let's just finish our tea and I'll drop you back at your place and we can just say whatever to get our parents off our backs. Okay? Sounds fair?"

Ayesha was taken aback. This kind of frankness was one of the last things she expected from the evening. She tried to say something but anything she said now would come out sounding like pity and she knew it. She had been rude. She had scarcely made an effort to make conversation.

The waiter returned with a blue folder. Inside was the bill and two foil-wrapped after-dinner mints. She reached over for her bag but

Aadil glared at her so she meekly put her bag down again. He pulled out his wallet, signed the bill and slipped his credit card into the folder. He waved at the waiter to catch his attention. Silence. Both tried to find something in the restaurant to occupy their attention so that they wouldn't have to make eye contact or conversation.

Ayesha smiled. "Why are you so irritated?"

Aadil glared at her but tried to mask his annoyance. "I'm not irritated."

Ayesha grinned cheekily. "I can see it on your face. You're irritated."

Aadil blinked slowly. He stared back at her. "Okay, let's see. Since we got here, you have smiled, nodded and looked at your watch as if it were going to disappear at any time. This is not my idea of an enjoyable dinner with someone I'd genuinely like to get to know a little better. In fact, this is not my idea of an enjoyable dinner, full stop."

Ayesha chuckled.

"So you think this is amusing?"

Ayesha shook her head. She was giggling.

"You think this is funny?" Aadil was visibly annoyed.

Ayesha found this even more amusing and as much as she shook her head to deny it, the more her giggling diminished her credibility.

"Let's go." Aadil stood up.

Ayesha reached out across the table and grabbed his hand. "Please sit down."

The giggling had stopped, although she was still smiling.

Aadil stood for a few seconds, looking around. No one in the restaurant was paying any attention. He sat down. "I think it is best we leave now." His voice was a controlled whisper.

"I'm not laughing *at* you."

Aadil's head tilted to one side, his eyes widening in disbelief.

"Well, not completely. It's just funny that we were both feeling the same."

Aadil's shoulders dropped as his mood changed from defensive to resigned.

"Look, let's start again, maybe really try to get to know each other. I mean it's still early and …"

Aadil interrupted her. "Thank you, but I honestly don't need your sympathy."

Ayesha's mood changed from frivolous to serious. "I don't give sympathy dates to anyone. I was just asking for us to start over. But suit yourself."

"I'm sorry. I wasn't thinking. Yes, I would like it if we could start over."

The doctor's face became softer. The couple got up when the waiter returned with the credit card. They walked slowly to the car. The conversation on the drive home was warmer and more honest than the dinner conversation and covered everything from music to politics to the Pakistani Moulana at the Moroccan Masjid. They laughed in between serious conversation about the different lives that they had both yearned for. The if-onlys increased until both agreed that their lives wouldn't be the same without the things they had endured. Ayesha shared a bit about her former husband and how madly in love they had been at university. How it all changed after a couple of years. Their jobs, their separate ideals, pressure from their families, everyone wanting them to have children. Aadil explained how he had been married once but that she had chosen wealth before love. He didn't mention his second marriage. He had given up and had poured himself into his work. He told her how his parents were nagging him to find a wife but he just couldn't see the point.

They arrived at the security gates of Ayesha's complex. She reached inside her bag and pulled out the remote. The gate whirred open slowly. Suddenly the car seemed congested. Awkwardness stiffened the atmosphere. What now? Aadil tried to work out what to do. They were just two adults out for dinner and he was dropping her off at home. He knew that if he tried anything and got the red light that would be the end of it. Ayesha would tell her mother, her mother would tell his mother and God knows who else. That's how things spread. Ayesha was in a similar predicament. As the car approached the front door she contemplated what to do. Invite him inside for coffee or thank him politely, shake his hand and say goodnight. It had been such a long time since she'd been on a date, let alone with someone whom she actually cared not to offend. What about the 'oh-no' look? If he gave her the oh-no look, she would be eternally embarrassed. The car stopped. Both tried to speak at the same time. Aadil insisted Ayesha go first.

"Would you like to come in for coffee?"

Ayesha couldn't believe how quickly the words had come out. If her mother could see her now, she would have told her she was being forward. Aadil hesitated. He could have said something about an early morning but that would sound clichéd and he *had* enjoyed himself since leaving the restaurant. He didn't want to hurt her. "Okay, one cup but I can't stay too long. I've got a heavy day tomorrow ... really."

Ayesha opened her door. "Well it's just coffee, nothing else." She rolled her eyes, realizing she had a talent for putting both feet in her mouth. She walked to the front door, opened the security gate and then the door, dashing inside to key in the alarm deactivation code.

Aadil followed. One awkward step after another. He positioned himself in a neutral position on the couch. It was a comfortable flat with an open-plan kitchen and a spacious lounge. Ayesha put the kettle on and told Aadil to make himself comfortable. She went upstairs to change her shoes.

They sat and spoke for hours, the coffee keeping them alert enough to chat animatedly. They forgot about their early morning appointments, opening up to each other. Ayesha talked about her divorce and the other woman, her miscarriage and what an asshole her ex-husband had become. Aadil spoke about his parents, growing up poor, how his parents had lost everything but tried to keep up appearances and how he'd made it his life ambition to ensure his parents lacked for nothing.

They lost track of time, before falling asleep on opposite ends of the couch, under the duvet that Ayesha had dragged from her bed.

Chapter 14

Slang and the two club bouncers walked into the warehouse ablutions. It was typical of all warehouse ablutions. Two toilets and one basin with the galvanized urinal shoved into a small corner. The small window cut into the wall was there because it had to be and for no other reason. Such facilities had been designed for the dregs who worked as non-skilled workers and who had long fed South African industry—functional, not aesthetically pleasing. For Slang, however, it was the perfect venue for his purpose. Poor ventilation, worse acoustics and located in an abandoned warehouse, far from prying eyes.

On a chair in the middle of the white-tiled bathroom was the barely alive first victim on the path to finding out the identities of the kidnappers. Slang had told his men about the kidnapping. What he avoided mentioning was the background to the kidnapping or that he was covering his own arse in the process. It wasn't as if the men cared anyway. They were here because it was a job. Slang was one of the few people who hired without papers. He paid them shit and got away with it. They had all put on industrial boots. The floor was an unholy mess of vomit and glue. Slang reached into his jacket pocket and pulled out three masks, the kind used by workers in high-dust areas. Not ideal but better than nothing. They slipped the masks on over their noses and mouths. The fumes from the confined space of the bathroom had had the desired effect, leaving the victim near death. He had started vomiting blood just before they came in but it hadn't killed him. Slang knew that he had his man, that he would soon have his name and the other kidnappers' identities.

"I'm not going to ask again. Give me the name of the person who hired you. I'll make all this stop."

The man in the chair was sobbing. His half-naked body was an inflamed red as if it would start bleeding at the slightest touch. His feet had been burned and cracked by the glue. His face was swollen from the beatings, his eyes mere slits. He had been vomiting, his mouth encrusted with dried blood and stomach acid. He wouldn't live long.

Slang nodded to one of the men who walked over to the window and punched out the taped-up wooden board, letting in the light and, more importantly, fresh air. The man whispered something. Slang looked at his men. He leaned over slightly, cocking his head, to hear what the man had to say. "You're gonna have to repeat that."

Again the man mumbled something barely audible. Slang looked at the man. He pulled out a knife, prodding it forcefully against the man's side. "One more time."

The man shouted out the information that would free him, maybe save his life. It came out like a primitive growl. "He's a drug dealer. They call him Sugaz. He works in Yeoville sometimes. His number is on my phone. He told me that all I had to do was make the calls. He would phone me and I would phone the old man. He gave me R10,000. That's all I know. I swear."

Slang stood up. "Cut his ropes. I said I would let you go when you gave me the information."

The man in the chair looked relieved. "I won't tell anyone. I promise."

Slang looked at him. "I believe you. Fire it up boys." He turned on his heels and strode out to the car.

The men lit a wad of paper that had been left in the corner, tossing it onto the sticky, half-dried glue. It ignited instantly, enveloping the man in the chair. He tried to scream but his throat only delivered a strangled gurgle. He tried to move, sliding from the chair onto the floor in an ungainly clatter. Black smoke from the burning glue quickly filled the air, clawing, choking, suffocating. The two men gathered up their things and left, closing the door behind them as if the victim were in some condition to escape. But Slang had ordered them to do that. No one questioned Slang's orders. They made their way to the car and drove off. Slang in the back. None looked back to confirm their handiwork.

The warehouse burned down and news reports speculated that the body found was of a young man who had probably tried to commit suicide or had accidentally set himself alight while "getting high on glue". The half-melted, empty alcohol bottles were a sign of debauchery gone tragically wrong.

Slang phoned the doctor on the clean number. "Ons is amper daar. Ek sal meer geld nodig. Die saak raak meer ernstig." *We're almost there. I'm going to need more money. This is getting serious.*

The doctor would drop off more money and Slang could then gather together some of the old team. He needed professionals he could trust, people who had a personal stake in these matters. Luckily he still maintained ties with some of his former 231 Battalion buddies. But they needed a bit of incentive to get moving. Besides, the money would be needed as a leash to keep them under control.

Chapter 15

Ayesha sat at her desk, gazing at the yellow post-it stuck on her computer screen. The director always made a point of using very big post-its so that you wouldn't miss them. He had obviously been in early while she was out at the clinic. Progress? A one-word question demanding information on the case. This was her first and only case since she had been back and she felt hopelessly out of it. The records at the clinic had turned up nothing. She had left an assistant investigator to comb through everything. The identity numbers were drawing a blank and she suspected the fingerprint record would also come up empty. The victim was still in her coma—his coma. She didn't even know how to refer to the victim. She tried to put it all together, thinking of the crime scene. Slowly she was adding up the bits of information. Something had to give. This wasn't random. The perpetrators knew the victim, that much was clear. The lab had found additional fingerprints. Three more sets as far as they could determine. Identifying them though was the problem. No criminal record. They had wanted to make the victim suffer, but why? They had wanted the victim to die slowly. But she—he—hadn't.

She reached over to the yellow manila folder on her desk. The folder itself was pitifully thin apart from the preliminary ME reports, the lab report and her own notes. Almost a week on and very little to show. She had to get her act together. She pulled out the evidence list, the list of items found in the victim's flat. Even the tools that had been extracted from the victim's genitals were listed. Ayesha searched the page. Something had to provide a lead. Near the middle was a small sub-heading 'Contents of handbag (found on floor)'. She read through the list: cell phone, lipstick, small mirror, make-up, notepad, pen, deposit slips, wallet, empty pill bottle (plastic). Ayesha clicked. Her regular GP. She jumped up from the desk and hurried to the evidence lock-up. Most of the victim's personal belongings had been sealed and locked away. The phone was important. It sat, charged, still on the duty officer's desk. There were no numbers on the phone other than work colleagues'. There were no next of kin listed, no friends, nothing. Since the identity had turned up false, it was hoped that someone might phone the cell and provide the real identity.

Ayesha retrieved the pill bottle. It was the plastic cylindrical kind, the type that pharmacists fill according to a prescription or mass-fill from bulk. She checked the label. Progesterone, Dr Wiley. There was a phone number. She smiled. This was a break. If she was lucky, she'd be able to establish the victim's identity and maybe get a lead on the perps. She dialled the number.

An older-sounding woman answered the phone. "The rooms of doctors Wiley and Vorster, how may I help you?"

Ayesha spoke slowly and very precisely. "Hi, I'm Investigator Mansoor. I'm phoning from the Special Crimes Unit. I'd like to speak to Dr Wiley please."

The woman on the other end hesitated. You could almost hear the cogs of her brain turning. "I'm afraid the doctor is busy right now. Can I take a message?"

Ayesha knew she was buying time. "Okay, could you ask him to please phone me back? It's extremely urgent." She read out her numbers, both office and cellular. She then double-checked to make sure that the woman had the numbers correct before asking her her name. "Meryl? Yes? Thank you, Meryl."

She replaced the receiver and almost immediately her cell phone buzzed. The caller ID displayed the director's number. "Morning?"

"Yes, morning, Ayesha, can you come to my office, please?"

"Sure, no problem. I'll be there shortly."

"Okay, see you now."

Ayesha gathered her papers together. The director would not be happy with her progress. He'd give her the usual speech about what the public expected from the SCU and what they deserved. And did she realize what her job description was? She was paid to cut through red tape and deliver results. She sighed. What else could she do? Her life was in turmoil. The events of the previous night still lingered at the back of her mind. Nothing had really happened. They had chatted until they'd both fallen asleep. Nothing more. This morning had been a bit awkward. But she liked Aadil. She thought she might see him again.

"There you go, my pretty friend," said Enrico Brandman, the head crime lab technician. "Freshly imported from Port Elizabeth."

"And what is this?"

"It's a hit on one set of the prints lifted from your crime scene. The other two are still being processed ... *and* your victim is classified. So you might have to speak to the boss about that."

"What do you mean classified?"

"Well, we checked the old SADF records like you asked but we've only got one match so far. Your victim is on there but her file is classified. Only one of the big dogs can access it."

Enrico had one of those perpetually rapid speech rhythms where it was entirely possible to miss everything he said because you were concentrating on the rhythm.

"Did you talk to the PE office?"

"Ja, I did, but you know how those guys are down on the beach?" He sniggered and left in his usual hurried fashion.

Ayesha considered the new evidence. She didn't know whether to laugh or cry. Ex-SADF. Both perp and victim. The victim in PE was also ex-SADF; also a transgender operation recipient. She would have to make contact with the PE office. Maybe they could exchange information. This wasn't coincidence. She breathed out deeply. The director was waiting for her.

Chapter 16

Ayesha knocked on the door. A cheerful voice told her to come in. She opened the door. The office was neatly stacked with piles of papers and files and filing cabinets containing even more important information. Bookcases lined the walls. Framed photos of the director with various bigwigs and the director accepting his appointment from the president, stared down from the walls. The director glanced up at Ayesha and motioned her to take a seat at the long, dark table in front of his desk. This is where most of the one-on-one meetings took place. The conversation was always direct and to the point. Usually he insisted on an agenda to work through because he didn't have the time to bounce around from case to case. He only really had one-on-one meetings with investigators working very high-profile cases, the kind the media fed on every day, and with the ADs, the assistant directors, who regulated the other investigators. The rest of his time was spent with politicians, parliamentarians and bureaucrats and at the unit's other offices around the country.

The director finished his call and shuffled around the desk, making his way to the long table. The table had six wooden chairs around it, though there were seldom that many people in his office at any one time.

"First things first. I met with the minister. I told him how far we are and he didn't seem too happy."

Ayesha tried to interrupt and explain herself but he waved away her attempt. "I know, I've been checking up myself. Let's see what progress you've made."

Ayesha shuffled through her papers. "Well, as you know, the victim is still in a coma. As I mentioned, the victim's ID didn't check out. All fake. The victim was also once the recipient of a transgender operation. I checked the transgender clinics, am still checking them, but so far no one has heard of her."

"So you're telling me you have nothing?" The director's eyes narrowed.

"I didn't say that. We did strike some new leads today. Firstly, I am waiting for her GP to phone me back. I managed to get his name off the empty pill bottle found with her personal belongings. And just before I came in, Enrico handed me this." She passed him the folder Enrico had given her. "We got a hit on one of the perps and we got a match on the victim but no identity yet."

The director scanned through the folder. He looked up, confused. "What do you mean no identity yet?"

"Well, I followed your advice and had the boys in the lab check through the old SADF records. They hit a match with one of the perps. They also hit a match with our victim. They are still checking out the other two sets. The criminal checks came up negative for all. However, the victim's file is classified. Maybe you can see what you can do about getting access?"

The director examined the file again, more carefully this time. He knew what Ayesha wanted of him. And he knew that the case had suddenly taken a quantum turn from a run-of-the-mill crime to a minefield of potential political and security ramifications. "Leave this file with me. In fact, leave the whole lot with me. I'll drop it off on your desk later this afternoon. Why don't you go and see that doctor? I'll make some calls ... maybe we'll have something by tomorrow morning."

Ayesha nodded. She didn't want to see the doctor just yet. But she knew that the director had some sensitive work on his hands. He continued scrutinizing the files. She stood up and excused herself. The director went over to his computer, a portable black notebook.

As she closed the door she saw him pick up his phone. She could imagine what was going through his head.

What was going on here, the director might wonder. Both former SADF. One the victim the other most likely her assailant. He would put good money on the other prints being former SADF. Both victims transgender patients. This smelt like a cover-up. Why? That was the problem with sweeping things under the carpet—they never stayed there. This was bigger than anyone imagined. And he could see where it was headed. It was a volcano of political mayhem waiting to explode.

Ayesha heard the muffled voice on the other side of the door. "I want the following files sent to my office immediately. Have you got a pen and paper? No pen and paper! Where the hell do they find you idiots? Yes, well take down this case number and deliver it to my office *now*, not tomorrow, *now*! I'm speaking to? Sergeant Tshabalala. Good. Sergeant, if that file is not here on my desk by twelve, I'm coming to get it personally. And you do *not* want me to have to do that. Do you understand? Good."

The director put the phone down.

Chapter 17

Slang sat in his car, studying the old face-brick, railway-worker house. This used to be a whites-only area. Government housing for government bureaucrats. The Nationalist government had made it policy that all whites, especially poor whites, had adequate housing—that's where the votes lay. All the houses looked the same, the same design on identically sized plots. Some of the original tenants had built brick walls in front, while others were content with the wire-mesh fence and matching steel gates that had long since rusted away. The area was blacker now. When the Group Areas Act had been scrapped—the statute dictating where people could live and own property depending on the colour of their skins—many blacks had moved into areas previously denied them. Most of the whites had sold up and moved out. The blacks who moved in could barely afford to relocate but they wanted a better life and living in what was previously a whites-only area gave them that illusion. The area deteriorated, not because there were now blacks living here but because the new owners had spent every cent they had in moving out of the townships into white suburbia. It was inevitable that some houses would fall into decay to be repossessed and auctioned off. There were still white people living in the area but it was essentially a black suburb.

Slang watched a black prostitute saunter past. Children played in the street with a plastic bottle. Black children and white children were chasing one another. The prostitute stopped by the car window, her top hanging low enough to display her wares. Slang looked at the orange top under the denim jacket, at the short skirt, the black marks around the neck of her loose-fitting top. She wasn't wearing underwear. Her eyes were bloodshot and she smelled of cheap wine, the kind of wine sold in foil bags and found on the floor of working-class liquor stores. Slang looked at her. She leaned over, further exposing her cleavage. She smiled, revealing bright pink gums and a gap-tooth smile.

"How much?"

The prostitute smiled broadly. She stood up straight, her one hand on her chest. "Twenty rands."

"No, too much." Slang pretended to lose interest. All part of the art of negotiation.

"I let you do anything. You can put anywhere."

Slang smiled. The prostitute smiled. The deal was almost done.

"I want to see money first."

Slang smiled again. He looked at her face. It was obvious that she had been in a transaction or two where she had not been paid. Maybe that's how she'd lost the tooth. Pimps on the street weren't interested in excuses and were merciless on their girls. It didn't matter if they killed them. There were more joining the trade every day; plenty more where they came from.

Slang pulled out his wallet and slipped out a twenty-rand note. He showed it to the prostitute. She tried to snatch at it as Slang pulled his hand away. "No."

She looked upset.

"I want you to go knock on that door. I want you to ask for Ricardo. When he comes to the door, you bring him here. When you come here, I'll give you the money. Okay?"

The prostitute nodded, but looked confused. She had been with many white men before, old ones, young ones, fat ones, thin ones, rich ones, poor ones, nice ones, and bad ones. This was the first time she'd be paid to do something that didn't involve sex. She didn't like it. Something was wrong. She nodded but she didn't like it.

Slang watched as she walked across the road to the face-brick house with the peeling white gutters and the rusted mesh fence. She kept turning back to make sure that he wasn't driving off without paying. He watched her walk tentatively up the steps and knock on the front door. He watched her wait as she watched him from the porch. The door opened. He could see her speaking to someone but he couldn't see to whom. A head popped out for a moment. The woman looked confused. She scurried from the porch, back to the car.

"I called him. Where is my money?"

Slang looked at her. He looked at the house. A curtain moved. Someone was watching. He handed over the money, started the car and pulled up in front of the house. He hooted once. A man came out with a jacket slung across his arm. He closed the door behind him and walked down to Slang's passenger door.

Slang wound down the window. "Jy vis nog nie in die donker water nie? Klim in, Ricardo, ek het werk vir jou." *Don't you fish in the dark water yet? Jump in, Ricardo, I've got work for you.*

Ricardo got in as they drove off, towards Hillbrow.

Slang nodded to himself. Just the other two now …

Chapter 18

The doctor's rooms were a converted house. Ayesha approached the receptionist. The meeting with the director had ended abruptly. Obviously there were phone calls to make but something was off. A woman was standing at the counter with her young son. The child didn't look sick nor did the mother.

The receptionist filled out a receipt and appointment card. "Well, we'll see you next month, okay, young man?" She had a thick Scottish accent, definitely not the woman Ayesha had spoken to earlier on the phone. "Okay, then. Goodbye." Turning to Ayesha, "Can I help you?"

"Hi, I spoke to Meryl earlier?"

"Ooh Meryl, I'm afraid she's off for the day, works mornings only. Maybe I can help you?"

"Mornings only? I wish I was that lucky," Ayesha said lightly.

"Well, we mere mortals have to keep things running you know. Now, how can I help you?"

Ayesha sighed. "Actually, I need to see Dr Wiley? It's very urgent."

Ma'am, these are doctor's rooms, everyone thinks it's urgent. Do you have an appointment?"

This was the part Ayesha hated. Why couldn't she be persuasive enough for people to simply accept at face value what she was asking. She reached into her coat pocket and pulled out her wallet, flashing her official credentials. "Police matter. I would prefer if I could speak to him now."

The big Scottish lady behind the counter was expressionless. She merely stood up and walked around the back. A few people in the waiting room looked up. Ayesha smiled politely, studying the non-existent artwork on the ceiling.

A short, balding man with thick spectacles came up to the counter. He looked about fifty. He appeared both bewildered and irritated at the same time. His face tightened as if trying to control himself. "I am Doctor Wiley, how can I help you?"

"Is there somewhere we can talk privately?"

The people in the waiting room pretended to read their magazines but were clearly trying to listen in. The doctor looked around. He too noticed the audience. "Sharon, show ... Detec ..."

"Investigator Mansoor," Ayesha corrected.

"Very well. Sharon, please show Investigator Mansoor to my office."

Ayesha sat down at the desk in the doctor's office. The doctor, still annoyed, took his seat. "Now, what is so urgent that you had to make a spectacle of yourself in my reception?"

Ayesha looked at the expression on the doctor's face and hoped that this wasn't his usual bedside manner. "I apologize for the inconvenience. I am working on a case that involves a patient of yours. I was hoping you could help me by answering a few questions."

"Let me warn you now that if it involves a patient, I cannot help you. They do still have the right to privacy."

"I know. But it could go a long way in helping me solve the case. It's about Ellen Fischer."

The doctor's eyes widened briefly. "What about her?"

"She was involved in a brutal rape. She's fighting for her life in intensive care. Her medical reports show that she was the recipient of a transgender operation. What do you know about this?"

"I don't know anything about the rape. And as for any transgender operation, well, that is privileged information, I'm afraid."

"I realize that. But, as Ms Fischer is in a coma and can't answer the questions herself, perhaps you could help us find out who did this to her."

"I don't understand. What does her status have to do with your investigation?"

"Okay," Ayesha let out a long sigh. "I'm going to share some very confidential information with you." She knew this might win his trust. "We believe that her rape had something to do with her status. We know that she didn't have the operation at one of the specialist clinics. That's all I can really tell you for now. What I need to know is how long you have been treating her and …"

The doctor cut her short. "This is not enough for me to share a patient's file with you. I'm sorry. If you want to access her file, you are going to have to get a court order first. Now if you don't mind …" The doctor stood up.

Ayesha thanked him. He still appeared irritated. She had got to him but he'd stood firm. She walked outside. Her phone buzzed. It was the hospital. Ellen Fischer had just regained consciousness.

Chapter 19

Director de Villiers sat at his desk. Across from him sat a man wearing a suit a size too small. He was a tall man with thin, greasy hair. He was perspiring so much that his skin seemed to be leaking. But he wasn't nervous. He was just one of those unremarkable men you wouldn't notice even if they walked right past you. However, the man sitting across the desk from Director de Villiers was not your regular government employee. It was his job *not* to be noticed. His job was simple—information. He was formerly a field operative who had worked in London for the NSA—the National Security Agency. Now he sat in an office directing more than three hundred operatives in South Africa and across the globe. Unlike his former colleagues, he hadn't lost his job when the new government took over. Speculation was that he either 'knew where the bodies were buried' or had worked both sides. Either way, he was the man you went to when you needed something or wanted something done.

"Director de Villiers, it's a sensitive issue." His voice was high and strained. His spectacles sat on the tip of his nose.

"All I want are the files. I have security clearance for them. I don't see why we have to have this conversation. The minister himself …"

"The minister, with all due respect, is second generation. He has no clue what has been done and what has to be done."

"I don't understand. All I need are those files. What's the problem?"

"This comes from the top. From the president himself. I don't really know what's happenening in your investigation but those files are off limits. That's the deal."

"Those files might be able to solve a vicious attack."

"Look, I understand your position, I really do. But you have to see the bigger picture here. If news were to get out, who knows what secrets would be leaked. And then what? Some people would lose their jobs, others would go to jail. The public reaction itself could bring the government to its knees. This may seem an important case to you but it's only a very small part of a very big picture."

"So what do I have to do to get to see those files?"

"I'll let you look at them but you cannot, I emphasize cannot, use them as evidence or to secure evidence. You may not utilize them or refer to them in any way whatsoever. You have to find another way. Do you understand?"

The director drew a deep breath, then let out a long, weary sigh. "Okay, when?"

The man reached into a tattered leather briefcase and pulled out several files. "The files .... as you requested."

"If you were going to give them to me, why the song and dance?"

"I wanted you to understand the seriousness, and the danger, of what you're getting into."

The man stood up, set to leave. He picked up his battered briefcase.

"Don't you want your files back?"

"No. Those are copies. I have more. I know you'll know what to do with them when you're done. I'll show myself out."

The man walked out of the office, closing the door behind him. The director looked down at the pile of manila files. String bound. He hoped he wouldn't have to use them but somehow he knew instinctively he would.

Chapter 20

Four men sat in the darkened room of Slang's office. CCTV monitors flickered. Occasionally he was lucky enough to spot a celebrity who, with a little encouragement, would take a girl up to one of the private suites. Showing them a copy of the videotape was usually enough to get them to cough up.

Slang had asked his bouncers to stand guard outside the office; he wanted no interruptions. The other two 'connections' had been almost too easy to track down after he'd found Ricardo. Firstly he'd found Mark 'Soutie' Simpson, an Englishman who had run off to the army because he didn't want to go to university. His parents, concerned that their son would not survive the army, tried every means possible to convince him otherwise. They even tried to bribe him. But he'd simply disappeared one day and they never saw him again. Soutie, although 'nat agter die oore'—*wet behind the ears*— when he arrived at training camp, proved to be a real find. It was inevitable that he would find his way into 231 Battalion. It was in the former homeland of the Transkei that Soutie, leading a group of no more than five men, went into a village and 'necklaced' everyone in sight. 'Necklacing' involved putting a tyre around a victim's neck, dousing it with petrol and setting it alight. The village was near the KwaZulu homeland border which meant that the act would further exacerbate tensions between the traditional Xhosa Transkei and the predominantly Zulu KwaZulu. Keep them fighting among themselves and hopefully they would have no time for mischief with the whites. That was the principle. Soutie loved the army but when things changed he found it difficult to adjust. He found himself frequently gazing at the bottom of a cheap bottle of whisky. When he did crawl out, it was to work as a security guard on Saturday afternoons at the rugby stadium. The money was just enough to last the week. As long as he was sober at work he was fine. The problem came in the off-season but he usually made a plan.

Wouter Verster had moved from 231 Battalion to the Security Police Special Branch. His speciality came in the form of torture techniques. In the army, captured guerrillas would be left exclusively to Wouter. His information-gathering techniques were believed to have saved many white South African lives. When the Special Branch heard of his exploits in South West Africa he was transferred to a desk job, to avoid an international scandal, but secretly, to impart his skills to a broader base. He didn't complain. He was one of those who believed you never argued with your superiors especially when you were fighting for your country and your people. A staunch Christian, he believed he was doing God's work in saving South Africa from the unholy. When everyone scattered after the death knell of apartheid, he was left with a set of ideals that were redundant. There were no superiors to report to. They'd all made sure they were clean, saving their own skins. He found a job selling second-hand cars for Ahmed's Quality Used Cars and became a part-time youth pastor.

Slang stood up, walked over to the VCR and popped in the tape that Dr Blignaut had given him.

"We didn't come here to watch videos. I thought you promised us jobs," Soutie said to the amusement of the others.

"Shut up. I said I had a job for you. Watch the video first and then we'll talk."

The men watched, silently, unmoving. The tape came to an end. Slang got up, addressing the men. "Twenty-five each. Ten now, fifteen when the job's done." He tossed three beige envelopes on the desk. The men did not react.

Wouter Verster spoke first. "Slang, I would like to help you. But that part of my life is over." Wouter knew exactly what they were being asked to do. "I would like to help you find these people but that's not my problem anymore. When everything ended we were left on our own. No one stood up for us. All the bosses ran away or made deals and we had to make our own way."

Slang nodded. "Ricardo? You're very quiet."

Ricardo looked up. He looked at Wouter. "I need the money so you can count me in. What do I have to do?" Something had changed in Ricardo. The resurrection of his old self, the slow mutation into someone he'd never forgotten but thought had long since disappeared. Slang recognized this. They had all suffered their share of demons but being resurrected was more painful. The things they had seen, shared, experienced, all of it filed away as if it were someone else's dream, someone else's nightmare. Now it was standing there in front of them. And they were scared.

"Soutie?" Slang asked.

Mark Simpson was a tall, lanky man. He wouldn't look out of place opening the bowling on a cricket pitch. He was silent for a moment. The money was what held his attention. He looked down. "Count me in."

Slang looked back to Wouter. "That just leaves you."

Wouter tried to say something but Slang raised his hand. "I know you've found your Christ. I know you've tried to make peace with the Lord over your previous life. But this is not government work. We are fighting for a helpless, innocent someone who was murdered by cowards. Fucking abomination. So you tell me you can just sit there as a good Christian with a clear conscience and know that you could have brought these killers to justice? That you could have done something for that poor baby, but didn't? We'll probably all go to hell for what we did but maybe, just maybe, we can save ourselves by doing something right." Slang fixed his gaze on Wouter.

Wouter felt like a hole was burning into him. "We aren't going to bring them to justice. This is not police work. You don't want us to find them and hand them over. You want us to kill them. That's not justice."

Slang interrupted, "Would you rather have them go to court and go free with the rest of the criminals? You read the papers. Rapists, murderers, they all go free. We deal with this in our own way. I need you on this. I need to find these people. The police are still looking for clues but they will find them in the end. I want to get them before the cops do. I need you."

Wouter screwed his eyebrows. "I need time. I have to think about it. I have a lot to think about here."

"You've got until tomorrow." Slang's tone was businesslike, his words cold and precise. "Come back tomorrow, Wouter. If you're not here at two, then I'll take it that you want out. I don't need to tell you all that this doesn't leave this room. We'll sort out the details tomorrow."

Slang barely glanced at them as they shuffled out. He had much on his mind, his priority being money and equipment. He picked up the phone. There was a brief pause. "I need one hundred and fifty and I need it by tomorrow midday. You know the procedure. We got names and I got a team. It will be done soon enough."

Now he only needed Wouter's buy-in.

Chapter 21

Ellen Fischer was conscious but she was nowhere near *compos mentis*. The nurse explained to Ayesha how she was on very powerful painkillers, that she had almost died. The trip was pointless. Ayesha knew that questioning her now would only lead to more frustration. Besides, she needed to get hold of a court order. Fucking doctor. She went to the door of Ellen Fischer's private ward. She peered in—wondering how someone so broken could have made it this far. What had Ellen Fischer done, or been, to have attracted such brutal attention? She stood awhile, watching the human wreckage in the bed. She thought about what her mother had said when she had learned of her husband's leaving. "Just remember, be grateful, there are always people worse off than you." At the time Ayesha had made a sarcastic comment about being thankful to God. She didn't feel particularly grateful and thought her mother was being her usual insensitive self. Now as she looked at the damaged thing with the stitches and the bandages, she was thankful, thankful for her own life.

Her phone rang. She reached for it and answered. A nurse glared at her but she ignored her.

It was the director. He was very brief. "Come here immediately. We need to speak."

Ayesha wondered what she had done. She got into her car. The buzzing phone vibrated restlessly. She reached for it. It was a message from Aadil. A man of few words, his message simply said, "What are you doing tonight? Supper? Call me when you have a sec. AM".

She smiled inwardly. She felt she had grown to like him, she had to give her mother that. The woman definitely knew her stuff. She started the car and drove to the office. She didn't know what kind of storm to prepare for. She had to phone Aadil but maybe after the meeting. She would probably want to speak to a friendly voice anyway ... after the director.

Chapter 22

It was after four in the afternoon and the office was almost deserted. The director's light was on, his blinds rolled down. Ayesha went to her desk and dumped her things. She gathered her thoughts for a second. There was no way of knowing what he would say or what the meeting was about. She tried to think of where she might have screwed up. She stared the door down. In less than a minute I will know what's going on, that's if I go now, she told herself. The call had made her nervous. Her director had said little but his tone had made her nervous. She took a deep breath and walked up to the director's door. She knocked and walked in.

"Come in, sit down." The director was facing his PC, a cigarette burning in his ashtray. The building was a no-smoking zone and for the most part the director didn't smoke but he'd been known to light a stick or two in the late afternoon.

Ayesha sat down apprehensively. "You said …"

"Yes, I'm glad you came. I'm pulling you off the case."

If the director had thought she'd go easily, her reaction was not at all what he'd expected. She looked straight at him. She showed no obvious disappointment but there was a simmering anger. With an effort she controlled her emotions, "Can I ask why or am I not allowed to?"

"I understand your surprise. You must be shocked."

The truth was that as soon as he'd read the files, he'd known that there was but one option open to him—pull Ayesha Mansoor off the case and hand it over to the professionals who would dispose of the case in such a way that it would never even make the papers.

She was not equipped to deal with the intricacies of the case. These men would eat her alive. That's what they were trained to do. Ellen Fischer was still alive. Imagine what they would do when they found out.

"I'm not shocked. I mean, what's there to be shocked about? You pull me off a case like this and don't even bother giving a reason. I mean that's not shocking. Not at fucking all."

"It would be better for you if you were removed from the case with immdediate effect. We can hand it over to a more specialized branch. Trust me."

Ayesha let out a sigh. "At least tell me why. You owe me that much."

The director reached to the side of his PC and pulled out the three manila files. "What I am about to show you is sensitive. Those fingerprints you pulled? They came up. As you noticed … classified. We know that they are ex-SADF and that's about all. I got these files today. These are the names of the owners of the fingerprints. Including our victims. It doesn't make for pleasant reading. And the one thing I have established is that these men are dangerous. I know them. I was one of them. This case is bigger than you can imagine and I don't believe our branch is suitably equipped to deal with it."

He passed the files to Ayesha. What he meant was that *she* was not equipped to deal with it.

"You can read them. But you cannot leave my office. Those files have to be destroyed before I leave this building tonight. I'll give you a few minutes." With that he got up and left the office. The cigarette burned itself out in the ashtray.

Ayesha began to read. What had started out as a brutal rape had now developed into a case with serious implications. They were not dealing with serial killings, they were dealing with assassinations. The case was actually older than she could have expected. From the fingerprints found at the scenes, she learned the identities of the victim at the crime scene in Port Elizabeth, the victim in Pretoria— Ellen Fischer—and of one of the suspects who had used the tools to torture Ellen Fischer in her apartment.

The director was away for over an hour. Ayesha read through military records, personal histories, current status and contact details. This was her case. No one was going to take it away from her. She owed that much to Ellen Fischer. She had to make a point of seeing her and questioning her as soon as possible.

When the director eventually returned she closed the files. He studied her for a reaction, something that would justify his rationale of taking her off the case. But there was a fire in her. He could see it in her eyes. "You're not going to drop this, are you?"

She shook her head slowly. "I think we both know how far this will go. Ellen Fischer won't get her day in court and these bastards will disappear. I think we owe it to her."

The director heaved a sigh, "Look, I am not promising anything. I still have to report to the minister. The final decision is his and his alone. I don't know how far up this goes. So you may be taken off whether you like it or not. Do you understand? Until then I am in charge. You report to me and only me. You discuss this with no one. Am I clear?"

Ayesha nodded. More than clear. The director sat down and Ayesha turned to leave. She was scared and excited all at the same time. She had to phone Aadil. Maybe they could grab a bite together.

The director watched her leave. He admired her courage but he knew they were playing a dangerous game. Maybe he *could* keep her on the case. Tighter control without letting her get too close. Protect her at the very least.

Chapter 23

It had been a week since the three men had sat in Slang's office after having been recalled for unofficial duty. Slang had told them that Dr Blignaut had increased their payment to fifty thousand each. He thanked them for doing what the police no longer did—protecting innocent people and dispensing justice to those who deserved it. They were given a cell phone and some money for expenses. He gave them the last lead he had. It was their job to finish things and make it look like the work of ordinary criminals.

The drug dealer had been short work. Sugaz had given up the names of his cohorts after Mark Simpson had cut off his toes with a pair of bolt-cutters. Wouter had persuaded Sugaz to phone the two 'worker bees', as he called them, and ask them to come over as he had another job for them. The two men duly arrived, were bound with electrical wires and shot twice through the back of the head. The flat itself was in a rundown part of Yeoville. Gunshots and screaming people were the norm. No one bothered calling the cops because most residents were there illegally and cops meant complications.

Sugaz gave up the names of his employers too. He spilled everything. How he didn't kill the baby himself, how he put the baby's body in a black bag with newspaper and had thrown the bag out with the garbage. But he didn't kill the baby. Greg and Ellen had. He'd sent the parcel. That was what he was paid for. Ricardo and Wouter beat him senseless afterwards and left him semi-conscious on the floor. He tried to mumble something but only bubbles of spit and blood came out of his mouth. Mark gave the order to burn the flat.

The men sat in the car across the road as the flat and then the whole building went up in flames, in one vast inferno. Winter fires were a regular occurrence. These buildings were old and no one would bother tracing the origins of the fire. The doctor and Slang had been very specific—leave no trace behind. And they had been around long enough to know that. They sat and watched floors collapse on each other. People screaming and fleeing. Another winter fire. People trying to keep warm. Arson investigations only happened in the movies.

They had spent two days driving to Port Elizabeth. Greg Swart, a local businessman, was one of the names that had come up. Slang told them he would get back to them with all the information they needed. They spent a couple of days cruising around Port Elizabeth, getting a feel for the place. They knew what they needed to do but not where.

Slang did get back to them. Greg Swart, former SADF member, discharged after a period at 1 Military Hospital. Slang gave them the address. The men drove to Swart's business and waited.

It was two days of following and waiting. They eventually caught up with him at a nightspot hangout. He was too drunk to walk really, let alone drive. Mark pretended to be an old friend and offered to get him home. No one noticed really. They walked to Greg's car. Ricardo and Wouter were waiting. All three proceeded to beat Greg. None uttered a single word. They picked him up and threw him in the car. Ricardo drove Greg's car. They drove along the beachfront until they found an abandoned building. Greg was dragged from the car and forced to kneel on the gravel. They stripped him down to his underwear. Greg's eye was half closed from the beating he'd taken in the car park. The three men spoke to each other, soft mutterings, barely audible. Mark and Ricardo walked up behind Greg. Greg said something about discounts. A double-tap through the back of the head. Wouter mumbled something into a cell phone and got into the car with Mark and Ricardo. Greg's body twitched on the gravel. A large pool of blood, matted hair and skull lay where the top of his head had been. The three men drove off.

Port Elizabeth had been cleaned. Now they knew who they were looking for and where she was. She would have nowhere to turn, nowhere to run. The three men had cut off her contacts. The final chapter was almost within sight. Sugaz had been very clear as to his employers' identities. He didn't ask many questions, but he did notice that Greg and Ellen looked odd for some reason. As if they were wearing disguises. But they had money. And he was certain they were the only people because he had only ever dealt with them. They made the decisions and they paid his expenses. They seemed to know what they were doing. They gave very specific instructions on how things were to be done. They asked for the tape to be included with the parcel that was to be delivered. Mark Simpson believed him. With his toes cut off, why bother lying?

For the three men who had for so long been hiding from themselves and society, they were now bloodily and gloriously reincarnated.

Chapter 24

They sat in the food court of the mall. Aadil was talking but Ayesha was still dazed after her afternoon with the director. What had she got herself into? The reality of the situation was slowly beginning to sink in.

Eventually Aadil asked, "What's the matter?"

The question seemed to surprise her, as if she had forgotten Aadil was even there. "I'm sorry. I'm not being good company."

"It's fine."

It was the kind of thing men said when they were anything but fine. Ayesha sensed his annoyance. She reached over and held his hand. It was an unexpected yet welcome gesture of concern and apology. Although they had become close and there was definite mutual interest, they were still to take this first big step. Holding hands. He was taken aback but tried to behave as if it was nothing out of the ordinary.

"You look like you've had a bad day. Why don't you tell me about it?"

She looked up at him. They'd grown closer than she'd realized. "I don't know where to begin."

"At the beginning?"

"It's not that easy. I don't even know where the beginning is anymore. My first case back is a lot more complex than I expected. It's draining having to keep it together when you know everyone is just waiting for you to crack. I *cannot* crack. Not on something like this. I know they want me off but I refuse to let them bully me. If you give up on a case, you'll never get anywhere. I can't afford it. I've told too many people that this is what I wanted and I cannot fail now."

The steely veneer she'd put on for her boss had disappeared. Aadil made her feel safe enough to let her guard down.

He reached across and squeezed her hand. They finished their supper and talked mostly about Aadil's work. Although Ayesha tried to make small talk, her mind was on the woman—or man—lying in hospital whom she would soon have to question.

They eventually left, long after they had finished their meal. He insisted on driving behind her to make sure she got home safely. And even though she told him she would be fine, he refused to take no for an answer.

She pulled into the driveway of her apartment complex as Aadil flicked his lights twice and drove off. Ayesha was exhausted. It had been a long day. Tomorrow would be longer. She undressed and stood in her underwear, rummaging in her closet for an old T-shirt. She slipped it on, unclipped her bra and jumped into bed, switching the bedside light off. She was about to nod off when she reached over to her cell phone. She made a 'missed call' to her father's cell. If he didn't receive the missed call every night when she got home he would have the cavalry out looking for her. She closed her eyes, thinking jumbled thoughts of what she'd read that afternoon in the director's office but sleep overtook her within seconds.

Chapter 25

An unmarked vehicle was parked across the road from Ahmed's Used Cars. More specifically, its occupants were watching a man by the name of Wouter Verster. There were several vehicles on duty in three teams—all doing surveillance work. They had come in early that morning. The office was in the process of getting a court order. One team was checking on incoming and outgoing calls from Verster's mobile phone while another was checking his banking records. Still another team was tasked with searching his house. They had enough evidence to convict him but it was obvious he didn't work alone. On the word of the director this case was more than what it seemed and involved multiple suspects—all of whom had the potential to flee — had one been arrested. Everything was kept deliberately low key.

Verster lived on his own. Like most men with his type of background he found it difficult to maintain a normal relationship. Or rather, partners found it difficult to cope with him. Many theorists dubbed it post-traumatic stress disorder combined with a male South African mentality that prevented them from getting help. The result was strained and broken relationships. This meant that Verster's type ground out an existence and lived on their own. No families, no wives, no kids. Not that they didn't have them but it was a past from another person's life; someone who was dead for all intents and purposes.

While Verster was at work, a team of specialists searched his house. The place was sparsely decorated, depressing, a single man's house. Wouter Verster had been married and had two sons. After leaving the employ of the South African government, the effects of alcoholism, stress, unemployment and depression had destroyed his marriage. One day he had come home to find his wife and children gone. He tried in vain to find her which forced him deeper into the bottle. He eventually gave up when the Sheriff of the Court delivered a restraining order barring him from contacting her, her family members or his sons. He could have appealed but he didn't bother. She remarried and moved to the coast. He eventually found salvation in a Christian outreach group. He tried to quit drinking only to lapse time and time again. The ministry helped him through his alcoholism and he found new vigour in his rediscovery of Jesus. He also came to accept the situation with his ex-wife and his sons.

The team scanned carefully through the house. They found nothing important. Scraps of burnt paper, an envelope with about two hundred rand stashed in a jacket pocket in the cupboard. They found several pistols and revolvers untidily hidden. The team leader was tempted to remove the ammunition in case they had to arrest him at some stage but decided against it. Verster would know that someone had been through his things. He would alert the others. They left the house as they'd found it.

Wouter Verster, though, had noticed the surveillance vehicles across the road that were changed at regular intervals. By lunchtime he had seen the same three vehicles several times—a mini-bus taxi without passengers, a municipal truck and a Telkom vehicle. It was obviously suspicious. He reached into his pocket and was about to pull out his cell phone but changed his mind. He walked inside the office, turning his back to the road. The receptionist was busy typing. Ahmed's Used Cars was not a showroom set-up. It was more a parking lot with brightly coloured prices splashed on the windshields of cars five years too old for conventional vehicle financing but Ahmed offered in-house finance at reasonable rates.

Verster took out his phone, shaking it and tapping it several times. "Ag, Sunette, can I use your phone to send a SMS to my landlady?

My phone is broken again."

The receptionist looked up at Verster. "Just don't make a habit of it. Airtime doesn't grow on trees, you know!" She reached into her bag and slid the leather-encased phone across the desk. She was about thirty but looked forty going on fifty. Apparently she had been quite a looker in her day. But years of smoking and drinking had left their indelible mark on her. Her blotchy skin looked like it was preserved by alcohol and her teeth were stained brown from a lifetime of smoking. She also wore too much make-up.

He picked up the phone, smiled and sent a message: "Hi, just to let you know that we have a new range of vehicles at affordable rates. Please come in today and inquire about our specials. Ask for Wouter".

He handed the phone back but not before deleting the sent message and the delivery report. "Thanks doll," he smiled at her.

He went back outside to see to a customer in the lot. The Telkom truck was now parked across the road. No technicians working on any lines. The truck was just parked there. He was being watched. That much he knew. Something was wrong. Obviously. He had to warn the others.

Across the road a technician and an operative watched Verster talking to the receptionist. The director had given the case a higher priority that morning but had given no reason. Band two meant that what they were dealing with was highly sensitive and suspects were to be treated as armed and dangerous at all times. So far Verster had not tumbled to them or if he had he wasn't acting like he had anything to worry about. He was a good salesman and had sold three vehicles that morning. So far the day had been bland. Nothing exciting. The team that had searched the house had come up with nothing—apart from some minor, predictable contraband such as the hand weapons.

Word from the director was that he had taken direct control of all operations. And their orders were simple. Watch everything Wouter Verster does and record it. Write it down, minute by minute. The next shift would take over in an hour. Time moved slowly during surveillance.

Chapter 26

Dr André Blignaut was a squat man with huge, bulging eyes. Slang thought he looked like he was about to explode at any second, almost apoplectic. As much as the doctor tried to dress down and look inconspicuous he just did not fit in with the surroundings in Slang's office. He pulled out two thick, brown envelopes and placed them on the desk. He was grateful for what Slang and his men had accomplished. His daughter, Marissa, and her husband had separated. Chances of reconciliation looked remote. André Blignaut didn't regret that. If there was anything good that had come from all this, it was the fact that his daughter would be rid of that husband. It was a terrible price to pay but the sacrifice wouldn't be without some reward.

Slang rambled on and on about what his team had done. Ellen Fischer had been one of the first in the programme. No, she wasn't dead. But there was no way she could survive, even in hospital. He had someone keeping an eye on her. If she did improve—it wouldn't be for long, he promised. Of course most people would have died after that sort of attack. The doctor didn't have to worry—she wouldn't talk—regardless. There was evidence of her involvement in the kidnapping if she did.

A light flashed inside the deep, dark recesses of the doctor's mind. What did he mean there was evidence to prove her involvement if she opened her mouth? She wasn't supposed to be breathing let alone talking?

The doctor stood up, his eyes set to pop out of their sockets. "I want you to finish the job I paid you to do." His voice was controlled.

The icy steeliness left no room for ambiguity or misunderstanding. "I don't want to take any chances with that cunt in the hospital." There was a white sliver of spit on his bottom lip. He got up, leaving the envelopes on the desk and made to leave. "And don't think I haven't protected myself either."

Slang sat down. The implications of what the doctor said were obvious. The doctor knew that Slang could have had him killed or have done it easily enough himself. He should have thought. Fuck— the sneaky bastard! His phone buzzed on the desk. He reached across and snatched it.

A text message from a strange number: "Hi, just to let you know that we have a new range of vehicles at affordable rates. Please come in today and inquire about our specials. Ask for Wouter."

Wouter? Something was wrong. Slang stood up and went to the cupboard where he kept a few changes of clothes. He pulled out an ugly red tartan jacket and a tattered cap. The cap had a picture of a Blue Bull standing on its hind legs with a ring through its nose. An old rugby supporter's cap. He kept clothes in his office for various reasons. Most of the time he used them to slip out the back door incognito. He picked up the brown envelopes, stuffed them inside his pocket and left. On the way out, almost as an afterthought, he grabbed a small pistol he kept behind the filing cabinet near the door. A throwaway. He paused. He looked at the firearm. It was a nine-millimetre Baby Browning. He stood for a few seconds, contemplating something. What if he himself was being watched? What if it was a set-up? There were too many questions and there was no way of finding out without getting closer to the action. He turned and went across to the desk. At the bottom of the three drawers was a smaller, almost unnoticeable drawer he had installed himself. He pulled it open. Two magazines and a nine-millimetre Beretta. There was also a black metallic tube. He screwed it onto the barrel. He slid one of the magazines into the gun and cocked it, aiming at the couch. The silencer's alignment was true. Good enough.

This was supposed to be a simple job. Nothing complicated. Now things were getting complicated, messy. He unscrewed the silencer and slipped the Beretta into his jacket pocket. He took the Baby Browning and dropped it into his trouser pocket. Things might indeed get sticky and it was best to be prepared. One could never be too careful.

Silently he prayed to God, asking him to simplify matters. He hoped Wouter was in one piece.

Slang approached Ahmed's Used Cars with caution. He could see the tacky attempt at a Las Vegas-type sign. He needed to park away from the lot. If Wouter was in trouble then he was probably being watched and, if he was being watched, Slang needed to remain as inconspicuous as possible. He sat in the car for some time, considering his next move, tapping the steering wheel. He removed the gun and silencer from his pocket. He screwed the silencer onto the barrel and put the gun back into the pocket. He needed to be prepared in case Wouter was setting him up, voluntarily or under duress, or if there were undercover cops involved, ready to pounce. He took a deep breath and got out of the car. He walked casually up to the lot, approaching with care. A municipal vehicle, one police van and a mini-van with a mother and some school kids were stopped at the traffic lights up ahead. There were one or two men trying to hawk black garbage bags and trinkets. Various cars and drivers. As yet he couldn't make out anything suspicious. He came to the lot but didn't enter at once. He scanned the immediate area. If there was something to worry about he would have been made already, in which case he would have to be on his toes. He noticed Wouter talking to a young couple by a white Mazda Midge. He approached and started looking at a Mitsubishi Colt single cab next to the Midge. The price tag read 'R120,000, low kms'. He studied the Colt. Who bought these things at such crazy prices? It was probably stolen. A young salesman approached him with a 'can-I-help-you-car-salesman' face.

"Just looking," said Slang. The salesman moved on immediately as if he'd expected the response.

Slang knew Wouter would spot him soon enough, if he hadn't already. He continued inspecting the vehicle, peering in through the windows. The driver's seat had loose stitching near the door. The dashboard was sun-cracked. Otherwise, it looked to be in reasonable condition. He ran his hands over the door. The alignment was out. Vehicle accident. The door had been replaced. He ran his fingers over the side. Fender and bonnet were out of sync. He walked round to the front. The right headlight looked good although it was a bit squint in comparison to the left. The pick-up had very obviously been involved in an accident and had been patched back together. He wouldn't be surprised if it was a code three, a vehicle involved in an accident and written off. Some second-hand car dealers rebuilt cars out of various wrecks and advertised them as regular second-hand vehicles.

"Can I help you, sir? Wouter Verster stood behind Slang like an eager salesman.

"Ja, I'm interested in this Colt. How many kays on the clock?" None would be any wiser on overhearing such an exchange.

"Hundred and twenty, sir."

Slang grunted.

"Sir, if you just give me a sec, I'll get the keys and we can take a look at the engine."

Wouter whipped back to the office. Slang turned briefly, scanning the road. A Telkom vehicle was parked on the far side. His right hand tightened on the weapon in his side pocket. That Telkom vehicle just wasn't right. He turned back to the Colt parked under the shade cloth. Wouter returned with the keys and opened the driver's door. He started the vehicle and then popped the bonnet. Wouter and Slang stood chatting over the engine puttering at the idle, a salesman and his customer inspecting the motor, nothing more.

Wouter reached in and tugged at something that caused the Colt's engine to roar. "There's trouble. The cops have been parked outside the whole day. No helicopters, just the surveillance across the road." The words hurried out of his mouth in a garbled rush.

Slang didn't look at Wouter. He moved away from the engine as if inspecting the vehicle's bodywork. "I want you to stay calm. They're still watching. But they've got nothing on you, just suspicions."

The truth, though, was that he knew the police had their man— and that man was Wouter. They were looking for the rest of the team. Wouter was the target. If he got caught he might turn or he might not. Was he willing to take that chance? Thoughts, options rocketed through his mind. He could feel the heat around his collar. His ears throbbed. His face felt hot. Something had to be done. Fast.

"Listen. Stay calm. You need to get out of town. I've got your money here in my pocket. Where can I give it to you?" Slang opened his jacket and pulled at one of the fat brown envelopes, displaying the tip of it to Wouter. Wouter swallowed hard, trying to think clearly among the jumble of thoughts in his head. Slang's mind was also racing—if he suggested they go for a test drive they might get away, but they'd certainly be followed. It was too much of a risk. It had to be done right here, on the lot. Now. While he could still blend in.

"I have a place. The workshop at the back," Wouter said, as if reading his boss's mind.

Slang walked over to Wouter and shook his hand. Anyone watching would have thought that Wouter had just made a sale. The two men spoke animatedly to each other. One happy customer to one happy salesman. They walked around the side of the building.

Once out of sight from the surveillance vehicle across the road, the two men hurried briskly to the workshop at the back. Wouter was sweating profusely. Slang followed him, his right hand gripping the weapon. They came to a small workshop that had been for the most part abandoned after the resident mechanic had decided he'd had enough. Ahmed had decided to close the shop until he could find a replacement. That had been two months ago. Wouter opened a side door and went inside. The main roller doors were closed and locked. Slang followed and closed the door behind him. There was a small office in one corner across from the three vehicle bays with their open pits. The tool racks were empty. There was a toilet on the other side of the bays, opposite the office.

Slang pulled out the brown envelope and handed it to Wouter.

Wouter opened it, his eyes widening when he saw the money. "Jissus, is this …"

"There's a bonus in there for you." Slang eyed the envelope.

Wouter was stunned. "I've never held so much money in my hands in my life!"

Slang smiled. "Now you know what to do. You go home like normal. Go home and eat something. Watch some TV and then go to bed. An hour after you switch the lights off, you disappear. Out the back door. I don't care where you go. Just go. Don't phone me. Don't contact me. You can't come back here again, okay?"

Wouter looked up from the bulging enevelope. "I understand. I'm a pro."

"Count it." Slang instructed him brusquely.

"I trust you." Wouter was hesitant to start separating the notes as if worried that the very act would wake him up from his current reverie.

"Count it! I don't want you coming back and telling me I *naaied* you," Slang snapped. It was an order not a request.

Wouter looked at Slang, sighed and carefully pulled out the stack of notes. He checked the envelope in case he'd left a note behind. "Phew, where do I start?

He stood with the bundle of notes in one hand and an empty envelope in the other, looking for a place to count it.

In a flash, Slang reached over and grabbed Wouter around his neck in a sleeper hold, tightening his grip every time Wouter attempted to inhale. Wouter dropped the envelope and the cash, trying desperately to break the lock. Slang's considerable height and size made it difficult, almost impossible. Each attempt to punch Slang in the kidneys from behind used up valuable oxygen.

"That's it. Fight me Wouter. Fight me with everything you've got," Slang hissed.

He had Wouter up in the air, off his feet. Two minutes without air. Wouter went limp. The wriggling stopped. A dead weight. Slang tightened his vice-like grip one more time and shook his victim. Wouter was unconscious. Slang dropped him to the floor. He picked up the money and put it back in the envelope, stuffing it back into his jacket pocket. He dragged the still-breathing Wouter round the pits to the toilet. It was a small room with a tiny washbasin and an old toilet pan. It appeared to have been built for a midget. Slang dragged Wouter inside, positioning him with his head over the bowl. He withdrew the firearm from his pocket. Wouter twitched slightly. Slang stood over him. He considered things for a few moments. Wouter would turn given the chance. He was all Christian now. Conscience. Jail. Something, someone would get to him. He positioned the end of the silencer at the base of Wouter's skull. He inhaled and squeezed off two quick shots as he exhaled. Two sharp thuds. Wouter's body slumped over the bowl, blood seeping onto the dirty white porcelain. Slang nodded briefly, forcing the door closed behind him. He took off his cap and pulled his jacket inside out. It was plastic inside with the label removed. The men in the surveillance vehicle wouldn't notice the stitching from such a distance.

He walked out of the workshop. There was a chill in the air. He strolled to the front entrance of the lot, his pace deliberate, measured. He wished he'd had more time to plan this all out more thoroughly. It was messy but at least this was one loose end tied up. Done. He made his way back to the car, slowly enough to mingle inconspicuously with the other pedestrians. He slipped into an alley. He took the gun out of his pocket and inserted it under his belt, pulling his shirt out over his waist. He took off his jacket and cap and threw them into a stinking garbage bin. He sauntered back out onto the main road, climbed back into his car and checked the road. It didn't appear he had been noticed, or followed.

In the surveillance van an operative noted that Wouter Verster had gone to the back of the car lot and was still out of sight. He and the customer had not returned. Other surveillance vehicles in the area were alerted. Wouter might have made them and escaped. He was to be picked up. Immediately. Suspect and any associates should be considered armed and extremely dangerous.

The receptionist called Wouter over the intercom.

Everyone seemed to be looking for Wouter.

Chapter 27

Ayesha sat at her desk kicking her heels. The victim was still in no condition to be questioned. Their suspect was still under surveillance. The search of his house had turned up almost nothing. She decided to do some background checks into her victim. She had the statements from the police. They had questioned Ellen's PA and everyone who'd been at the bar that night. They had interviewed her apartment building superintendent. If Ellen was being watched, no one had noticed a damned thing. Definitely pros. She needed to check the file again.

She went over to the director's office. He had taken control of the case and Ayesha now played second fiddle to him. He was out but she let herself in and closed the door softly behind her. She began searching for the file, by process of elimination, trying to figure where the director might keep it. She checked his drawers. Nothing. Perhaps he'd taped them under the desk? Nothing. She got up, about to leave when she noticed that the framed picture of the president looked off centre. She went over to straighten it when something clicked. She unhooked the picture. Behind it was a plastic harness with three brown folders neatly strapped in. She took the folders out, put the picture back and made her way back to her desk. If she read one file at a time, hiding the other two, no one would be any wiser. She had seen something earlier in those files that had troubled her. She couldn't yet put her finger on it but she was sure that whatever it was was in there somewhere.

She read through the first file. Greg Swart was actually Nina Gertruda Swart, born 1965 in Despatch in the Eastern Cape.

Conservative background. Her father was a policeman, her mother a housewife. Nina had left home when she was eighteen and had joined the army in 1983. Two months into her training she was transferred to Pretoria for psychological assessment. She was placed under the care of a Dr A. Blignaut. She was released in February 1986.

The file ended abruptly. There were no details for the two years from her transfer to Pretoria until her release in 1986. How did Nina become Greg? It was disturbing. Two ex-SADF members had had sex-change operations but nothing showed up in any of the clinic registers. Both had lived by themselves. Ayesha made some notes. She needed to shoot through some questions to the provincial office in Port Elizabeth. Hopefully someone had questioned the family members—that is, if they were privy to such information.

She put the file in her drawer and pulled out Wouter Verster's. His file would have read like that of an exemplary career soldier were it not for the small fact that he had worked for the apartheid government. The files contained summaries of operations into neighbouring countries and former homelands. Being summaries, however, the information was sketchy at best. A more detailed personnel file was probably stored in some deep, dark archive in the new South Africa. She scanned further. Everything seemed regular. Treated for post-traumatic stress disorder six months before joining the Security Police, a maverick unit comprised of sadistic killers. Their job was primarily 'neutralization' of political dissidents—never to be seen again. The file didn't give any details about the trauma that Verster might have experienced before he joined the Security Police. He had not been treated at a military hospital.

It was frustrating—the files were not proving very useful. Up-to-date summaries of people that left more questions than answers. She made more notes. She tapped her pencil on the desk. The answer was in front of her—she knew it—but for some reason she couldn't put her finger on it. She felt like screaming. She could almost taste what she was looking for. She put Greg's file away and pulled out Ellen Fischer's file. She looked at it. Would it give her some insight into the pulverized wreck of that human form lying in that hospital bed? Would it shed some light on who had been involved in the attack? One person had died in a similar crime. What was the link? Three people—one perpetrator, two victims—all linked to the SADF.

Ayesha read through the file. Allan Edgar Fischer was born in 1966 in Port Elizabeth. He came from a middle-income family, his mother a mornings-only administrator, his father a teacher at a local technical high school. Allan Fischer matriculated and applied to Rhodes University Port Elizabeth to study Accounting. Never registered. Refused to join the SADF. No political affiliations at the time.

Ayesha found herself drawn deeper into the file, uncovering more about the beaten, bloodied woman found near death a fortnight before. There were a number of formal exemption requests entered into his record in an attempt to avoid conscription. He was granted a temporary stay on the grounds of an impending marriage. December 1983. Instructed to report to the national service registration office by 1 February 1984. Second formal exemption request. University acceptance and preliminary attendance. Exemption request denied. Allan Fischer to report to 1 Military Hospital in Pretoria on 1 April 1984. Allan Fischer discharged after serving the mandatory two years' national service.

The records ended abruptly there. Similar to Greg Swart's. No accounting for the two years while in SADF service or how both had become recipients of sex-change operations. As she closed the file something unusual grabbed her attention. She took the files to the photocopy room. She copied the covers of each file as well as the contents. She managed to slip the files back into the hiding place behind the president's portrait. She looked at the picture. She wondered if she should leave it straight or the way she'd found it.

What if he had deliberately left it tilted? She shifted it slightly. The president smiled back at her as she tipped him to the left. She stepped back and studied the effect. The president appeared to be listening to a voice on his right-hand side while still smiling at his audience.

Chapter 28

Director de Villiers threw his silver attaché case onto the back seat. He took off his jacket and tossed it over the case in the back. He got into the car and switched his phone on. He made a habit of only switching on his phone once he was in his rented car or if he was being picked up, in his hotel room. He waited a couple of minutes. Several messages came through. Some were text messages. Three were from the same number. Two were voicemail notifications. He had left Johannesburg at noon; it was now two. Sometimes he wished he could just switch off from the rest of the world. He checked the three messages.

The first one said everything he needed to know: "We've got a problem. Call me as soon as you get this".

He tried to dial his voicemail. But he instinctively knew who would be at the other end and what they would be saying. If there was a problem now it had to be very serious. His call was interrupted by an incoming call from the same person who had sent him the text message.

"Ja! What! You know I just left the fuckin' office, what's the problem now?"

"I'm sorry, boss. But we've got bad news."

"Okay, out with it. I've got meetings and I'm running late." The director was in Port Elizabeth for a meeting with the regional office. He was also on a mission to check through any files relating to Greg Swart. Maybe they'd picked up something and had inadvertently forgotten to pass it on to Ayesha or maybe they'd overlooked something obvious; it had been known to happen.

Now this. Bad news. Bad news from the surveillance team on his lead suspect.

"It's Verster, sir, We've just found him dead."

"What do you mean you've just found him dead?"

"We found him shot twice in the back of the head in one of the toilets at his place of work."

The director drew in a deep breath, bit his bottom lip, suppressing his anger. "I thought you were watching him? That's what you were supposed to do."

"I know, boss. I'm sorry, but he went inside with a customer and didn't come out again."

"Did you see the customer come out?"

"No, boss."

Okay, meet me at my office with all your surveillance reports tomorrow at ten. Photos, video, everything. And I want a report on my desk by the time I get in. Understand!"

He ended the call and drove to the offices of the Port Elizabeth Special Crimes Unit, his fury catching in his throat, his bottom lip near bleeding.

Part II

Chapter 1

September 1983

Allan Fischer got dressed for school. Before the end of next month he would be done with uniforms. It was annoying having to wear a collar and tie every day. The teachers said it was preparation for the real world. His father agreed. He would—he was also a teacher. And, of course, his mother agreed with his father. That's what his mother did. She did whatever his father asked; he'd never heard them disagree or argue over anything. Allan stood in front of the mirror and folded and tucked in his tie until the knot was a perfect triangle. His mother usually made him take it off at breakfast and would do it again for him. His father would watch and shake his head. He'd usually make a sarcastic comment, asking Allan what he'd been doing all that time in his room that his tie was still not done when he came down to breakfast. This was the price you paid for being an only child. Although you never wanted for anything, you were always within the radar. There was such a thing as too much attention.

In little over a month, Allan Fischer would be writing his final matric exams. The rumour around school was that all pupils with guaranteed university acceptance would be exempt from national service for at least the duration of their degrees. So everyone studied particularly hard. And when you graduated you could usually get in as an officer or on some specialized course and not end up in the bush. Of course, if you were a qualified doctor you were sorted. You were paid decent money, you were immediately commissioned as an officer and you didn't have to fight. The only real hardship was the initial couple of months basic training.

The 'border war' had gone on long enough for every white South African high-school student to understand what it meant to go into the army. Some said it was South Africa's own Vietnam. Many tried to prolong their university studies, becoming professional students in the process, learning the tried and tested delaying tactics to avoid the unavoidable. The truth was that the army had your number. Even the insane were called up. It all depended on the type of school you'd attended. The liberal English-medium schools tried to encourage many of their matriculants to study further. Even if they did end up in the military, they'd become specialists or officers. They had a better chance of coming back normal. Coming back alive was not the only goal—coming back 'normal' was important. You wouldn't get a decent job if you were abnormal. Even in parochial Port Elizabeth everyone knew someone who had fought in Angola or South West Africa. So and so's father's cousin killed himself only two weeks after being discharged. Everyone knew someone ...

Allan arrived at school and glanced at the boys milling around in their brown uniforms. Almost all schools had a cadet programme. Schoolboys in brown uniforms would practise every week, drilling, PT, endurance marches, carrying logs. They would wear their brown uniforms to school every Friday, and subject to a rigid inspection. All the preparation needed for your future in the army. If you were lucky you made corporal and gave orders to the juniors. On Founders Day you would take part in the parade to honour your school, your country and, most importantly, God. The fact that most boys hated the two years of cadets—standards eight and nine—was not important. Everything was preparation, as if your whole life up until that stage was a dress rehearsal for the battles ahead. Waiting in formation.

Allan was very glad that those days were now behind him. The year had been tough enough as it was, with cadet training undoubtedly the most horrible experience he'd endured. Awful in every sense. Some of the boys took to it naturally. For Allan it was onerous, brutal, debasing. He did not miss it in the slightest.

"Hey, loser!" Jacky Vermeulen was Allan's mostly on-again girlfriend. He turned to see her coming towards him, bag half slung over a shoulder, hair freshly dyed.

"Nice hair. They're gonna give you shit for that. Again."

Jacky was constantly transgressing school rules. Her regular excuse was that she didn't realize her shampoo was also a hair colourant. Likely.

"What are they going to do? Expel me with less than a month to my valedictory? I don't think soooo!"

Allan smiled. Jacky walked up to him and grabbed his hand. She was standing so close to him that it was almost impossible to see that they were holding hands. He looked at her. She always joked about how she was taller than him. And she was. Just. He smiled, squeezed her hand and then let go. Getting caught holding your girlfriend's hand at school was more embarrassing than being caught committing a crime.

Jacky was one of the school's leading academics. She had received merit awards since primary school and as such it was difficult to discipline possibly the brightest pupil in the school. Teachers tried appealing to her maturer side. That didn't work. The other clever kids, egged on by the teachers, tried inviting her into their group. That didn't work either.

Allan believed that it was because she was so bright that she deliberately tried to rebel, to get under everyone's skin, to make a statement of sorts. She didn't want to be pigeon-holed as a nerd, preferring the concept of the rebellious intellectual. She had once corrected the English teacher and then proceeded to ask if a re-mark was not in order as there may well have been other mistakes. The teacher was not happy but Jacky had a point.

Most of the time Allan and Jacky were on as boyfriend and girlfriend. When they were off it was usually due to the fact that Allan lacked what Jacky had by the bucket-load—confidence. She simply didn't care if there was a test or an exam looming or if her future depended on the results. This bothered Allan. On his best day he couldn't come close to Jacky academically. This irritated him. The truth, though, was that he was madly in love with her. It was overwhelming. She was everything he wished he was and *then* some. She was also an only child but that was where the similarities ended. He parents were local celebrities. Her father was an attorney and her mother a doctor. Well-to-do socialites in demand, their fundraising activities made them the darlings of the city. Jacky was as carefree as Allan was restrained. Yet somehow they worked well together. They had come to the school from different primary schools, they had been put into the same class and somehow ended up sitting next to each other. Like most adolescent boys Allan tended to turn bright red and look down at his shoes whenever in close proximity to a female. And that's how he spent the greater part of his first year sitting next to Jacky. He tried to make conversation but his comments, once out of his mouth, had sounded better inside his head where they should have stayed. He tried to explain the concept of fishing to her one day. "It's all in the wrists" but the hand gesture looked obscene. Jacky had just laughed.

That was what he loved about her. No matter what he said or did she was always the same. On their first Valentine's Day in high school he felt awkward giving her a card but he knew she would think it odd if he didn't. A hundred other boys in school would also be sending her cards. He agonized whether to sign it 'Love Allan' or simply 'From Allan'. He opted for the former. There they sat in class, all of fourteen years old, boys and girls dressed in cheesy costumes, sending each other tinselly cards in white and red envelopes. There was even the occasional plastic rose. You needed guts to send someone roses, even if they were fake. Allan sat and waited for the lanky Cupid to call out Jacky's name. Everyone got a card. Even if you didn't get a card from an admirer, you'd get one from your teacher. It would be signed 'Anonymous' but everyone knew where it came from. Allan got two. One was from Jacky. She looked at him and smiled. The lanky Cupid read out more names and dug out more cards from the black bag.

"Jacky Vermeulen, you're very popular!"

Allan kept his eyes on the desk as the class, a bunch of temperamental, hormonal fourteen-year-olds, went quiet. He focused on some graffiti scratched on his desk—'Press button for teacher to explode'.

He looked up. Jacky was standing. She was red with embarrassment. She took a neatly wrapped bundle of cards amid a chorus of oohs and aahs and sat down. She crammed the pile into her bag and mumbled something about it all being so childish.

Allan wasn't in Jacky's next couple of classes and didn't see her again until after break. She hadn't said anything to him after she'd received her cards. He wondered whether she'd read his and whether it had upset her. Love Allan. What was he thinking? Now would be a good time for a fire drill or a bomb scare.

The bell rang and everyone took their places. Allan sat down and started hauling out his books.

Jacky leaned over as he straightened up. "I love you too, Allan Fischer," she whispered.

Allan turned crimson. Jacky sat at her desk, staring straight ahead as if nothing had happened. She didn't giggle, just sat there looking at the front of the class with a huge grin on her face. It was then that Allan knew that without any doubt he was madly in love with her. They were a couple throughout high school. In their yearbook they were voted the couple most likely to get married first.

With the exception of English and Afrikaans, Allan and Jackie seldom got the chance to sit together in class. They spent their breaks together though, and were closer friends than the average high-school couple. Everyone in the school knew they were a couple and when anyone else sat next to Jacky in one of her classes the teachers would jokingly say they'd mention it to Allan.

Most of their free time was spent studying. They usually talked on the phone for one or two hours over the weekend. In an effort to spend more time together they sometimes studied at each other's house. Although Jacky actually did very little studying, she tried to give the illusion that she was taking her matric exams very seriously. Allan's mother was home in the afternoons and after a few weeks of observing them working diligently together, she stopped worrying. It was clear they were good for each other. Matric exams were an absolute priority, if only to delay conscription.

It was one day at Jacky's house that Allan's life changed forever. He was to enter a world that most people didn't know existed, let alone ever experienced.

Chapter 2

October 1983

The weeks blended into a singular blur of discussions, notes and past papers. In between it all was talk of next year, the holidays and making it the best time of their lives, as if there was no tomorrow. In a very real way this was your family and as close as you were you realized that this was the last time you might all be together, carefree and with futures, with hope. Some guys were keen to enlist. Many believed that it was their duty and that if they died it would be for a noble cause. Others jumped at the mouth-watering prospect of guns and war and making sure the 'kaffirs' didn't cross the borders into South Africa. Even some of the girls were wanting to enlist in the SADF. The hype was not limited to one particular gender and, in spite of the bad press, there were still a few girls and boys who could not envisage a life beyond the army.

One week before the valedictory, the matriculants were summoned to the school hall. The headmaster had, for the most part, cancelled the concept of study leave for matriculants. Instead, they were split into groups according to their subjects with the normal school day becoming an intensive revision session. Only later would they be allowed a week off before the first exam.

Matrics were exempt from school assemblies or any other compulsory school function. They were at school primarily to study so that they wouldn't hang around at home, wasting time. Everyone figured they were being summoned to the hall because someone in the Standard Ten class had pulled off a prank like the previous year when drunken matriculants had taken a grudge out on some staff cars with shaving foam.

The matriculants shuffled their way to the gallery, their privileged seating area earned by virtue of their having made it to Standard Ten. The headmaster, Mr Friend, was wearing his grey suit, his face a mottled, reddish colour. He was in a bad mood. Next to him stood a tall, lanky man in crisp military browns. He wore a beret similar to those of the cadets. What on earth could he want? The cadets were in standards eight and nine? The headmaster summoned the students down from the gallery into the main body of the hall.

"Sit down and be quiet, please," Mr Friend said sternly. "We have a guest today and I would appreciate your attention."

After a few years you got used to Mr Friend's little outbursts. At least he cared about his pupils. A fifty-year-old bachelor, Mr Friend had devoted his life to teaching and this school in particular. He stepped forward to introduce his guest.

The man next to him was tall, ramrod-straight, his hands clasped rigidly behind his back. He had a moustache that looked straight out of a Spaghetti Western.

Mr Friend addressed the group. "Good morning, everyone. I apologise for interrupting your studies. Unfortunately, there are some other matters deemed more important."

Allan looked across at Jacky sitting on the other side of the hall with the girls. She shrugged and faced the front again.

"Ladies and gentlemen, may I introduce Commandant Victor Basson." Mr Friend motioned for the ramrod-straight, moustache-sporting soldier to step forward. "Commandant Basson."

"Good day, boys and girls."

Allan looked at Jacky. She was staring directly ahead. Although he tried to come across as friendly, the commandant's smile seemed rehearsed.

"You have to forgive me. I usually go to the Afrikaans schools, not the English ones. If there is anything you don't understand please stop me and I will try to explain better. I am from the local SADF recruiting office. Does anyone know what that stands for?"

A general murmur rippled across the hall.

"Boys and girls, I am from the South African Defence Force. It is my job to make sure that we can live in peace without having to worry about our enemies coming and blowing up restaurants, our post offices or our electricity plants. Now, I am sure you have all heard or read about the bombing that took place recently at the Wimpy restaurant. Yes? You look like bright kids so you must have heard about it. That, boys and girls, was the work of enemies of our fatherland. Communists. They want to take over this country. They want to see chaos in our country. They want to stop you from going to school, stop your parents from going to work and take away the things your parents have worked so hard for. They want to take it away and give it to the blacks in the townships.

"The reason that I am here, boys and girls, is that I want you to think about something. You are at a very important stage of your life. You are young men and women and one day, maybe soon, you will have your own children."

There was some giggling and one or two snide comments. Mr Friend stepped forward and glared at them. Everyone went quiet. Jacky looked at Allan and smiled. They had spoken a couple of times about marriage and kids. Jacky always joked about how she hoped their kids would have her looks.

"Now, some people will tell you that the situation in South West Africa, Angola, Mozambique is not our war, that we should just leave them to kill themselves, that if the blacks kill themselves everything will be better. The truth is that we have many enemies who want to see our beautiful country brought to its knees. There are people out there who want every white person in South Africa banished or dead."

The commandant's diatribe continued relentlessly and after a while the murmuring stopped, the matrics slowly warming to the subject. Duty, Honour, God. The SADF was so much more than simply being a soldier. It was the difference between being proud of your calling and of shaming your family and friends. You could make a good life in the army. In fact, if you wanted to study and become a doctor or a lawyer, the army would help you. The army also helped its own with houses, schooling, job security.

"If you are proud to be a South African, you'll do the right thing," the commandant concluded his address. "Please would everyone stand for the national anthem."

Everyone shuffled obediently to their feet for *Die Stem*. Mr Friend thanked the commandant for giving up his valuable time to visit the school before dismissing the matrics. As they filed out, soldiers in brown uniforms at the door handed out recruiting pamphlets which were in Afrikaans.

Jacky and Allan walked out together. Break was in about five minutes and if they walked slowly enough they wouldn't have to go back to class.

"Oh God, can you believe that rubbish?"

"Well, he had a point, you know." Allan was trying to be see both sides.

"Oh please, give me a break! That was such propaganda bullshit!"

"Easy tiger."

"Oh, I can't believe you fell for that shit! Are you that dumb?"

"Well, we can't all be as clever as you!" Allan turned to storm off.

"Allan?" Jacky called after him.

Allan stopped. "What?"

"I love you."

Allan smiled. Even when he was angry with her, she instinctively knew how to make him smile.

Chapter 3

Victor Basson sat in his office and looked at the papers in front of him. The situation on the border was becoming increasingly desperate. It used to be easy to encouarge men to join the army. Offer them a chance of a nice house, a stable job, pride—yes, most importantly, pride—and they served their basic training and made a career out of the defence force. Even with conscription and the threat of jail to dissenters, Basson was forced to visit schools and persuade young adults—no, children—to sign up. The war was a never-ending meat grinder. Who were they kidding? South Africa was fighting the entire continent and it couldn't go on forever. Even if women were allowed to fight on the front lines it couldn't last. The army would eventually run out of children. Even those who were sent into the townships came out a complete mess. Although it was his job to convince the children, the conscripts, the soldiers that it was total war, what could he do when soldiers on duty in the townships deserted their armoured Caspirs and Buffels and sneaked home at night? How could they believe that this was total war when less than an hour's drive from the fighting and shooting and killing, they were sitting down to a suburban family supper or a braai or a movie. The situation was fucked up. And in spite of Victor Basson's reservations the war would grind on. It was his duty to do the best he could with what diminishing resources there were.

He sat at his desk and pondered. The white kids didn't want to fight anymore. How could you entice them with a housing subsidy when most of them knew someone who had been killed in action or who'd come back from the bush suicidal? Basson feared the worst.

Maybe this generation would sign up and still feel they were doing their duty. But what about the next generation? It was unlikely. The end was near. Eventually, they would run out of reserves, there would be no reinforcements and they would have to pull back from the borders, out of Angola and South West Africa, out of Mozambique and the surrogate homelands that had for so long acted as buffers against the red tides and the black tides from the north. Every white would be looking over his shoulder, forced to retreat from the townships like cowards. It was only a matter of time before the whole country was overrun by murdering black communists.

There were some proposals on the table. A large number of young white males were being lost through migration. The government had tried to discourage emigration by instituting strict foreign currency restrictions. Even the issuing of passports had been slowed, deliberately, to a trickle. In spite of international sanctions and foreign travel restrictions, Western countries welcomed the droves of qualified, degreed South Africans who'd earned a reputataion abroad for hard work.

Basson scribbled down some notes. Cut down or cut out the number of boys going directly to university. Offer correspondence courses instead, in the army, of course. He wrote boys. It was intentional. He strongly believed that the army was no place for a woman. Unless there was something wrong with her. Yes, wrong was the right word. Women had no place in the services. Except maybe as nurses. But even then. He summoned a corporal to his office and instructed him to type it up. This would be the best tactical move since he'd proposed visiting the schools, direct recruiting. Basson was a master tactician. He knew it. He'd developed the training strategy around recruiting. He hoped his new proposal would be implemented soon. That it would be accepted was a given—of that much he was sure—just when?

Chapter 4

Allan sat with a glass of water in his hand on the sundeck overlooking Port Elizabeth and Algoa Bay. It was evening, with yellow-white lights flickering across the bay. Jacky was in her room, studying. Her mother had gone out, saying she'd be back soon. He loved Port Elizabeth on evenings like this. It was truly amazing. No wind. The air was cool but not cold. And you could smell the ocean. He felt two warm arms wrap around him

"This is a long break, mister." Jacky kissed him on the cheek.

"Damn maths won't sink in. Thought if I came and sat out here maybe something would click."

She sat down on a deck chair next to him. Her mother had still not brought out the yellow and white striped cushions, usually left outside during summer, coming in occasionally when it rained. During winter they were wrapped in plastic and stashed in the garage.

"So, tell me, what are you so deep in thought about?" She hooked her arm around his, pulling herself closer to him.

"I was just thinking about us and what's going to happen next year. I mean, you're going to Cape Town and I don't even know where I'm going to end up."

"Well, you did apply to Rhodes for next year ..."

"Ja, but I haven't told my parents yet."

Jacky held him tighter.

"And it's not just that. You're going to be miles away in Cape Town. I mean, why can't you just stay here? So we can be together?"

"I told you to come with. We've both been in PE too long. I'm sick of this town. I need change."

"Are you tired of me?"

"Oh, I get where this is going. What if I meet someone else?"

"I didn't say that."

"Well, that's what you meant."

"You didn't answer my question."

"Allan, do you know why I'm so in love with you? Why I've been in love with you since Standard Seven? Because, of all the boys out there, you are the only one for me and the only one I can ever see myself with."

Allan sat quietly. He fretted about losing Jacky. He looked at her. She was gorgeous. Even when he was with her other guys hit on her. And even though he tried not to show his jealous side Jacky knew when he was upset. She normally dealt with it very well; she was proud that Allan was her boyfriend. She loved him because he was so different from the other boys. He stood out from the rest, even though his lack of confidence and insecurities bubbled to the surface occasionally.

He leaned over to kiss her. Their lips touched gently.

A loud bang interrupted their reverie. It was so unexpected, so sudden, so jarring, that Allan could hear his own heartbeat pounding in his head. There was shouting coming from downstairs. They hadn't heard anyone come in. They got up softly. Allan cautiously led the way, squeezing Jacky's hand. There was a commotion downstairs. Surely it couldn't be burglars? They were making too much of a racket. Allan looked around for something to use as a weapon but there was nothing.

"Jacky? Allan!" a voice bellowed from below. It was Jacky's father. There was an edge, alarm in his voice. Something was wrong. Jacky called back, let go of Allan's hand and rushed down the staircase, with Allan following right behind.

Downstairs in the kitchen, two black men and Jacky's father, Paul Vermeulen, were manoeuvring a badly bleeding man through the door. Jacky's mother screamed at Jacky to go up to her room, her hands clasped to her face. Jacky's father screamed at Allan to give them a hand. Shock gripped Allan as he stood there. Frozen. Jacky's father shouted again, snapping Allan into action. He hurried across to help, struggling to get a grip on the injured man, slippery with blood and sweat.

"Open that door!" Paul Vermeulen yelled.

Allan opened a door leading off from the kitchen, down a small flight of stairs to what appeared to be the basement. He reached for the light-switch cord dangling in the doorway. The three men manhandled the wounded man towards the basement, grunting and heaving as they struggled down the steps. Allan was in front, without any way of letting them pass.

"Allan! Come hold him here," Jacky's father shouted. He was covered in blood.

Allan wormed his way among the writhing bodies, locking his arms around the man's leg. Mr Vermeulen, sweating, breathing heavily, grabbed a key from his pocket. He shouldered a steel cabinet aside which revealed another door. He unlocked it as Allan and the two men followed him in with their groaning charge. Paul Vermeulen switched on the light to reveal a dank room, sparsely furnished with a bed, a washbasin and a toilet. There were no windows as this section of the basement was completely underground. They placed the bloodied man on the bed.

Paul Vermeulen checked the man's vital signs. He was still alive. "You two need to get out of here. Hang on, I have some spare clothes. You can't go anywhere like that. Allan, you stay here. Watch him. I'll send Jacky's mom in just now, but just keep an eye on him. Please." With that he departed with the two black men.

Allan stood there, confused, disbelieving, looking at the black man on the bed drenched in blood. It looked nothing like the stuff you saw on TV. The man moved slightly. He mumbled something and then went silent again. Allan froze. He then tentatively approached the bed to see if the man was still alive. He didn't know what to check first. The man's chest moved erratically as he struggled to breathe, gasping, spluttering, salivating.

Jacky's father returned a few minutes later. "I need you to stay with him. Here. Jacky's mom needs to get some things from her surgery and I need to drop the men off." Mr Vermeulen was wearing fresh clothes, the soiled ones obviously in the black bag he clutched in his left hand.

"But I need to get home. My parents …"

"It's fine, you can spend the night here. I'll phone your mother and tell her something, okay? Please. I really need your help."

Allan couldn't refuse. He nodded dumbly, his mouth dry.

"Thanks. You're a good man, Allan. Just keep an eye on him. Keep him warm. I should be gone for an hour or so and Jacky's mother should be back soon. But I need you here just in case. Oh, before I forget. Don't answer the door or open it for anyone … under no circumstances whatsoever. We all have keys so you just stay right here. Okay?"

Allan nodded again, silently.

He pulled up a chair and looked at the man with the bloodied body struggling to breathe. He didn't know what he was supposed to do. He wasn't a doctor. He vaguely heard Jacky's father on the phone telling his mother that Allan had nodded off to sleep in the study. It was too late to wake him up and bring him home. The poor boy looked exhausted. Rather let him sleep over. He was really sorry. No, he didn't mind Allan spending the night. Not at all. In fact it was a pleasure. He would drop him off at school in the morning. Yes, he was sending Jacky's mother over to pick up some clothes.

Then he heard Mr Vermeulen instructing Jacky's mother to stop at the garage on her way. "Tell them that there's a horrible noise when you drive. Open the bonnet, look around to see if you are being followed. If you are, come home immediately. I'll make a plan to get the stuff you need from the surgery. Just pick up Allan's clothes on your way back."

The house was now eerily quiet. All Allan could hear was the gurgled breathing of a man who clearly appeared to be dying. He had never seen that much blood in his life. It smelt sweet, metallic. Sickly so.

Allan instinctively knew that he was now somehow involved in something bad, something sinister, something dangerous. The fact that they were hiding a black man in a white neighbourhood after dark meant serious trouble if they were caught. Black people were not allowed out of the townships after dark, except domestic maids.

He couldn't even begin to hazard a guess as to why he was here, in this position, watching over a dying black man ... nor was he really sure he wanted to know.

It was all so surreal.

Chapter 5

Victor Basson was addressing a group of men seated around a boardroom-type table. He was delivering his proposal for the future of the South African Defence Force.

"The truth is simple. Our white kids are finding ways out and don't understand the gravity of the situation, especially the English-speaking ones. We have no other option. Yes, some of my proposals might be considered .... radical ... but we must now draw on the Indians and Coloureds to fight, to boost our numbers."

One of Basson's assistants clicked a new slide forward on the projector. A list of financials in bullet points appeared on how money could be saved and how additional troops could be trained.

A murmur of approval rose from around the table.

A tall man with thinning grey hair in a black suit and wearing black-rimmed spectacles then stood up. The room fell silent. "I'll take this proposal to the minister but approval should not be a problem." He turned to Basson, "Thank you for your commitment and your vision, commandant. I'm sure you have a promising future ahead of you if you carry on like this."

Basson smiled to himself as he came to grips with the fact that his most controversial proposal had for the most part been accepted and would be implemented soon enough. He *was* making a difference. Surely such measures wouldn't go unnoticed?

Chapter 6

Late November 1983

A look of utter astonishment came over Allan Fischer's face. He just stood there, dumbfounded, as the supercilious recruiting sergeant eagerly delivered the news. The sergeant motioned for the next recruit to approach the desk, dismissing Allan with an irritated wave of the hand. Allan turned and walked away slowly. He could feel the eyes of the sergeant and the boys in the line burning a hole into the back of his head.

Since that evening in October when he had discovered that the Vermeulens operated a 'safe house' for the underground movement, the liberation struggle, everything had changed. His whole world had been turned upside down. The discovery that Paul Vermeulen was actually one of the 'terrorists' that the government was fighting had steeled his resolve *not* to join the SADF. Well, that and the fact that he'd never intended doing military service anyway. He had a reason now, a God-given, justifiable reason. He'd told his parents about his decision to go to university instead of the army. Of course, this was a standard delaying tactic. It was common knowledge that the majority of the army was comprised of working-class conscripts—and those without the aptitude or money to further their studies. The wealthier candidates had university plans or trips overseas or anything else they could conjure up to avoid the army or at the very least delay it, which would hopefully buy enough time to return when things were different. Allan's parents were disappointed, apprehensive and most of all worried. They knew that their son was bright enough to go to university but they simply couldn't afford it. Allan had showed them the letter granting him provisional acceptance pending his final results and a letter granting provisional financial assistance pending his full acceptance by the faculty. But their reaction had disappointed him. They really wanted him to join the army. They believed it was every white South African male's duty.

As Allan walked away from the recruiting office, shoulders slumped, he could feel his anger boiling up inside. How the hell could this be? First his parents, now this! He wanted to scream. Instead he went over to Jacky's house. Only her father was home when he arrived.

"What's wrong?" Paul Vermeulen stood at the door, concerned. They had not spoken about what had happened that evening in the basement. Jacky and Allan had only discussed it briefly a few days later. She had implored him not to mention a thing to anyone.

"Nothing," Allan answered Mr Vermeulen, as he turned to leave. "Can you ask Jacky to phone me please?"

"Allan, I think you and I need to talk. Why don't you come inside?" Paul noticed the letter in Allan's hand.

Allan stood outside for a few seconds, staring at the ground. He lifted his gaze and stepped inside.

They sat down in the lounge, Allan's head bowed dejectedly. The destruction of his plans by the stroke of a civil servant's pen was too much to bear. The smirk on the sergeant's face as he'd handed Allan the letter, gleefully explaining the contents.

"Okay, you first. What's in the letter?" Paul could see it was futile to talk about 'that night'. The boy's mind was on other things. He needed to let it out.

Allan passed the letter to Paul. Tears welled in his eyes. He daren't speak. Paul took the letter.

Dear Mr Fischer
Re: Application for exemption
    You are hereby advised that under an amendment of the Conscription

Act of 1968 of the Republic of South Africa, you are no longer classified as persons eligible for exemption except on grounds of: University admission to complete studies in pursuance of a Medical Practitioner's qualification; Marriage; Mental Illness.

You are reminded that it is an offence to fail to complete mandatory national service under any of the Republic's Government Institutions.

You are to report to your nearest conscription office with your Identity Document and a Medical Clearance Certificate at the date and time as indicated in previous correspondence. Please also ensure that you complete the attached form of good character, duly signed by your local minister.

H. Viljoen
Commandant

Paul read through the letter again, his brow knitting with growing concern. Allan was on the verge of tears.

"Look, just relax. It's going to be fine. We just have to be clever about this."

In the days and weeks that followed Allan and Paul tried everything. It became clear that Allan wasn't alone. Thousands of young men had lost the opportunity to attend university because the government had decided to cancel the financial aid schemes for degrees not considered relevant to the cause. Financial assistance was now only offered for those courses relevant to careers in the military.

The truth of it was that everyone had begun to see the effects of the government's war against the '*Die Swart Gevaar*'—The Black Peril. Boys were being sent to fight in Angola. Boys were being sent to fight in South West Africa, surely soon to be Namibia. Boys were being sent to fight in Mozambique. Boys were being sent to the townships to fight alongside the police. Body bags were coming back. Sometimes they came home with a letter of regret. Sometimes a letter came back on its own. Sometimes nothing came back. The military was a white institution. But the government had started running out of white boys to send to the army. It was now necessary to have every available body on the borders to defend the country against the communists, against the black peril, against the terrorists who would see South Africa brought to its knees.

Allan seemed to be at Jacky's house more often than he was at home. Exams came and went. He began spending more time with Jacky's father than with Jacky. He told his parents that it was still his intention to go to university and thereby hopefully put off his national service for the next four years. His parents loved him and deep down they didn't want their son to fight in such a futile war but his duty was his duty ... and they had their reputations to consider. Conversation slowed to a trickle in the Fischer home. For Allan it became a place where his parents lived and his clothes were kept. Most nights Paul would phone and ask if Allan could sleep over.

In December Paul made a suggestion that Allan would never have thought of in a million years. Jacky had gone out with her mother. In fact, Jacky and her mother had planned to be out of the house on the premise of Jacky helping her mother at her surgery—to allow Paul the opportunity to present Allan a proposal.

"Allan, you know I said I would try to help you with this problem of yours?"

Allan sat across from Paul, curious. He had not been sleeping well since that letter. All his plans had been destroyed by that one piece of paper, that letter. His parents weren't aware of it. And here was Paul offering to help. Hopefully, he wouldn't suggest leaving the country and going underground, into exile. Allan didn't want that. He knew he'd never be able to come back. Paul was involved with the underground, providing safe houses, safe passge for the movement's operatives, the cadres, the revolutionaries. It would be simple enough for him to get Allan out of the country but Allan didn't feel it necessary to go to such extremes, not yet anyway.

"Yes?" he said, hesitantly.

"I've been thinking for a while now. I've had a chance to read through the letter and speak to a few people I know. As it stands, you will have to serve your two years and then you can go to university. You might, I say might, then qualify for financial assistance. However, the ways things are going, there is no guarantee that anything will go according to plan."

Allan knew exactly what he meant. Usually, your mandatory two years were made up of six months' basic training and eighteen months in the bush, on the front line, on the border. Or ... dying in the bush, on the border, something that was becoming more and more prevalent. Living or dead, few came back the same.

"I've had a chance to speak to some friends who know about these things," Paul started hesitantly. "What I'm going to suggest is not going to be easy and I want you to think very, very seriously about it first before you give me your answer. There are other options but I think this is the best solution ... for the moment."

"I'll try my best." Allan wanted to tell him to spit it out, say it. This must be why Jacky and her mother had made an excuse to leave for the afternoon. Paul needed some space.

"Well, I know how fond you are of my daughter. And well, there is one loophole that will be able to buy us time until we can think of an alternative. Hmm ... there is no easy way to say this. Will you marry my daughter?"

Allan sat there, stunned. There was an awkward silence. Of all the things he'd prepared himself for, this was certainly not one of them.

"I know this is a bit sudden but if you get engaged, you only have to present the authorities with a letter from a minister with the proposed date of the marriage and the reasons for needing to get married. You will have a six-month exemption period from the date of marriage. This will buy us some time."

"And what'd be the reasons for such an urgent marriage?"

"That Jacky is pregnant." Even suggesting this seemed to upset Paul. "That doesn't mean that you and Jacky should … you know what I mean." Paul was finding it difficult. Was he the concerned father or the concerned friend?

Allan wondered what Jacky would have to say about such a thing. Did she even know that her father was selling her virtue to save his life? Like other teenagers, Allan and Jacky often got carried away while making out but they'd always stopped short of actual penetration. The risk of pregnancy was just too high. And now he would have to tell people that he'd made Jacky pregnant. He could only imagine what his parents' reactions would be when he told them they were going to be grandparents. How was he going to start *that* conversation? He would have to think about it very carefully.

"When the authroities see there's no baby we'll say she had a miscarriage or something. I know a doctor who can arrange the necessary. Right now, all you need to do is say yes. And then we can try and sort out this mess."

"I need some time to think about this. I mean, I am going to have to tell my parents. And well …"

"I know. But when you make up your mind, you phone me first. Don't speak to anyone about this. Not even Jacky, not just yet. You just make up your mind. But you better do it soon. By tomorrow. We're running out of time."

Allan lay awake that whole night. Getting married so soon had certainly not been in his plans. But neither was going to the army. He was too young to get married. But he was also too young to die in the army. Something had to be done. He wished the whole world would just self-destruct, tonight, right now and spare him the agony of having to make the decision. He thought of how many other boys were sitting at home, champing at the bit, eagerly awaiting their chance to fire real guns and kill real people. There were probably as many other boys sitting at home nursing the same shattered dreams as his. As he tossed and turned, trying to sleep, he knew he'd made up his mind. He knew it when Paul had first suggested it. The only cloud was how to tell his parents.

Marrying Jacky. He smiled to himself. Maybe things weren't as bad as he'd first thought. Maybe things were going to get better. Yes, they were young but he loved her deeply and well, he would just have to grow up a bit faster. He wondered what she'd have to say.

*****

Paul Vermeulen was a member of the South African Communist Party. He had helped many Party operatives escape from South Africa into exile. He was a vital cog in the underground. He could have helped Allan escape from South Africa, but as an eighteen-year-old white boy, what would his options be? A military training camp in Angola or Tanzania or Zambia? Allan was not military material. Besides, he would simply be swapping one uniform for another. It would have been simple to get the boy out of the country to join the liberation struggle but Allan would not survive that. It wasn't about the cause. It was about giving a boy the best opportunity he could.

They lived in a society where boys were forced to become men before they had fully experienced childhood. Marriage was a serious alternative, not something Paul took lightly for it concerned his daughter. But it was a chance to save a young life and he had a soft spot for the boy.

Perhaps Paul was trying to compensate for the loss of his own son, Jacky's older brother, Brian, who had died when Jacky was six months old. Maybe it was that—the son he'd never had. Whatever the reasons, Paul felt obliged to try and help Allan. It was part of who he was, it was part of his work. Apartheid couldn't last forever and with international pressure mounting, how long could the government continue to feed the meat-grinding machine with the bodies of young white boys?

Ironically, it was because of the mounting international pressure being exerted on the South African government that it felt the need to send more boys into the military. Dissidence and unrest were spreading across the country at an alarming rate.

Perhaps it was the looming of a last stand, a scorched-earth, to-the-death, bloody stand.

Chapter 7

Victor Basson sat in a meeting with the dour, stubborn, old warhorses—all ardent supporters of fascist nationalism, the fatherland and apartheid. He couldn't believe his luck when they'd transferred him from his Port Elizabeth office to Pretoria to act as adviser to the Union of Commandants, an elite, exclusive group who made the real decisions that steered the government's hand. The prospect had excited him. He felt honoured. But this meeting had opened his eyes to the reality of the situation. The Americans had their Vietnam. South Africa had the entire African continent.

A burly man with the look of a Springbok front row forward stood up, his moustache glistening with crumbs from the pie he had just eaten for lunch. His face was florid and its condition was not helped by the confinement of the stuffy room.

"We have no choice but to put this recommendation to the minister. May I remind you gentlemen, we are on the African continent, surrounded by Africans. We are the final barrier between civilized government and complete anarchy. Anarchy lies around the corner. The Soviets are pouring billions into the terrorists' coffers. The terrorists have money, they have guns and they have the international media taking up their cause. They have no law to abide by, no accountability or responsibility to anyone. If we withdraw—throw in the towel—our boys will die for nothing. Our people will be the laughing stock of Africa."

He sat down in a huff. He'd deliberately emphasized 'laughing stock' to underline the seriousness of the position, to goad them into action. He suspected it would work.

The chairman, a silver-haired man who had served under the former prime minister, cleared his throat to signal his intention to speak. "Gentlemen, we have a sensitive situation before us. On the one hand, we have massive negative publicity overseas which is now filtering into the country. As much as we might try to impose censorship and control the press, there is only so much we can do before there is no news left to impart, except that we are a government who is afraid of our own shadow. We cannot deny the fact that our supremacy on the continent is being challenged and we are being stretched to our limits. We all know we have the military power to take Zambia and Mozambique or Angola and South West Africa and anywhere else we might choose, but we mustn't lose sight of why we are committing our troops to the conflict. To protect the borders of our republic. But what about protecting our country against internal elements? Brave men have died for our fatherland. Sorry, if anyone thinks we are just going to hand it over to the first bunch of communists who threaten us, then they are sadly mistaken."

The stuffy room with poor ventilation and short tempers became deathly quiet. The old man had been silent for most of the meeting, generally directing traffic from one opposing argument to the next. But he'd heard enough.

"My second point is something we ignore at our peril. And in some respects this is more important. Very simply, our pool of reserves of good fighting men is fast drying up. The troubles in the townships are sucking us dry. We are running out of troops. Gentlemen, I urge you to think about Commandant Basson's proposal very carefully. We have discussed the pros and cons *ad nauseam* so now we shall put it to a vote."

Victor Basson sat back and watched the older men scribble down their votes on scraps of paper. He had presented his recommendations earlier in the meeting. It wasn't necessarily his personal doctrine, only what the situation called for. Basson was practical. And times like these called for practical solutions. Yes, the SADF military machine could take Luanda or Harare or wherever else they so chose on this godforsaken continent, but at what price? The war machine was running out of fuel. It was time to be practical.

Basson had told the group, "We need to look at how our white South Africans are avoiding their national duty. Marriage, homosexuality, university. Simple. As you will see from my arguments in the proposal in front of you, we cannot afford to withdraw from the continent. We would be playing right into the hands of the Soviets who would then use the so-called Frontline States as a springboard from which to launch their invasion of the fatherland. We cannot afford to show any weakness whatsoever. I have outlined the measures we must adopt to increase our efforts here and north of our borders."

That was enough to get the ball rolling. Those who had served in the field knew the price they would have to pay to keep the republic alive. The older, more radical supporters of Nationalism had other ideas. Brought up during the Depression with the Jews and the English dominating politics, the economy and every facet of their lives, their bitterness at the subjugation of the Afrikaner race was to grow into the laager mentality of apartheid, separate development. They could not imagine a price too high for protecting their right to self-determination. To them, this was more that just white against black. This was about the triumph of the Afrikaner 'volk' over the adversity of imperialism, communism and black nationalism. In 1961, Dr Verwoerd had removed South Africa from the Commonwealth and established the Republic of South Africa. They had not succumbed to the British or the United Nations and they would certainly not succumb to the blacks who would undoubtedly turn their homeland into yet another African disaster. There was no future for the Afrikaner people in a South Africa without control of their own destiny.

It was a secret ballot. Basson did not have a vote. In fact, if he'd had the choice, he wasn't too sure which way he'd vote. It wasn't that he didn't believe in the republic. On the contray, he had committed his life to his country but he had made a conscious effort to utilize every opportunity before him to advance his own career. He was particularly adept at strategy and intelligence. Knowledge was power. As he excelled his career progressed with other broader, more important opportunities presenting themselves and therefore his proposal was nothing more than a 'practical' solution.

The silver-haired chairman gathered up the slips of paper. He proceeded to open each vote and placed them in separate piles. 'Yes' for the new programme, 'No' against the proposed programme and a phased military withdrawal from foreign soil.

The vote was decisive, with two generals abstaining. The programme would be implemented with immediate effect. The ramifications would have a devastating impact on the life of Allan Fischer.

Chapter 8

Allan moved in to Jacky's house. His parents had not reacted the way he'd hoped. He'd expected them to be concerned, supportive, but they were angry, hurtfully so, excessively so. Had he lost his mind? He was too young to get married. He wouldn't go to the army but he was going to get married? Did he know what it took to support a wife? Was he going to rely on his wife to support him? Or worse, his wife's family? He wanted to tell them he was getting engaged only to delay his call-up, that he was only doing this because he didn't want to join the army, that he wasn't ready to get married. But Paul had warned him. Do not tell anyone anything, not even your parents. Only Jacky and her mother knew the real reasons.

Allan sat in the back seat of the car behind the driver's seat, staring out the window. Jacky held his hand. She could see what this was doing to him. She was trying to reach out but he kept a part of himself distant, his own private world of torment. She squeezed his hand. He didn't squeeze back.

Allan wondered how it had got to this point. He was not interested in the army. He was not interested in being a glorified cadet. He had seen the reality of it at school, the brutality of it all. It was pathetic; men bullying boys who would grow up to bully others because that was the way of things. He felt Jacky squeeze his hand. He wanted to squeeze her back, he wanted to turn to her and look into her eyes and tell her now how much he loved her. But he didn't. This was not how he'd thought he'd be getting married. His parents' only child on his way to the courthouse, without parents. If only he could explain it all to them, explain that he didn't want to come back like Willem

Botha who had stumbled into an Angolan minefield and was now in the wheelchair at the corner café. He didn't want to come back like Gordon Shaw, who had been his neighbour for so many years and his senior at school, who was given a red sports car for his eighteenth birthday, who was selected for Eastern Province Craven Week, who was now a quadraplegic, who couldn't talk and   didn't even know who he was anymore. He didn't want to come back like that. How could he explain that to his parents? He didn't want to kill people, he didn't want to be killed. He wanted to go to university, he wanted to become someone, an accountant maybe, he wanted to live his own life. He wanted to marry Jacky. One day. Not now. Not like this. But he had run out of options. His financial assistance had been cancelled. There was no way he could go to university. In fact, since he wasn't able to afford to study further, he was expected to report for national service in January. Marriage was his only option right now.

The court ceremony was short and cold. A legal formality. None of the lump-in-the-throat stuff you saw on TV where the groom wears a tuxedo and the bride wears a flowing white dress with bouquets of flowers. No people throwing confetti or rice. No ladies in big hats crying, no friends hustling to congratulate you. Just some clerk of the court with ink-stained fingers mechanically stamping, reading and questioning. Jacky was pregnant and hence the marriage. Both bride and groom were under twenty-one but a child on the way permitted marriage without parental consent. That solved Allan's problem. For now. Jacky's parents were the witnesses. Jacky was dressed in a dark blue skirt and a white blouse. Allan wore his best church clothes, a white striped shirt with tan pants and brown shoes. The clerk stamped and certified the documents, congratulating the couple with rehearsed civility.

They went back to the house. Paul tried to make conversation in the car but the newlywed couple was mostly silent, wrapped up in their own thoughts. Although they were now legally married they occupied separate bedrooms. The next day Paul would be going to the United States via London. That was what his ticket said. Actually, he was to collect money in the UK and deliver it to the ANC training camp outside Lusaka in Zambia. He carried several passports; it was necessary. He was being watched. He knew that. He suspected the house was now wired. Nothing important was discussed in the house anymore.

The newlyweds barely spoke that first night. Allan was distant. He wasn't sure if he'd done the right thing. It all felt so strange, so alien. Paul had tried talking to him out in the garden where it was safe. Allan declined.

Allan slept restlessly. He kept going over his parents' reaction. His mother crying at the door, his father turning his back as Allan stood in the doorway with a suitcase. Almost eighteen years old and he'd left with only a suitcase. His father eventually came to the door and pulled his mother away. He glared at Allan and slammed the door. Allan felt his emotions welling as a tear rolled down his cheek. Thinking about it made him feel sick to his core. Why couldn't he just go to the army? Why couldn't he just sacrifice those two years? He would please his parents, make them happy. But the answer was obvious. He was not the type. It was not what he wanted. He'd never wanted it. Why did life have to be this hard? He sobbed silently in the darkness, drifting off to sleep, his pillow wet with tears.

Chapter 9

January 1984

The local recruiting office of the South African Defence Force had a separate section for people applying for exemption. You had to fill out a yellow form and bring along the required documentation. Paul was still away. Allan had tried to call his parents on Christmas Day. His father had answered but when he heard his son's voice had put the phone down. Allan knew that there was no point in trying to visit. Christmas had been special with his new wife, even if they were still the kids in the house. Jacky's mother had taken him along and introduced him as Jacky's husband at all the family functions. It sounded odd to be introduced as her husband. Of course, they knew what people were saying, that she was pregnant, that she'd had to get married. The 'baby' was due sometime in May; they were sticking to their story. The two of them laughed about it now, whenever someone asked how she was doing and when the baby was due. How everyone at every get-together seemed to know was a mystery, but then Port Elizabeth was still a small town in many regards. Everybody knew everybody.

Allan sat waiting on the uncomfortable government-issue plastic chair for the man with the short-sleeved shirt and blue tie to call him. He was holding a clipboard. He wore black horn-rimmed glasses. He looked every inch the professional bureaucrat.

"Meneer Fischer?"

Allan stood. He'd brought a copy of his marriage certificate and the doctor's letter confirming that Jacky was indeed pregnant.

"Kan jy asseblief vir my volg?" *Can you please follow me?*

Allan followed the man to a cubicle. There was no exchange of pleasantries, the atmosphere cold and formal. Allan handed over the forms and the man asked a few questions while scrutinizing the accompanying documents. He got up with the forms, telling Allan to wait, that he would be back shortly.

Allan sat thinking about Paul. Why had this man done so much to help him? His own parents didn't even begin to understand his reluctance to do his national service. What he didn't know was that after his chat with Paul that day, after he'd received that letter, Paul had talked to Jacky about him. Paul and Jacky had always had a close and open relationship. Well, as open as parents and children could be. She told her father how much she loved Allan, how he'd planned to go to university, how he hated the idea of going to the army, how the idea of fighting appalled him. She'd asked Paul to help in whatever way he could. Paul would have been reluctant had it not been for his involvement with the movement. But it was what his daughter wanted. And this was the best solution he could think of.

Allan waited. The bureaucrat with the blue tie returned and sat down without a word. The yellow form had been stamped and signed. He filled out a section at the bottom, tore it off and handed it to Allan.

"As you can see, you have been given an exemption, backdated to the date of your marriage," he said coldly, in a thick Afrikaans accent. Allan was relieved. The pencil-pusher had been away for so long he thought there might be a problem.

The clerk leaned across the desk. He pointed with his pen to the date that had been stamped in red ink. "This is your reporting date." The voice was void of any malice.

Allan was taken aback. He was confused. "I don't understand."

"It states so quite clearly over here. You must report to the Grahamstown barracks on the fifth of March 1984. It's quite clear."

"I can see, it's very clear, but you don't seem to understand. I just got married. My wife is going to give birth in May."

The clerk looked up and peered at Allan over his black horned-rimmed spectacles. "Mr Fischer, that is why you are only reporting in March and not January like everyone else."

"But I thought that married meant …"

The clerk didn't allow him to finish. "Meneer, you must take up your concerns with your commanding officer as soon as you report for duty."

"But …"

"Thank you, Mr Fischer." The clerk sat motionless, shepherding Allan towards the door with his eyes.

Allan realized it was pointless arguing with him. He got up, grabbing the papers. He felt sick. This was not how it was supposed to be. He should have been enjoying his summer holidays with Jacky on the beach. His only worry should have been thinking about Jacky leaving for Cape Town in a month's time. He had intended to move to Cape Town with her, perhaps get a job—Paul was going to help him out with that. Jacky would attend university and Allan would work until they all figured out the next move.

He walked out of the office. Grahamstown—it was about an hour and a half's drive from PE. He had no idea how he was going to get out of this. He needed to see his parents. His parents first and then Jacky. He needed to tell his parents that they'd been granted their wish. He would be going to the army. He was becoming a troopie.

He approached the house slowly. As he drew closer his steps became slower, more hesitant. He was nervous, afraid. But he needed to see them. Maybe they would be happy. Maybe he could take something from this. He dragged his feet the last few paces to the short brick wall in front of what used to be his home. He wanted to turn around and run. Run back to Jacky. Run back to his new home. Forget that his parents had closed the door on him, forget that he was going to the army, forget that he'd never go to university. He opened the gate.

He walked up the path to the front door. He didn't know whether to ring the doorbell or knock. A stranger in his own home. He could feel the pounding of his heart in his chest, the sudden heat in his face and the beads of sweat forming on his upper lip. What if his parents wouldn't open the door? What if it were like Christmas Day when they'd hung up on him? Worse than a reaction was no reaction.

He rang the bell. The silly chime seemed to mock his anxiety. Everything seemed to be happening in slow motion. He could hear movement inside, a chair scraping across the wooden floor. The radio was on and he could hear the volume being turned down as someone approached the door. The steps were heavy, brisk. His father.

Time stood still. The door opened with an incongruous suddenness. His father in the doorway, looking old and tired. He was a tall man, but he was stooped, weary.

Allan tried to smile.

"What do you want?"

This was not how he'd imagined it when he'd played out the scenario over and over in his head. His eyes misted up but he held back the tears. He could feel the lump in his throat. He handed his father the yellow piece of paper that the bureacrat with the black-rimmed spectacles and the blue tie had given him.

"Go show it to your new father."

He slammed the door.

Allan stood, immobilized. His head drooped. He was sorry he had embarrassed his parents. He was sorry he hadn't been the son they wanted. He wanted to cry. His world was collapsing. He was losing control. He turned away from the door before he started to cry, before he lost control and showed his pain. He walked back down the path, the tears now rolling down his cheeks, the piece of yellow paper in his hand crunching as his fist tightened.

Slowly, as he walked out onto the street, his hurt turned to anger, a pain-fuelled anger, a driven and helpless anger, a futile anger. He wanted to scream, to hit something, anything. He walked the few kilometres to Jacky's house in a daze. The tears dried. His face felt dry, starchy, stiff—his cheeks burned.

As he approached the house he began going over the afternoon's events, trying to make sense of it all. He had enough to deal with as it was; if his parents couldn't be there for him because he embarrassed them, then so be it.

Jacky opened the door, surprised to see him.

Allan looked at his wife. He hadn't stopped to think about what that meant yet. It had just been a means to an end. But here she was—his wife.

"Honey, are you okay?"

Allan forced a smile. "I love you."

Tears welled up again.

Chapter 10

March 1984

Allan had retreated into that dark place in his mind. A world where he tried to deal with his life, such that it was. His relationship with Jacky had deteriorated. She had tried to reach out to him, to tell him she would wait until he was done, when they could live together like a proper married couple, like lovers. But by mid-February Allan had grown even more distant. He woke up early and only came back in the evening. As his call-up date grew closer he grew further away— from the only family he had left in the world.

The government had gone into overdrive. Civil unrest was unfurling into naked violence, everywhere. There were bombings and riots as soldiers in brown uniforms, clutching R4s on the back of Caspirs and Buffels, patrolled the city. The war was no longer confined to the border. It was no longer in faraway townships. It was no longer the maid's story of a victim, a 'sell-out', having a tyre set alight around his neck for being an informant. It was no longer people building barricades and starting fires in the streets and young soldiers and policemen firing rubber bullets into crowds of protesting people. It was no longer the stayaways that left the factories and cities deserted. It was civil war.

Fear shrouded South Africa like a blanket. The UN implemented international sanctions against the country. The US government had suprisingly led the call for sanctions, against the very wishes of its own president, Ronald Reagan, the man who had used the South African army as his surrogates to fight his Cold War battles in Mozambique and Angola.

This spurred the movement on; the end was was near, victory was soon to be theirs. But it was only the calm before the storm. The government had been making cosmetic changes; blacks could come into urban areas after dark and a sham of political representation had taken shape in the form of the Tri-Cameral Parliament. Apartheid was still alive but under different guises. Blacks were still not allowed political representation of any substance. Violence escalated. Soldiers were visible on the streets in areas that had previously been considered safe. Bomb blasts in bars and post offices and fast-food outlets became common. Children were taught at school how to identify an explosive device. The president would soon implement a a State of Emergency. This was the total war; it had come to South Africa.

Allan had come to accept his fate. His mother and father had abandoned him because of his perceived cowardice and his assumed political stance, because of his lack of respect for the right way of life, because of his lack of respect for his country and his parents. The irony of it all was that he was now on his way to do his duty—his national service—but they were still ashamed.

Paul had very seldom been around the house. Since the unrest had escalated, he had been visited several times by the Security Police. Once or twice he had been hauled in for questioning. The problem was that you never knew if he had been taken in for questioning ... or worse. Whether he would come back. He went away often. He called it camping. The truth was that he was getting more and more involved with the struggle. The liberation groups were pooling their resources as the fighting intensified. The police stopped coming to the house because Paul essentially no longer lived there. He'd sometimes stop over in the middle of the night and be gone by morning. His wife did not question him or ask him to stay. Allan once came across her sitting on the side of her bed, quietly sobbing. He wanted to comfort her like he would his own mother. But he didn't. He just walked to his room and closed the door. Soon he would be gone and then what? She didn't need that. He didn't need that. With everything the way it was, Allan was reluctant to ask Paul to get him out of this. He knew there was nothing Paul could have done anyway. As far as the government was concerned, they needed as many white bodies as possible in the armed forces; time was running out and there would be an all-out bloodbath should the country fall. Pressure had to be met by immovable force. And excuses and exemptions were no longer acceptable. The government could not afford to show any sign of weakness; it would be exploited by the enemy. This was the age of paranoia.

At six-thirty in the morning on the fifth of March 1984 it was unusually cool. The weather matched Allan's mood. He stood at the kitchen window staring into space. Jacky had told her mother she wanted to take Allan to the bus stop herself. There was a pick-up point where he would be collected and then taken to the army base in Grahamstown. Their conversations had been reduced to hostile responses of yes and no. Neither had made any effort to reconcile or make things better in the short time they had left. They didn't know how.

Jacky came downstairs. She was wearing a tracksuit. Her hair was tied up in a ponytail. "Are you ready?" Her tone was precise, void of emotion.

Allan noticed it. He had been thinking about this moment for a long time. "Ja, I'm ready," he said, pointing to his single black bag. He hadn't packed much. He was going to the army, not on holiday.

"I'm gonna get the car. I'll meet you round the front. You can say goodbye to my mother in the meantime."

"I said goodbye to her last night." He hadn't seen Paul in over two weeks so hadn't had the chance of saying goodbye to him.

"Fine. Well, you can meet me round the front." She turned. They had avoided each other for so long that now, as the seconds slipped away, neither knew what to say that would make this any easier. But it still didn't diminish the pain inside.

Jacky closed the door. Allan wanted to tell her that he was sorry, that he loved her, that he was going to miss her but something prevented the words from coming out.

The drive was silent and awkward. The bus was scheduled to arrive at seven-thirty. They were early. Allan had hoped they wouldn't be. He loved Jacky. He loved her so much. But he had seen what this mess had done to his parents. He didn't know what it would do to her. He didn't want to think about it. He just wanted it to go away. They sat in uncomfortable silence. Time stopped.

"You know, Allan, I love you, and I have never loved anyone as much as I love you." Her voice shattered the silence with a suddenness that shook him.

His mind raced.

"But since January you have pushed me away. I have tried to be there for you but you kept pushing me away. I have torn my hair out trying to get through to you but you just don't seem to care. You think this is only affecting you? What about me?"

She began to cry. Allan reached across to hold her but she pushed him away. His nearness only seemed to increase her tears. She began to sob loudly.

"I love you so much and you don't even see it, Allan. I was going to put off going to Cape Town for you. But you don't care. Fuck you, Allan. Fuck you for making me fall in love with you."

"I'm sorry. I am so sorry," Allan whispered. He didn't know what to say. He didn't want it to end like this. He tried to hold her. She pushed his arm away.

"Fuck off. Get out of my car. Just please get out." She was screaming.

Allan knew there was nothing he could do. He reached into the back seat and grabbed his bag. He got out and closed the door. The bus hadn't arrived yet. Jacky started up the engine and drove off. She didn't look back.

It was the last time they would see each other.

The bus arrived at seven-thirty on the dot. Young men filed into the seats with nervous anticipation. They were going to the army. They were going to shoot people, they were going to use guns. Allan took a seat next to a large eighteen-year-old whose face looked no more than that of a fourteen-year-old boy.

Allan stared out the window. The city gave way to thorn trees and prickly pears with occasional herds of cattle and scattering flocks of sheep and goats. There were several stops before they reached their destination—the small, colonial, frontier town of Grahamstown.

He had nodded off to sleep.

Chapter 11

Allan Fischer was no more than two weeks into his basic training of early morning PT, constant drill and constant abuse, all in Afrikaans of course, when he was ordered to see Minister van Wyk. The minister was there for the recruits' spiritual guidance but also happened to be a qualified psychologist. He was a balding man with a wiry build. He usually wore an open-necked white shirt and dark brown trousers but in summer he preferred a green safari suit. He wore spectacles and at times he could be found swabbing the sweat from his face and his glasses in the dry Grahamstown heat. He had been with the base for a number of years, having been personally recruited by ministerial adviser Victor Basson who also happened to be from the Eastern Cape. The minister was not just a man of the cloth who dispensed psychoanalysis and the word of God, he also made recommendations on recruits who might be unfit for combat and needed 'adjustment'. This was a euphemism for a witch-hunt—sniffing out political dissidents, homosexuals, the insane, cowards—effectively anyone considered unfit for combat in defence of the fatherland. The recruits trusted the minister. He was therefore able to identify the malcontents that perhaps the authorities couldn't. That was his job, to gain the recruits' trust. To avoid conscription, many young men claimed they were either homosexual or insane. But the army and the government needed the numbers. Every conceivable loophole had to be shut down. However, confessing openly would be akin to an admission of failure, so counsellors were used to weed out the unfit. With proper treatment some men could be 'fixed' and declared fit for combat. For others, the mere prospect of 'treatment' would discourage them from feigned excuses.

Allan Fischer had endured two weeks of hell, so when the drill sergeant thrust the piece of paper in his face with the instruction to see the minister, he wondered what he'd done wrong. Or perhaps this was a lucky break ... it was too much to hope for.

He was ordered to report immediately to Minister van Wyk's office. He wanted to ask where that was but he'd quickly learned that questions merely invited the wrath of the instructors. Asking questions was considered mutinous.

The whitewashed building that housed Minister van Wyk's office was situated near the main administration block, a hodge-podge combination of clinker brick and prefabricated structures.

He walked up to the free-standing building on stilts with three concrete steps leading up to the door. He knocked hesitantly. Nothing. He knocked again. The door opened. A tall, balding man opened the door. The minister stood aside and gestured Allan to enter. His mouth was full. Allan walked into the office. It was sparsely laid out—a desk to one side, a tray on the table with tea and a large sandwich on it. There were posters of soldiers with Afrikaans slogans. There was a steel filing cabinet. Utilitarian.

"Asseblief Meneer Fischer, sit. Koffie? Tee? Ek het nou net ontbyt begin." *Please take a seat Mr Fischer. Coffee? Tea? I've just started breakfast.*

"No thank you, sir. I got a note from the sergeant, um… that you wanted to see me?"

Minister van Wyk looked at Allan Fischer, slightly bemused. He'd replied in English, another mutinous act. The drill sergeant had said that Fischer was a loner. He kept to himself and rarely spoke. He sat on his own in the mess. He'd received no mail from his family or his pregnant wife. It had been only two weeks but most new recruits had received some mail after their first week. In those two weeks neither his wife nor his family had not tried to contact him. Most peculiar considering he'd applied for exemption based on being a new husband and an expectant father.

Van Wyk led Allan to a tatty couch with foam-rubber stuffing sticking out and invited him to sit. Allan removed his beret and sat down while the minister made himself comfortable in an easy chair on the opposite side of the coffee table.

"Allan, I noticed that you applied for exemption based on your recent marriage. Do you want to talk about that?"

Allan had half expected this. He must have earned a black mark against his name and now they had grown tired of waiting for him to come to them, begging to have his case reconsidered. He'd thought about it but knew it would be a waste of time. They had him now, good and proper, in their clutches. There was nothing for it but to bite the bullet and try and salvage a glimmer of purpose from the whole unsavoury experience. Make the best of it and all that.

"Yes, I did, but there's nothing really to talk about."

"I notice from your file that you were not happy with the outcome?" Van Wyk's expression had suddenly become serious, not worryingly so, but enough to cause Allan to be on his guard. This was not the man at the door of a few seconds before. This was the counsellor. Concerned. Professional. Something else?

"Well, I expected something else." Allan's tone was flat, almost void of emotion. As if he were hiding his contempt, his contempt for being forced into something he found distasteful, contempt for the system. He wondered if it showed.

"What were you expecting?"

"I didn't expect to be joining the army."

"Interesting." Van Wyk scribbled down some notes on a pad on his lap. He looked up again. "You didn't want to be here? Why not?"

"I didn't say that." Allan knew better than to argue. Or to state the obvious. "I thought I would be at home when my wife gave birth to our first child."

"Interesting." The minster made more notes. "Your wife, how is she?"

"I don't know. We had a fight just before I left and I haven't phoned her yet." He was beginning to feel uncomfortable.

"But she's pregnant. Don't you want to know how your unborn child is doing?"

Allan could feel the blood rush to his cheeks. Suddenly he felt pressured, almost cornered. Were they onto him? Why were they questioning his motives?

"Are you okay, Allan?"

Allan nodded dumbly.

"Okay, Allan, I will admit we've noticed in the short time that you've been here that you haven't called home once. We check on these thing simply because we're concerned for the troops' welfare. If they have personal problems, we want to know about them. That's why I'm here." The minister smiled a humourless smile. "Is there a problem you would like to talk about? You don't seem to have many friends either. You know, I *am* here to help. You are at a difficult time in your life. It's tough being young, you have just left school and now you are here, away from your family, thrown into this tough environment. And you're married, expecting your first child. That must make it even more difficult for you."

Allan nodded again. "Thank you, but I'm sure I'll be okay. I'm just going to have to get used to everything."

"Allan, you know the army is not suited to lots of people. Maybe this place is not for you. Maybe if you really don't want to be here I can help you with your problems. It's nothing to feel bad about. There's no shame attached to this. Anything you tell me here is between you, me and God. I can help you. I *want* to help you."

Something clicked in Allan's head. Maybe he could still get out and get back home, back to his parents. Back to Jacky. Maybe then they could be a proper married couple.

"Allan, I want you to know that you can always come to me. Whenever you want, with any problem, with anything that's troubling you." The minister had a genuinely benign look of concern about him.

Maybe he was sincere. "Thank you, sir."

The minister nodded, indicating that their meeting was at an end. Allan stood up and thanked the minister.

The minister jotted down some more notes. He took the sheet from the pad and slipped it into the file. He would need to see Allan again. It was hard enough having to be every boy's mother and father but now he needed to quality-test every new recruit. Allan displayed worrying signs. He was married yet had made no effort to contact his wife, his pregnant wife. And he hadn't even mentioned his parents. Very worrying indeed.

The minister picked up the file and began reading through it again. Something in there about his father-in-law, one Paul Vermeulen, that seemed out of the ordinary ...

There was of course always a possibility that he was hiding something.

Chapter 12

Allan had been visiting Minister van Wyk's office once a week for over a month. The minister had initiated the mandatory sessions under the guise of being concerned for the young man's mental and emotional well-being. Van Wyk knew that Allan's parents were not talking to him and wanted nothing to do with him. He tried to get it out of him but Allan always clammed up. He didn't talk much about his wife either, or his unborn child. Van Wyk noticed that Allan clammed up on anything related to his family or his wife. He had his suspicions confirmed by an intelligence report sent to him, on his request, after one of his sessions with Allan.

According to intelligence reports, terrorist-cell cadres were making contact with young white South Africans and converting them to the other side, the communist side, the side that would bring the South African fatherland to its knees. The wrong side. And some of them, deliberately or not, found their way into the armed forces. Dangerous, bad for morale. It was not something the government could afford.

Allan displayed all the signs and symptoms of a white South African who could be a spy, a traitor, someone who might compromise his unit, compromise miltary security, or worse, someone highly trained who might turn and use his skills against his own.

His family had no contact with him. He had married soon after school. He had applied for a university exemption but had been turned down. He had applied for exemption because of his wife's alleged pregnancy. He had been granted a temporary stay. And now, here he was. Alone. The last bit of evidence, although unproven and circumstantial at best, was suitably damning. Perhaps he wanted to lash out at the government, wreak revenge. Perhaps he was one of those lunatics who'd go beserk on the shooting range and mow down his instructor and half a dozen fellow recruits. It had happened before. Maybe he was angry enough to join the other side, treacherously so. At least, that's how it might look. Whatever it was, it was patently obvious that he was hiding something. He had to be. He kept to himself and he had no known friends.

Allan's wife, Jacky Fischer, was the daughter of one Paul Vermeulen, someone who had been flagged by the Security Police as having links with known terrorist organizations. A suspected member of the banned Communist Party, it was believed Paul Vermeulen was a key member of the underground's hierarchy in South Africa. He had been questioned before but never detained or charged. He was a lawyer and so couldn't easily be intimidated. They didn't have any evidence but they knew he was guilty—without doubt.

Van Wyk could see it all quite clearly now. No man would sit calmly by and let his brand-new marriage fall apart, especially when there was a child to consider. Unless there was no child. Unless Allan was not really married and all that he was doing was trying to shirk his duty. It made sense. There was probably more to it, though.

He sat at his desk and began his report, including all his observations from his weekly counselling sessions. Finally, he included his recommendation for Allan Fischer: "The candidate should complete his national service training at 1 Military Hospital Voortrekkerhoogte. The candidate displays clear signs of delinquent behaviour and should be considered subversive. Further testing is required to ascertain value of candidate to SADF."

He attached the required form. It required some signatures. Van Wyk signed in two places—the one section titled 'Chaplain/ Predikant/Minister' and the other 'Base Counsellor'. The fact that he was both minister and counsellor made things so much easier. He'd heard of stories of ministers whose recommendations of relocation to Voortrekkerhoogte were blocked by certain counsellors. Some of them just didn't understand. They could not marry the idea of God and science and still do the right thing, still do their duty. To allow such behaviour among the honourable, the God-fearing, would indeed be a sin, intolerable. He shook his head when he thought of the possibility of Allan being an enemy of the state. He liked the boy, he was a pleasant boy but then you couldn't trust someone who had no sense of duty to his country and van Wyk knew he had a job to do. He stapled the report to the official transfer form. Once the commandant stamped it, Allan would be on the next transport to Pretoria. One way or another they would find out what his real intentions were and hopefully save him. Maybe that was all he needed. To see the light.

It must have been about a week later when the corporal delivered the innocuous, brown windowed envelope to Rifleman A. Fischer. Allan was on kitchen duty at the time, peeling potatoes. He wiped his hands on his apron before opening the letter.

He was to report to the transport office at six o'clock the following morning with all his belongings. He was being relocated to Pretoria and was relieved of all his duties with immediate effect.

He didn't know what to think. He hadn't made any waves since he'd arrived. He'd had an initial run-in with the drill sergeant but that was because he'd responded in English instead of Afrikaans. He somehow sensed his meetings with van Wyk had something to do with this. Perhaps van Wyk had instigated this.

Later that day, after he'd packed his meagre belongings into his army-issue duffel bag, he tried to visit the minister. He was met by a notice on the door. Minister van Wyk was away for a few days in Port Elizabeth attending a conference. That was it. No contact details in case of emergency, no apologies, nothing. Allan went back to the barracks and lay down on his bunk. Something felt out of place.

He didn't want to be here. They knew that. But why was he being sent to Pretoria? No one would furnish him with any information as to where he was going or why. The staff sergeant in the main administration buildings said that he should take it up when he got there. All they knew was that Allan had to be on the next train to Pretoria and that they were to make sure he got to the station and onto the train.

Allan didn't go to the mess hall that evening. He didn't have supper and he didn't say goodbye to anyone. The uncertainty surrounding his relocation was only countered with a certain nervous excitement, excitement about the possibilities. Maybe van Wyk had recommended him for a different kind of training. Was it naïve to think that?

The next morning, in his brown uniform, his head shaved and sporting his beret, Rifleman Allan Fischer boarded the train. By seven the following morning he would be in the Transvaal, in Pretoria. He was moving farther away from Jacky. But in the weeks that had passed he had already moved on in his mind. She had made her feelings clear, that it was pointless continuing. The marriage, if you could call it that, had not worked. He hadn't heard from a soul since the date of his enlistment. He was on his own. Moving on was for the better. He had no one. He needed no one. That's what he kept telling himself.

*****

Paul Vermeulen had taken a trip to Mozambique with his family. He went out one morning, leaving his wife and daughter in the hotel. He was supposed to meet up with some of his comrades. By lunchtime, he had not returned. By evening, they knew something was wrong. Jacky and her mother did not return to South Africa, applying instead for political asylum in Britain. Paul was never found. He was officially listed as missing, suspected dead.

Chapter 13

Allan Fischer could not have imagined the reception he'd receive when he reached Pretoria in the early hours of a cold autumn morning. There was sunshine on the platform but it was a cold sun. Two military policemen approached him. He couldn't see their rank but he stood to attention anyway.

"Allan Fischer?"

"Yes."

"Come with us."

The two men looked like brothers. Hair shaved short under their stiff berets. They got into the front of a white Toyota Cressida with military plates. They didn't bother looking at their charge, nor did they open a door for him. They were there to pick him up, that was all. Allan got in without a word. The men in the front were silent.

He felt tired. Twenty-four hours on a train without proper sleep. He'd dreamed of Jacky in his half-sleep, he'd dreamed of his parents. Something was niggling him but he couldn't put his finger on it.

Dr André Blignaut was head of Ward 22, 1 Military Hospital. A psychiatric ward, it had the look of the fictional type of facility seen on television, with armed soldiers patrolling the grounds and guarding the exits. Patients dressed in white robes were permitted limited movement within the building. They were not allowed into the grounds as they were considered dangerous, and a flight risk. The patient roll comprised a cross-section of members of the South African Defence Force. Some were troopies from the border who for various reasons could no longer be trusted to point their rifles in the right direction. It was part of Dr Blignaut's job to decide whether these conscripts were faking or if they really were lunatics. In the event that they were diagnosed as unstable, Dr Blignaut would decide the appropriate treatment. In the hospital, he was God. Although he held the rank of commandant, he was always addressed as doctor. Dr Blignaut was a firm believer in the policies of the National Party and the government. He resented the label of right-winger. He preferred nationalist, someone who was playing his part in protecting South Africa from its enemies. He might not be on the front line with a rifle but his work ensured that no malingerers, malcontents or any other mental cases polluted the crack soldiers on the border. He was therefore invaluable. He still had his reservations about women in the military. If Marissa, his daughter, ever grew up wanting to join the army, well, he'd certainly forbid it in the strongest terms.

Although he ran the entire psychiatric ward and held sway with the most powerful nationalists in the country, including the State President, he still kept his finger on the button, acutely *au fait* with every single case and patient under his jurisdiction. He refused to delegate total control to any one of his subordinates. He ran the assessments for the Security Branch as well as assessments on returning soldiers or those applying for exemption due to mental illness. Too often he found it was an excuse, an excuse to shirk your duty, to abandon your obligation. How it troubled him. Boys as young as sixteen would be willing to do their part, to fight the communists, but there were educated men, doctors for example, who thought they could escape the net, avoid their responsibilities.

He was on his way to a special treatment session. A young woman from East London's army base had been referred to Ward 22 by the local chaplain after it emerged she had wrongfully accused fellow soldiers of rape. In subsequent counselling sessions she admitted to being a lesbian. This outraged the good doctor's sense of morality. The godless lives of today's children. They cared little about anyone, anything, let alone their own lives. The nation was morally bankrupt.

Where were the parents of these children? A lesbian!

He had tested her to see if she was possibly faking. He had to. It was not unknown for objectors to enlist to avoid imprisonment and then, a few weeks or months into training, 'develop' a condition, a condition that would prevent all further involvement with the army. It was an old scam but Dr Blignaut was always several steps ahead. Rumours spread like wildfire. One recruit might be successful with a particular trick and it would spread. Within weeks you'd see more than a few conscripts exhibiting the same symptoms. Everyone knew that homosexuals were not allowed in the army. It was a fact that tough fighting men could not rely on homosexuals in combat. They also had a negative influence on the rest of their squads. The rot, the cancer, the infection had to be removed before it spread to other units.

Nina Swart was a stout, androgynous woman with short hair. If you didn't know her gender, you could easily have mistaken her for a man. Dr Blignaut looked at the woman strapped into the chair. What must her poor parents think?

"Môre Nina." *Morning Nina.*

Nina mumbled something but the gum guard that had been inserted in her mouth for 'her protection' by his assistant, Trudy, impeded her speech.

"Nina, we are going to run a few tests, something to help you with your problem." He peered at her through his spectacles as he took his seat next to her chair. Electrodes were attached and strapped to her arms and head. Nina had been referred to the hospital after she had charged three fellow soldiers with rape and sodomy. The defendants had alleged that after a heavy drinking session Nina had invited them to participate in group sex, which is what Dr Blignaut read when her counsellor and base chaplain had referred her for 'special treatment'. The chaplain had actually persuaded her to confess she was a lesbian. Nina had felt confident in divulging her sexuality in order to contest the 'not guilty' verdict at the sham trial. The chaplain realized that he was nowhere near qualified enough to diagnose the validity of such a claim. He had heard many a soldier claim to be homosexual. But as Dr Blignaut had instructed them in a nationwide memo addressed to all chaplains, ministers and base counsellors, homosexuality was an epidemic threatening the very core of Afrikanerdom. Whether Nina Swart was feigning homosexuality in order to receive a discharge was unlikely as it was commonly known that women were not encouraged to enlist, but the chaplain had made the necessary arrangements and she was transferred.

Dr Blignaut always made the assumption that claims of lesbianism and homosexuality were spirited efforts to avoid military duty. Upon this premise he managed all his initial interviews. He had been around long enough to know how to spot the difference between a fraud and the real thing.

After three sessions he had realized that his patient was unashamedly lesbian. A deplorable condition. A shameful ailment. A disgrace to everything her white Afrikaans skin stood for. How it disturbed him to see the youth in such a state of rebellion, of moral degradation. Such deliberate antagonism towards authority and everything pure and right was ungodly, a crime against humanity. They didn't know what it meant to be marginalized and treated like dirt as had the Afrikaners of the Depression. They didn't know what sacrifices the great visionary, Dr Hendrik Verwoerd, had made in 1960. They took it all for granted. Too much freedom was a bad thing. They'd had unlimited chances to prosper, yet they involved themselves in sexual deviancy. How it sickened him. He had seen it all. Drug abuse. Belligerent protesters with no idea of the torment of combat. Spoiled and selfish youths with no idea of the realities. Everyone was quick to call for an end to apartheid, even the white youth, without the vaguest idea of the consequences, too horrible to contemplate. It was not merely his job to ensure proper mental care but his duty to ensure that the youth were cured irrevocably of such abominations.

He looked down at his patient. Her future was at hand. A husband and children. There were other alternatives. But this was his preference. To return a daughter to the way that God had intended.

He raised his index finger. Trudy was sitting at a control desk that operated, among other things, the lights, a screen and projector and the transformer that fed the electrodes attached to Nina's body. The room went dark. Nina was struggling, wriggling to free herself from the straps. She mumbled something. With her head bound to an elevated head rest, enough for her to view the screen in front but unable to turn away, her words came out as salivating, animalistic grunts.

"Just relax, Nina. I told you I am here to help you. If you relax it will be easier on you."

Nina knew she was in trouble. She wanted to scream in terror.

"I'm going to show some pictures. You will feel some mild discomfort at first." His voice was calming, reassuring. He had done this many times before. He knew what to look for, the signs that the patient couldn't take anymore.

Black and white pictures of naked women appeared on the screen, alternating with more graphic images of women masturbating. Yet more showed women engaging in sex, one couple performing oral sex in the 'sixty-nine' position.

The doctor's soothing voice encouraged Nina to fantasize. "I want you to look at these pictures. I want you to think about what you are seeing. Think about what you'd like to do to these women. Think about how much you want them."

The heart monitor was showing signifantly elevated levels. The doctor studied the tickertape; her breathing was increasing, her heart rate was increasing. He nodded to Trudy who reached across the desk and turned a large white dial, calibrated to ten, up to level two. Nina's body jolted violently. The shock was instant but didn't last more than a second. The machine was calibrated so that the higher the level, the longer and more violent the electric shock.

The doctor was talking in a low, controlled tone. "Notice her hand on the other woman's clitoris. Imagine that's you, that your lover is bringing you to climax." His language was designed to arouse. But his clinical tone instilled fear, however; only arousal was recorded on the charts, not fear.

He signalled for Trudy to up the dial another level. This time there was a more noticeable effect, lasting several seconds. The doctor droned on with his narration. Two women were kissing each other with single-minded depravity. He signalled for the dial to be turned up another two levels. Trudy twisted the dial, trying to block out Nina's distorted screams as the electricity surged through her body. The light of the screen illuminated the ugly, contorted face, the body that stiffened and bucked grotesquely.

Trudy was scared but she knew better than to question the doctor's techniques. After what seemed an eternity, he motioned for Trudy to switch off and replace the images. She replaced the slides in the projector with a new set—colour pictures of a heterosexual couple appeared on the screen. No lesbians, just a happy man and woman, holding hands, smiling. The man was tall and handsome with blond hair. He wore a red jacket. The woman was shorter and had shoulder-length brown hair under a pink woollen bonnet. The couple was in the midst of a loving embrace, the man gazing adoringly into his blissful partner's eyes. The couple kissed. It was a wholesome kiss. Lips locking. None of the lascivious behaviour of the previous images. The new set moved in sequence, telling a story. They were leaving a church. The man looked strong and confident, with the woman wearing a white dress, veil tossed back, bouquet in hand. People milled around the church door. The bride looked joyous.

There was no shock. No electricity. Trudy knew the drill. She had been through this before with some of the male patients. The pictures were obviously different but the technique was the same. Dr Blignaut was narrating in a more cheerful, loving, fatherly type of voice. The images continued. Nina's heart rate and breathing levels were still high but they were dropping steadily.

A few more weeks of this and they'd hopefully begin to see meaningful results. Nina would start to realize that she also had her duty to fulfil, subconsciously ... and consciously. At every level. And if this didn't work there were always other methods, more radical, more drastic. It was a shame that proud Afrikaners, proud white people, had to suffer such indignities but they needed to be returned to God's flock ... for the sake of the fatherland.

The session eventually came to an end. Trudy removed the electrodes and administered a sedative to Nina before unstrapping her and wheeling her back to the ward.

This was the first session in a series. It would take over a dozen sessions to determine progress. Not every patient responded to the therapy. There was of course the final solution ... surgery. But that was a way off yet, if at all.

André Blignaut checked his watch. He had one more session for the day. But not in Ward 22. It was for another programme on which he was consulting. Hannes 'Slang' Wessels had called him and asked him to pop in to check progress. He needed to get his bag before the helicopter transported him to Groenfontein camp. It was a forty-minute chopper ride, the camp barely accessible by road. Groenfontein was the treatment centre for the drug addicts, a common problem among troopies. After a programme of rehabilitation at the camp, patients were generally declared ready to return to combat. Slang Wessels ran the programme. Groenfontein also happened to be a fertile recruiting ground for his Security Branch operations.

André Blignaut took off his white coat and slipped into a sports jacket, curious about what surprises Slang had lined up for him.

What had the border sent back this time? What dregs of humanity? The helicopter was waiting as Dr Blignaut made his way to the chopper pad.

In a locked room within the ward, in a sedative-induced daze, Allan Fischer heard a helicopter take off.

Chapter 14

Allan Fischer was escorted from his room by a burly man wearing a light-brown, open-necked shirt and slacks. He was taken to another room and directed to a chair. The man stayed, standing watch next to him. His head was spinning. He had been given "something to help him sleep", as the nurse put it. Two small white tablets and a glass of water. He'd had to stick out his tongue at the nurse to show he'd swallowed the tablets. A few minutes later he was asleep. He dreamed of Jacky.

His beautiful Jacky. She had her back towards him. He tried to call out to her but she kept walking. He tried to reach out to her but she kept moving away, just far enough, enticingly, out of reach. He felt a heaviness in his chest. He was running. He could feel the fear driving his muscles to the point of combustion. He couldn't stop running. He saw Jacky and started running to her. She turned around. Towards him. Facing him. He stopped to tell her how much he missed her, how much he loved her. Instead, she looked past him and started shouting, screaming out, directing whoever it was chasing Allan, toward him.

A heavy hand shook him. He could feel himself being shaken back into reality. He could feel the weight on his shoulder. He turned, struggling to open his eyes, eventually opening one eye and focusing on the small figure which he assumed was the nurse, and the monster in brown who'd had been shaking him. He was told to get up. He had to meet the doctor. He wanted to ask a question but couldn't.

Groggily, he tried to pull himself together. His head felt heavy, he struggled to focus. He closed his eyes and took a deep breath. As he exhaled, he opened his eyes and again tried to focus. Nothing. He felt like there were millions of tiny hammers trying to break their way out of his head. His mouth felt dry, his mind out of sync with the rest of his body.

The door opened as he felt the bodyguard grab him around the arm and hoist him from his chair. He turned to meet a slightly balding man. A man with large, bulging eyes in a white coat. He looked like a doctor. The man mumbled something and Allan looked around. He was in an office. There was a desk and a few chairs, windows laced with convincing burglar-proofing looking out onto the ochre landscape of the Highveld. This was a military institution; the bars to keep people in, surely. Allan took a seat at the desk, slouching. The world was starting to feel normal again. Maybe the doctor would give him some answers. Maybe he would tell Allan why he was here. He wasn't sick, he didn't need to be in a hospital.

The man in the white coat sat down in front of him. He smiled, an insincere, sinister smile. "Good morning, Mr Fischer. Can I call you Allan? Yes? Well Allan, my name is Dr Blignaut and I am here to help you with your problem."

Allan was confused. He didn't have a problem. "Doctor, I don't know what … what I am doing here, but …"

"It's okay, my young friend. I've had a chance to look over your file. I've read about your alleged wife and your parents. I want to ask you some questions. If you don't mind."

"I don't know why I'm here. I was told to come here but no one has told me why." Allan knew he was sounding whiney. He thought his heart might explode, like his chest was going to cave in. He was scared. For the first time in a long time he felt terrified. He had been here in the hospital for three days, or was it four, perhaps five? He could remember taking the tablets. He could remember everyone telling him to wait for the doctor.

"Allan, just relax," the doctor insisted, a little too forcefully. "We are going to help you. I just need to ask you a few questions."

Allan nodded.

"How do you know Paul Vermeulen?"

Allan hadn't thought much about Paul since he'd left for the army. He'd tried to forget about everyone. Jacky. His wife Jacky.

"He's my father-in-law."

"When did you last speak to your father-in-law?"

"I don't know. I can't remember. It must have been before I went to Grahamstown. He was away when I left."

"Do you know where he went?"

"No, he never told me."

"And your wife?"

"I don't know if he told her but we never talked about it."

Dr Blignaut listened carefully. He noticed Allan Fischer's reaction when he said the words 'your wife'. He knew well enough that his wife had not been to visit her husband. Unusual behaviour for newlyweds. And his own parents hadn't had any contact with him either, even though he was their only child.

Allan's record indicated that he might be one of those deluded whites who thought that ending apartheid was a noble cause. The young recruit's file from Grahamstown was detailed but it didn't include any hard evidence of Allan Fischer holding the same views as his now-missing father-in-law. He looked at the youngster. Eighteen years old and they thought they knew it all, that they could change the world.

"Mr Fischer, Allan, when last did you hear from your wife?"

Allan heard the question. He was feeling almost normal again. But he couldn't mask his reaction. "I haven't seen her since I began my training," he blurted out.

"Yes, we know, Allan. According to your files you haven't made any effort to see your pregnant wife. Do you want to talk about it?"

"No."

"I didn't think you would. But I might have a solution to help you talk more openly about your feelings."

The doctor stood up and walked across to a table in the corner. Above it was a small cupboard. He opened it and took out a vial with what looked like a metallic syringe.

Allan turned to face him, alarmed.

"Mr Fischer, sorry, Allan, I want you to relax. I'm going to give you something to help you ease your mind, to help you relax. Maybe we can get to the bottom of why you find it so hard to be a part of the solution."

"What are you are giving me?" He felt bile rising in his throat.

The doctor was tapping the syringe as he slowly withdrew the needle from the vial. He squeezed out a few drops to ensure there were no air bubbles in the syringe. He took out a thin rubber hose as he approached Allan. "Now, Allan, we can do this the easy way or I can call Braam to help me. The choice is yours. I am only trying to help you. You must understand that."

Allan could feel the adrenaline surging through his veins. He could hear his breathing become heavier, laboured. He felt his legs trembling. He felt like running. But where to? This didn't feel right. It felt wrong. He stood up.

"What is that?" He wanted to stay calm but it was difficult after so many days on his own in that room. The questions. Now an injection? He still didn't know why he was here. He turned to the door. It was panic. He didn't know why, he just needed to get out of there. Something was wrong. He didn't hear the doctor shout out for Braam. He opened the door and received an unexpected punch to the face. He felt something reset in his mind, blackness clouded his vision as he felt himself falling. He heard something crack as his head hit the tiled floor. He couldn't open his eyes or move his body. A boot connected with his face. He heard distant voices. Two men talking. He was drifting off. He start to lose consciousness.

Dr André Blignaut came to the door and stopped the burly orderly from inflicting further damage on the boy. A couple of punches were usually sufficient to subdue an eighteen-year-old boy. He administered the injection and instructed Braam to take Allan to the treatment room, to strap him in. He would be there directly.

What followed was three days of a drug-induced haze for Allan Fischer. He thought he was speaking to Paul and Jacky. He lived in a blur, drifting, swimming, between sleep and the doctor's incessant questions

"Yes, I saw that black man. He was bleeding. He looked like he was going to die. He had been shot."

"He stopped in Zambia once but that was to drop off money."

"I didn't want to be in the army. I tried so hard. I even got married but that didn't work. My parents weren't happy."

He sounded like a loquacious drunk. He cried a lot. And he told them everything he knew about Paul Vermeulen, his mother-in-law and his wife Jacky. He told them about the trips to England, the fake medical certificate stating his wife was pregnant, how she wasn't really pregnant, how his father-in-law had arranged it all.

For André Blignaut the information was unimportant. It was merely confirmation of what the Security Police had known for some time, the reason that Paul Vermeulen had gone missing in Mozambique, the reason the rest of the family had gone into exile.

*****

Paul Vermeulen had gone to meet his contact. The only name he had was the name Ismail. Working in this line, you met all types of people of all races and you were never sure who your comrades were, nor did you know who your enemies were. Your most loyal comrade could be a spy. It wasn't a case of not caring, but with the country the way it was, you hedged your bets. Something along the lines of it being better to rule in hell than to serve in heaven. Heaven was too far off now. Probably a fable. But people like Paul did what had to be done. They carried money and arranged weapon drops, passports and meetings, things that had to be done.

As he waited for Ismail, he knew he was taking an undue risk. But it was something that had to be done. He didn't deserve to call himself a South African if he turned a blind eye to the injustices of the system. His window was rolled down.

He didn't hear the footsteps approaching the car. He heard something cut through the air but he turned too late, as the dart sank into his neck. The effects were instantaneous as he slumped onto the passenger seat, across the fresh bread rolls he'd just bought. He vaguely felt hands grabbing him, dragging him into the back seat

In all, the whole operation had taken less than a minute.

The immigration officials authorities didn't ask too many questions of the sunburned South Africans in transit through the Mozambican border post. They had nothing to declare; besides, their rands kept the country going—prostitutes, drugs, hotels, food, deep-sea fishing in the Mozambique Channel. The country survived because of white South African tourists. No one else came to the civil-war-ravaged hellhole.

As they approached the South African border gate, the three men flashed identification which made it very clear who they were and what they were capable of. The South African Police and immigration officials waved them through with barely a glance.

Wouter Verster, Mark Simpson and Ricardo Texeira sped on to a deserted roadworks camp they'd secured before leaving for Mozambique. The blue hardtop Ford Cortina came to a dusty stop beside a rusting railway container. The men pulled out the limp form of Paul Vermeulen; they'd given him two injections since picking him up. He was strapped into a chair and given another injection. They left him while they busied themselves changing number plates, stashing weapons in hidden compartments. Then they were ready.

Paul Vermeulen had his fingernails removed with the help of a pair of pliers and his testicles squashed in a vice-grip. Each man took turns at punching and kicking him but Paul was a strong man and the interrogation continued longer than usual. He was stripped naked, his arm was broken, he had lost an eye when Mark Simpson used an awl to gouge it out so that he could study the trickle of blood and vitreous fluid run down his cheek. Paul stopped screaming ... eventually. He tried to look up. His remaining eye was swollen shut except for a slit. He laughed at them. His wife and daughter were safe; they could do nothing other than kill him. He wouldn't break. They took turns clubbing him until the laughing stopped.

At the Truth and Reconciliation Commission hearings many years later, a deeply penitent Mark Simpson declined to name the other perpetrators involved. He sobbed as he recounted how Paul Vermeulen's body was dragged to an open pit where it was doused in petrol and set alight. They'd stayed all night, drinking around the smouldering remains to ensure it was totally unidentifiable. Mark Simpson had used a hammer to remove the teeth.

He was granted amnesty.

Chapter 15

Jacky held his hand. They were running. He couldn't recognize the surroundings. Open veld. Dust between his toes. She was laughing, excited. She was dragging him, pulling him across the veld, excited.

"There's something I want to show you."

Allan thought for a moment that the army, the hospital, had all been a dream, a very bad dream. He couldn't remember how he'd got here. She let go of his hand and he couldn't keep up with her. A voice was shouting at him. It was somewhere in the distance. He couldn't see where it was coming from. Jacky, where are you?

Allan was choking. Water. Someone was throwing water in his face, rudely waking him. A tall man with a thick moustache now lifted him out of the bed by his collar.

He was thrown onto the floor. He looked up. André Blignaut, wearing a safari suit, stood next to the tall man. There were soldiers, unarmed, standing behind the two men.

"Staan op!" *Stand up!*

Allan was still groggy. His head hurt, his face hurt. He felt detached from reality but not the pain. He glanced up and a powerful punch connected with his cheek. He heard the sound of his cheekbone cracking as he fell flat on his back. He tried to reach up and touch his face but his limbs weren't responding.

"Ek het gesê jy moet opstaan!" *I told you to stand up!*

He was being kicked. A boot was placed on his throat. He could feel pressure building in his head. He opened his eyes and coughed, choking, spluttering.

"Maak hom opstaan!" *Make him get up!*

He felt two pairs of strong hands grip him under his arms and effortlessly yank him up. He hung there between the two human crutches, his head lolling uselessly down onto his chest. The tall man was bellowing something at him. He lifted Allan's head and studied him. Allan felt warm, wet liquid dripping down his face. A few reddish-black drops stained the dusty floor. He looked at the man. There were tiny red veins on his forehead.

The man was angry. "Gooi him in die stort!" *Throw him into the shower!*

"Ja captein." *Yes captain.*

Groenfontein was a military camp in the middle of the bush, intended for the rehabilitation of drug addicts undergoing national service. It was situated near the Kruger National Park and was only accessible by air. With no roads in or out, supplies were delivered by air once a week. Every month, new 'patients' were delivered into the care of Captain Hannes 'Slang' Wessels. He had been nicknamed 'slang'—the Afrikaans word for snake—because of the particular manner in which he'd killed a terrorist in South West Africa. The captive had been stripped and tied to a chair with his arms strapped behind his back. He was beaten and tortured with wet pillowcases, jumper leads and car batteries. Eventually Hannes had taken a young puff adder and slipped it into a pillowcase. He made sure to do it in front of the man in the chair. He wanted him to see what he was doing. He then took the pillowcase and placed it over the victim's head.

André Blignaut and Slang Wessels watched as the soldiers dragged Allan Fischer to the shower outside, a cold-water pipe attached to a showerhead. The wooden cubicle stood in the middle of an open patch of sand, loose and dusty. Allan could feel his bare feet dragging through the sand before being propped up against the wall of the cubicle. It was early in the morning; the water was freezing cold. He gasped for air. André and Slang stood by watching as their two 'pit bulls' took turns slapping Allan, forcing him to stand up. The combination of the effects of the injection and the beatings he had received made conscious choice impossible.

"You didn't say what this one did?"

Dr Blignaut turned to Slang. "I know this is a drug rehabilitation clinic, but I thought it could be useful to break him, maybe get him to give us more information. Stuff that he might know."

"So he's a spy?"

"Well, we did some checking into his background. His father-in-law was Paul Vermeulen. He tried to get out of the army. First it was university, then he was getting married and then the wife was pregnant. If she was pregnant, then so am I." Blignaut chuckled.

Slang looked at him. "So what do you want me to do with him?"

"The usual, maybe some extra attention. What I'm particularly interested in is what motivates him, what drives him. He doesn't appear the cowardly sort and yet he tries to duck out of his military service. Nor does he appear to have been indoctrinated. So, it's not political, he's not yellow and he's not a homosexual. What then?"

"But why here?"

"Because who is going to help him out here? A bunch of drug addicts?"

Groenfontein, although labelled a rehabilitation centre, was also a laboratory of sorts. Dr Blignaut's involvement was more than just an adviser or observer. Men, and now women, who made it here were considered the dregs of society, barely worth the effort. Generally they were incarcerated until they'd completed their national service when they were released to become someone else's problem. For Dr Blignaut it was a case of mental toughness. People resorted to addiction because they were mentally unfit to deal with life's challenges. They'd never learned how to handle adversity and therefore had not developed the scar tissue needed to deal with life's challenges. So they resorted to narcotics. He knew that it was possible to cure these soldiers of their dependency, but Fischer? Now there was a challenge ... intriguing.

Slang Wessels would not have been out of place with a bullwhip in hand, lashing slaves. He was a brute of a man who'd trained most of the Security Police operatives. He'd once beaten an informant to death with a sjambok—a hippo-hide whip—because he'd given him poor-quality intelligence. Those around him at the time genuinely feared for their lives. But he'd drifted restlessly from assignment to assignment, never sticking with one operation for too long. His manner offended his superiors, perhaps the reason he'd been posted to the middle of nowhere, heading up the drug rehab programme where he could hone his skills on the narced-up wretches without prying, bureaucratic eyes watching his every move. He'd worked closely with the doctor over the past year; the doctor appreciating the almost endless supply of laboratory specimens.

"Do you think it will work?"

"I'm not sure, but I want you to push him to his limits then tell him his wife and family have all disappeared. He will go berserk but he might tell us what we want to know."

Allan Fischer leaned barely upright against the wall of the cubicle. He wiped his face with his hands, the water stained pink. He was bleeding. He tried to collect his thoughts, looking up at the brute who was screaming at him. A punch met him square on the jaw. Another smashed into the bridge of his nose, shattering it. His mind went blank but he didn't drop. More punches, more kicks, interminably. He lost track of time ... of space ...

Chapter 16

It took two weeks of physical torture and mental anguish out in the veld before Allan broke down completely. He'd lasted far longer than most, even Slang grudglingly gave him that. The constant beatings, the survival exercises that saw him dropped naked and barefoot in the middle of the bush with nothing but a knife and a compass, the persistent screaming, the death of a youngster who'd been peddling mandrax and finally the death of a married couple.

Big Joe had just turned seventeen when he arrived in the camp, having joined the army at sixteen. The entrepreneur in him found a steady demand for narcotics and contraband. He'd made a very healthy profit before being caught and despatched to Groenfontein. He was dropped off in the veld, alone, naked and barefoot but failed to make it back to camp. Three days later, a stretcher with Big Joes' corpse, or what was left of it—the jackals and hyaenas had got there first— was ferried out by helicopter.

Allan couldn't take it anymore; there was a real chance he would die here. You got beaten if you spoke English. You got beaten if you took too long to reply. Most of the time it was the two pit bulls who carried out Slang's commands; from time to time he'd get involved himself, but only out of sheer boredom.

A patrol had picked up a couple, a black man and his wife, trying to cross over into Mozambique through the Kruger National Park. Mostly it was the other way round, illegal immigrants desperate for a new life away from the ravages of civil war. But some fled South Africa—criminals and, inevitably, would-be freedom fighters. The couple had been captured by a night patrol. They were brought to the camp, roughed up and half-dead from thirst. The soldiers trundled into the killing ground as it was called, the bare square of sand near the shower cubicle, like opportunistic predators smelling the scent of fresh blood and fear in the air. The man had blood all over his face, his one eye swollen shut. Allan looked at him. Blood always looked redder on black skin. He remembered the man he had seen in Jacky's house. It seemed like a lifetime ago. The man was pleading, trying to shield his wife cowering in the sand behind his legs.

Slang stood off to the side, observing with mild curiosity.

"ANC?" a pit bull screamed.

"ANC?" howled another.

The couple tried to deny it. Someone shouted they had been caught with communist propaganda, trying to cross the border.

Slang turned to the group of recovering addicts. He told his pit bulls to stop and bellowed across the dusty square. "Here! We have the enemies. Kaffirs! Kaffirs who come into your house and kill you while you sleep. Communist kaffirs who steal what we work for and kill us while we sleep. Dirty, stinking kaffirs who rape our women and bayonet our babies ... What are we going to do, men?"

There was stunned silence. For most, this was the first time they'd come face to face with 'the enemy". They looked harmless, innocuous, ordinary people.

"This is the problem with you wankers. That's why you're here, because you're weak. Your minds are weak. Spineless, that's what. You think the enemy is weak?" He walked over to the black man cowering on the ground, trying vainly to protect his wife. "What do you think he'd do if he and a bunch of his comrades came across you and your defenceless wife? This filthy, stinking, rotten, skelm KAFFIR! Huh? If you can show me how strong you all are, I might just let you go back home." His voice reached a crescendo. In this camp there was no other authority. There was no other god; Slang was omnipotent. He could make your life easy or he could take your life away.

He turned to the quaking pair on the ground, "You're in for it now, kaffirs." He smiled and sauntered off into the wings.

It didn't take long for someone to react. A rock hit the man in his chest. He turned to look where it'd come from. He saw one man, then many, rushing at him, their faces contorted by their own fear and hatred. They saw Satan. They could smell his sweat, his blood. They attacked the man, kicking him, punching him. He tried to crawl away, away from the carnage. His wife was screaming in terror. Someone grabbed her from behind and threw her to the ground. She tried to get up as one of the brutes kicked her in the stomach, winding her, rupturing something inside. It became a screaming, bloody mêlée of hate, the crazed, atavistic mob out of control.

Allan Fischer stood quietly in the shadows, caught up in the horror of the scene, unblinking, unable to summon the tears.

"What's wrong with you, Fischer? Don't you want to get out of this place?" Slang glared at him. "Or are you too much of a moffie? A fucking homo? Huh?"

Allan didn't reply. He simply stared, transfixed by the spectacle in front of him, the basest of human depravity.

Slang was angered by what he perceived as Allan's challenge. He strode over to the bloodied, moaning woman on the ground. The pit bulls stood over her as they looked at the unmoving body of her husband, flesh a sodden, reddy pulp, the dusty earth around him drenched with dark, seeping pools. The woman sobbed quietly as Slang approached, whimpering pitifully as he grabbed her arm and dragged her to the shadows. She pleaded, screaming for mercy as Slang dropped her to the ground in front of Allan.

"Fuck her!"

Allan's eyes widened in disbelief.

"Are you fucking deaf? I said fuck her!"

Allan had never had sex before. He looked around. The mob turned from the corpse, leering at the spectacle unfolding before them. Allan felt his chest tighten. The woman looked at him. There was blood dribbling from the corner of her mouth. Her eyes were filled with terror. Her face was covered with sand and grit and blood and tears. He looked at her. She was about thirty, with light brown skin, her hair tucked in what had been a brightly coloured scarf, now nothing more than a filthy rag.

"Fischer, I'm giving you an order!"

Allan looked at Slang for a long time.

Slang unholstered his pistol. He put it against Allan's temple. "I said do it, or you can join the kaffirs."

Allan didn't blink, didn't move muscle.

Slang cocked the weapon, pressing the barrel hard into Allan's temple.

Something snapped in Allan. He slowly turned his head to face Slang, the muzzle of the gun grinding against his forehead. He still didn't say anything. The violence, the chaos, the brutality, the murder—it made him sick to the very core of his being. He could take no more.

He leaned his forehead against the gun, pressing harder and harder, forcing Slang to brace himself, willing him to pull the trigger. Do it now! his eyes screamed silently into Slang's.

"You think I am going to let you off so easily?" Slang hissed, not quite as confidently as he'd hoped, as he dropped his hand and pointed the gun at Allan's stomach. "It won't kill you, but you'll wish you were dead.

Allan's eyes bored into him.

He waved the gun at the mob, without taking his eyes off Allan's. "Now finish this bitch off!"

The mob rushed at her, tearing at her clothes, ignorant of her terrified howls for mercy, her dead husband stared unblinkingly from the centre of the dusty square, unseeing. Hate spewed from their very being, every movement, every action an affirmation of their recovery from mental weakness. They were willing and able to follow orders—to do their duty. See Slang! See now!

Allan trussed up by the pit bulls, was forced to watch with Slang's pistol stabbing into his gut. He tried to close his eyes but the pit bulls forced open his eyelids with the tips of their bayonets. Allan watched the men with whom he'd shared the same tent, sacrifice their humanity forever. She passed out several times but was doused with water to bring her to.

Eventually they pulled up their pants, sidling off into the shadows, almost embarrassed, leaving the sodomized, brutalized wretch whimpering pathetically in the sand.

Slang walked up to her and shot her in the head. One shot. The body bucked once and then was still. He ordered the bodies to be taken away and dumped across the game fence in the national park. The lions would feed well tonight.

He instructed the pit bulls to put Allan in 'the box' to be sent back on the next plane. Allan spent three days in 'the box'—a six-cubic-metre steel box with only five small ventilation holes. He was being flown back into the care of Dr André Blignaut.

Chapter 17

Allan's failure to obey orders was enough evidence for Dr André Blignaut. He decided to begin corrective procedures reserved for homosexuals within the South African Defence Force.

For the doctor it was patently obvious. Allan was indeed trying to avoid the army. Allan was in all likelihood homosexual. He wondered why he had not considered it before. All the evidence now made sense—his parents having no contact with their only son, Jacky Fischer's lack of a medical record other than a preliminary report confirming the bogus pregnancy, the marriage a sham and he a mere boy, no more a spy than the doctor's own daughter. Hadn't all his fellow recruits said they thought he was, well—different?

Allan was started on the same programme as Nina Swart. In fact, there were a number of patients being subjected to the same procedure. Only a week earlier one desperate soldier had hanged himself in his room, using his pants as a noose.

In the days and weeks that followed the treatment intensified. After every session Allan would be sedated and taken back to his room. He tried to control his mind, to escape his body. He felt he might be losing his mind. He had never before witnessed such things, such perversions. It was a living nightmare.

After a month of sessions, Dr Blignaut visited Allan in his room one morning. No Braam bearing sedatives, just the doctor in a brown suit, his black horn-rimmed spectacles folded neatly in his jacket pocket. He pulled up a chair by the bed. Allan was awake and alert enough to be aware of the situation, even though his head was swimming.

"Allan, we have been going back and forth for a month now. I simply want to help you. I know you are a homosexual. And you know you are a homosexual. Everyone knows you are homosexual. The South African Defence Force has no place for your kind, but here you are."

Allan looked at the man. The man with the calm voice, the man who controlled everything. His face throbbed, swollen; he could feel the tightness of the skin. He grimaced, testing his own pain threshold. He felt a cracking, a tearing. Dr Blignaut looked at him and passed him a handkerchief. Allan took it and wiped his face, looking at the drops of blood and pus from the cracked scabs where the electrodes were regularly positioned. He offered the handkerchief to the doctor who declined with a wave of his hand.

"Allan, I can help you get out of here. I know you don't want to be here. You've done everything in your power to stay out of the SADF, but I *can* help you. All you have to do is sign these documents admitting that you are a homosexual and you'll be free to go."

"What's the catch?"

"No catch. I don't want you here anymore than you want to be here. If we can help each other, then why not? I mean, it's obvious that my treatment is not working. You still have over a year to serve before your time's up, then what? For the next ten years you'll have to do your Citizen Force camps. You don't plan to go through this again, do you? I certainly don't."

Allan was silent for a minute. He thought about the months that had passed. He had lost Jacky, his parents and his future. Getting out a year earlier would maybe give him a head-start in making things right with Jacky, with his parents. It was never too late. Who cared what it said on your record anyway. He would be out.

"What do I have to do?"

"Sign this document admitting you are a homosexual, that you pose a threat to your fellow countrymen and are unfit for duty. The law doesn't permit homosexuals in the SADF."

Allan took the document from the doctor. He read the first few lines, took the pen, initialled each page, then flicked to the back and signed at the bottom.

"When can I leave?"

The doctor took the document. "Well, I need to process this first. Braam will come and get you when we're ready. However, tomorrow morning, latest, everything should be wrapped up. You'll be free to go."

He smiled as he looked at the boy grinning on the bed. He hadn't seen him smile since he'd arrived.

The doctor left the room, making sure the door was locked behind him. He strode down the sterile passageway to reception. The nurse on duty smiled up at him from behind the counter.

"Get Rudolph on the line for me, sister."

The nurse dialled a number and slid the handset across the counter. "It's ringing, sir."

"Hello, Rudolph? Dr Blignaut here. Yes, I am well, thank you." He spoke softly. "We have two more for the programme. How soon can we start?"

Chapter 18

Allan was left alone for what seemed like an eternity. His meals were delivered to his room and Braam brought him more sedatives. Allan tried to ask the nurse what was happening but she didn't answer him, averting her gaze. This went on for a week. Left alone. He tried screaming but was threatened by Braam. His sleeping patterns changed. He slept more heavily and for longer.

One evening, having just fallen asleep after the sedatives had kicked in, he felt hands gripping him forcefully and lifting him onto a gurney. He sensed himself being wheeled down a corridor before losing consciousness. Voices—loud vibrations—unintelligible.

He was moved from the psychiatric ward to a top-secret specialist unit within the hospital. When he finally woke he discovered he was strapped tightly to the bed, a drip in his arm. The nurse said it was for his own protection. He was in pain, his whole body in agony, the pain between his legs excruciating. What had they done! He tried to explain that he was supposed to be going home, for the nurse to speak to Dr Blignaut. He blurted out he was homosexual, not supposed to be here in the first place. Armed guards entered and he went quiet.

Allan would never see Dr Blignaut again. Well, not in the hospital, not as Allan Fischer and not until many, many years later. He, along with thirty other conscripts that year, had received corrective surgery, surgery espoused by Dr Blignaut as a curative measure for their homosexuality. Allan had received the first in a series of surgical procudeures. His immediate thought upon regaining consciousness was that he was dreaming, that this was all a horrible nightmare gone wrong, but the pain was too real, even through the barrage of sedatives and painkillers. His thoughts eventually graduated to a kind of reality and the full weight of what had happened began to take effect. Dr Blignaut never came to see him again. Another doctor came in and told him that it had been done for purely practical reasons.

" … and you won't be able to have children."

Allan prayed for death, like the one patient who'd managed to get hold of a scalpel, ramming it into his throat. Allan had no such recourse. His wrists were chained to the bed, as were his ankles. They even changed the linen under armed guard.

He was eventually released. He had been counselled, warned, threatened. It took him a year to force himself to look in the mirror. The SADF paid for his monthly hormone treatment. Every month he'd have to visit a government doctor at 1 Military Hospital. Every month he'd receive a cocktail of medication, some temporary, the rest permanently, for the rest of his life.

"… don't let this ever run out," the doctor told him during an earlier visit, tapping a bottle of blue capsules.

He even tried committing suicide on several occasions. The antidepressants didn't work. Finally he retreated into himself—into his own hatred and self-loathing.

And so Allan became Ellen. In time he completed a correspondence degree through the University of South Africa. It took his mind off things and into a different world. He was becoming Ellen Fischer. He still considered taking his own life, but the seeds of vengeance had taken root. He would not let them win. For that alone, he lived.

In later years he met Nina Swart at a veterans' support group. They were not veterans of the bush war but veterans of a different sort. Some who attended never came back. Suicide. Everyone in the group thought about that option, most on a daily basis. Some didn't want to be involved, they didn't need the support, they had bought the illusion. They'd had to. Adapt or die, nothing more.

Ellen considered herself luckier than most. Some of her support group had been left in a state of limbo—botched procedures had left them neither man nor woman. Suicide rates were high. Ellen was lucky, in spite of the overwhelming, black depressions.

As the years went by, she paid for additional surgery to complete the process. If she was going to be a woman, at least be a proper woman.

In 1995, a group of former patients instituted a class action against the doctors and staff involved in the former Ward 22, 1 Military Hospital. The allegations were laid out in camera at official Truth and Reconciliation Commission hearings in Johannesburg, Pretoria, Port Elizabeth and Cape Town, but the doctors and staff were never officially charged because of lack of evidence. There were no dockets, no direct proof. In fact, to the contrary, several private practiners gave evidence they'd performed various sex-change operations at the behest of the complainants. The TRC knew they were onto something but the matter was never heard again and those implicated quietly smiled to themselves and got on with the business of adapting to the new dispensation. The past was over—now to move on.

But Ellen Fischer could not move on. Every suicide in the support group was a bitter reminder that fuelled her desire to see justice done, vengeance. Greg Swart had become a close friend but he moved back to Port Elizabeth.

She stopped the counselling sessions. They were pointless. Nothing remained now but one single point.

Part III

Chapter 1

Director de Villiers sat in his car trying to figure out his next plan of action. Wouter Verster was dead, right under the nose of his own surveillance team. Greg Swart's death had confirmed what he'd suspected from the time Ayesha had stumbled upon the gender reassignment of Ellen Fischer. The top-secret files he'd had access to were unremarkable, more left unsaid than actually written down. That much was obvious.

He picked up his cell phone and made a call. "I'm on my way back. I need to see you in my office. I don't care what you said or who you're answerable to. Be at my office at six."

He phoned the office. He left a short message with his secretary. He wanted to see his surveillance team in his office the next morning with full viewing equipment and surveillance report.

Director, as you can see, the procedure was never completed. Most of the sexual organs were removed. The breasts were also removed. As you will see from my report we found scarring on the shoulder, the hip, the inside of the thigh. The scarring on the shoulder indicates a skin graft. From a medical perspective this is all I can tell you. The injuries sustained are plainly obvious. The victim died due to severe trauma suffered to the head. No signs of sexual abuse. I really can't tell you any more than this.

He was spitting. He hadn't told Ayesha the full extent of his suspicions. He hadn't told her because he didn't think he had the courage. He'd be forced to face his own demons ... his own contribution. Things were different back then. What they did back then seemed necessary. There was a shit-storm brewing, that much was clear but he had no idea how far up this would go. Someone was eliminating these ex-servicemen, soldiers that the former government was convinced they were helping. There was medical proof that they could be cured ... that was all they'd been trying to do.

The director was angry. Why was this all being resurrected now? The scarring, the military background? There was someone who knew, the man he was going to see later that day, Victor Basson.

Chapter 2

Ayesha had just said goodbye to Aadil at the coffee shop. He was her escape from the stresses of work, of this case. The news that one of their suspects had been killed while under the unit's surveillance had created much tension. Director de Villiers had sent sharp memos to everyone involved, including her. She was nowhere on the case. She felt she'd lost control, humiliated that the director had felt it necessary to take over. She'd sat up the previous night going over and over the facts, again and again, over and over. One name kept coming up. Dr André Blignaut. Wouter Verster had served two weeks at Voortrekkerhoogte under the care of one Dr André Blignaut. Both Greg Swart and Ellen Fischer had been under the care of Dr André Blignaut. The files were sparse on detail but that shouldn't pose a problem with the director coming back into the frame. He could open doors, he had contacts.

A buzzing on her desk as the phone jarred her thoughts. A private number. She picked up. Her eyes lit up as she recognized Dr Johnson's voice. Ellen Fischer was awake and well enough to answer a few questions. Five minutes only.

Her drive to the hospital was fevered with scenarios. She couldn't picture what the victim would look like now, awake. The whole situation had shocked her to her very core. Ellen Fischer had been raped, assaulted, mutilated and left for dead. Now, two weeks later, she was conscious and well enough to talk. It was highly likely that the doctor would monitor the conversation to ensure Ellen didn't undergo any further stress. She'd have to be careful. It was a delicate situation.

She took a seat in the waiting room. She'd brought her digital voice recorder and notepad along with her. Dr Johnson approached, determined to let Investigator Mansoor know exactly who was in charge here, and motioned for her not to get up.

"Good day Ms Mansoor. Ellen Fischer has been conscious for a few days now but I didn't inform you because I felt that she needed the rest. I can't put my patients at risk, you know?"

Doctors and police often had this strained kind of relationship. Different priorities—one recovery, one justice.

"I understand exactly where you are coming from, doctor" Ayesha smiled, reassuringly. "But understand me now. I would not for one second jeopardize her life. I need to make that quite clear. She is critical to my case. I need her alive. But just as you have a job to do, so do I. I have to find the person or people responsible for this. I won't take up a lot of her time."

"You've got five minutes." The doctor wasn't convinced.

The doctor led her to Ellen Fischer's private suite. The woman lying in the bed looked barely human. Her hair was combed flat against her head, matted, greasy. There were bandages, dressings on her face stained red with Mercurochrome and blood. Open cuts and abrasions around her face and neck, blue and purple, healing now, were swollen with dried pus and crusted blood. Her body was covered with the hospital bedding but Ayesha had read the crime scene and medical reports when she was first admitted. She could only imagine what the rest of her looked like.

The mottled human mess in the bed turned to face her. A purple protrusion on the cheekbone had forced the one eye shut. Ayesha stepped up to the bed. She was apprehensive. She had never questioned someone so brutalized.

"Hi, I'm Ayesha Mansoor. I'm from the SCU."

"I know who you are. Dr Johnson told me you'd be coming to ask me some questions." Ellen spoke without emotion, her voice low and flat. As if she'd prepared herself. Her voice was gravelly, hoarse, unused to speech for over a fortnight.

"I want to ask you about your attack ... if that's okay with you?"

"Well, what do you want to know? Did I see the people who did this? Do I know why they did this to me? I can't tell you anything."

"I'm sorry. Really I am. But please understand, we want to find the people who did this. There have been other, similar attacks. Your assitance will be invaluable."

Silence.

"Ms Fischer, can you tell me how many people there were?"

Ellen Fischer squinted at Ayesha through the one eye, dully. "Three. There were three men."

"Can you tell me more about them? Were they white, black, tall, short? Anything you remember."

"No. All I know is that there were three men. It was dark. They spoke Afrikaans. I think they were white."

"Is it possible you knew any of them?"

"No." Her voice was starting to tremble.

"Ms Fischer, I know this is difficult ..."

"No, I don't think you have any idea. Look, I'm feeling very tired."

"Just a few more questions and then I'll be gone."

"Please. I need to rest. I can't."

Something had switched in Ellen Fischer. Perhaps Ayesha's questions had brought it all back—the attack, the assault, the rape, the invasion ... the tools.

Ellen closed her good eye as a tear spilt down her cheek. The kidnapping and the cruel murder of the child, they had lost all hope, they had lost what little they had left of their humanity. She deserved this, it was her final punishment, what had she been thinking, why didn't this woman detective just go away and leave her to her own living hell, there was nothing she could do—she couldn't turn back the clock—rewind history. She was so tired—so very, very tired.

A sob as another tear slid down her cheek. She tried to turn her head away from Ayesha and away from the world.

Ayesha knew that she needed to persevere. She reached out for Ellen's hand, but Ellen snatched it away.

"Okay, please, one more question. Please," she implored. "How do you know Dr André Blignaut?"

Ellen's eyelid fluttered briefly.

Ayesha could see that she'd struck a nerve. She had her opening for the next time, though she couldn't risk pursuing the issue any further today. Ellen would shut down, perhaps forever.

She picked up her recorder and switched it off as she stood to leave. "Thank you, Ellen," she said softly. "Thank you."

She got into her car, staring into nothingness. There was a link with André Blignaut. It was very clear. She'd go over the files again. Sometimes your eyes skipped over the obvious.

From a distance, on the other side of the parking lot, a man in a car jotted down some notes. As she pulled away, the man started up his engine and slowly followed her, at a discreet distance.

Chapter 3

Ben de Villiers sat in his office waiting for Victor Basson. The offices were empty. Everyone had knocked off. For most of the staff this was just a job. For Ben, this was who he was. He had been fortunate to find employment under the new government, considering his past involvement with the apartheid regime. Some had labelled him a traitor for switching allegiances.

He went over the notes he'd made during his recent trip to Port Elizabeth. Some of the holes had been plugged but he needed to find out why there'd been holes in the first place. The whole thing stank of a cover-up.

There was a knock at the door and the lanky figure of Victor Basson entered. There was no exchange of pleasantries as Basson sat down in front of the desk.

"I do not appreciate being told what to do, de Villiers."

"When I asked for those files, I certainly didn't expect you to pitch up here with them. Your involvement raised my suspicions. I should have known better," Ben de Villiers said, coldly.

"Look, when I came in here, you said you needed to identify your suspect. You identified him. What happened to him afterwards is not my problem. If you don't know how to capture a suspect alive, maybe you should try another line of work." Basson was playing the same game. He didn't know how much De Villiers knew. He needed to tread carefully.

"I want the complete, unadulterated files. The victims, the dead suspect and any other information you might have." Someone else was monitoring the case. Keeping tabs. Someone a lot higher up.

Years in the business told him as much. Where there was smoke, there was almost certainly fire. In this case, at least.

"I gave you everything I have. Now, if you don't mind." Basson stood up to leave.

"Sit down, I'm not done," de Villiers snapped, tossing a bunch of photographs on the desk, photos he'd been given by the ME's office in Port Elizabeth, .

Victor Basson glanced at the photos and sat down. De Villiers had more than he'd first thought.

"Do you want to read the report?"

Basson recognized the photos of the body of Greg Swart. He'd seen them before, right after the medical report had been done. He knew what was in the report. Against his better judgment, he'd decided to do nothing, to leave the report as is. A big mistake. How had de Villiers linked the two attacks?

"So what?" His expression was ambivalent. He knew his carelessness had cost him, though. He'd slipped up.

"So what? So what you say! Basson, you forget I worked ops with you. I was there too. I know what happened to this man. There have been two attacks on two of your patients from that programme. One fatal. So ... why don't you sit back and tell me what the fuck is going on? My main suspect is dead. You are aware of that. And I want the original files. Not this recycled bullshit you keep fobbing off as official."

Basson smiled. "Dear me. You've really forgotten how all this works? Why I handed over the file? Why you're still sitting in that chair? You should know me better. I've given you what you wanted. Everything you need is in those files. But you didn't look properly. More than that, I can't help you with. If you don't like what I'm saying, why don't you ask your boss what he thinks? See if he agrees with you? Or maybe this is something that the Special Crimes Unit should drop ... as unsolved. Because that's what it is ... unsolved.

You'll be lucky if you still have a job when this is all done. Such a brutal attack and the head of the operation himself doesn't know what happened. How do you think your boss will react? So, Meneer de Villiers, do not threaten me or make demands of me, especially if you don't know what's going on."

"Fuck you."

"I think our business is finished here." He got up to leave. At the door he turned. "Maybe you'll have better luck with your surveillance tapes. Hmm?"

De Villiers sat, unmoving, contemplating the situation as calmly, as rationally as possible. It wouldn't do to react, to get angry. A cool head was required, especially now. It didn't matter what he knew, how much or how little, he was being set up for a fall in order that a dark, grotesque secret could stay just that—hidden from the world forever. He checked the time, scribbled something on his deskpad and packed up his briefcase—his decision made.

It was time to bring out the big guns.

Chapter 4

Ayesha and Aadil sat next to each other on the sofa. Aadil was talking about his practice, patients and the endless government regulations. Ayesha was finding it difficult to concentrate. She felt drained. She snuggled up to him and pulled his arm around her shoulders. This took him slightly by surprise. They had become very close recently but they had not yet been intimate. He didn't want to rush things. He knew that Ayesha was still fragile after her divorce. He didn't necessarily approve of fix-ups or match-making but in this case he'd been pleasantly surprised. He prattled on about his work but she wasn't in the mood for talking. She looked exhausted. He could smell her hair, her head resting on his chest, tucked under his chin. She smelled good. She felt good. He felt like kissing her but he was apprehensive. He knew he could try to and let the cards fall where they may, but he didn't want that. He wanted to ask her what she thought, if she thought that there was a future.

"You awake?"

She moved slightly. "Yes. I'm listening to you."

"I think we need to talk about stuff."

"Stuff?"

"Yes, stuff."

She sat up and faced him. "What stuff?"

"Well ... us. You know ..."

"That's not stuff. That's us."

"I know. I'm just saying."

Ayesha smiled. "Relax, I'm just messing with you. And what would you like to talk about Doctor Munshi?"

"Well, I think we've become really close lately, that we've, sort of ... well, you know ..."

She grinned as he spluttered his way through what was very obvious.

"And I just wanted to know whether you felt the same way I do. You know, where you feel our relationship is going."

"How do you feel?"

Aadil blushed heavily. "Well, I think it's obvious how I feel about you."

"Is it now?"

"Yes, well I care about you. I really like you."

"You-like-me," she mimicked in a singsong voice, Aadil's declaration amusing her. She had felt them getting closer. In fact, sometimes at work she felt the need to phone him just to hear his voice. She hadn't expected it, least of all with someone who'd been 'arranged'. But there was a serenity about him. And she needed calm in her life, she needed someone she could escape to after work. It had been less than a month since she'd returned to work and she felt like a rookie again. The case was causing her a great deal of stress. Something about the apartheid doctor was niggling her. She was missing something.

"Aadil! I like you a lot. And I know we've become very close and I'm grateful for that. But I don't know if I'm ready yet for a serious relationship. There's a lot of stuff I have to deal with first and a lot of baggage to get rid of before I can commit."

She noticed that Aadil's nervous expression had given way to disappointment. She'd hurt him with her response. Honesty was not always the best policy. She wanted to say she didn't mean it, that she'd meant something else. But she knew that nothing she said would help the situation. He wasn't stupid. She sighed.

Both sat in awkward silence. Ayesha wanted to apologize. But she'd told the truth. She would be betraying herself if she said otherwise.

And anyway, he'd know she was lying to ease what was essentially the truth.

Aadil felt like running away. He wasn't ready for this, this whole relationship thing. Maybe the old people were right. Maybe it was better to find a younger girl, see whether you had similar interests, whether you were compatible and then get married. At least both'd know where they stood. This dating game was draining. He wanted to get up. He needed a face-saving excuse. What could he possibly say that would allow him to leave without things getting complicated? The longer he waited the more awkward it would become.

Ayesha's cell phone rang, an abrupt intrusion. She looked at it, at him, unsure what to do.

"Answer it." Aadil's voice was low, controlled.

"I'll get it later." She switched the phone to silent. "Aadil, you're very quiet. Please talk to me."

"I am not talking about some dating thing. I mean, what do you think about getting married? Or at least getting my uncle to go see your folks to get the ball rolling?" It was a spur-of-the-moment thing. This is what he had been getting to. But now ... just out with it and say it. Like it was.

Ayesha sat up and looked directly at him, seriously. Marriage. She hadn't thought about things going that far. She should have. She was out of touch with the way things were done. She had forgotten. She had only recently got used to the idea of having someone in her life. This was too quick. Things were moving too fast.

"I don't know, Aadil. I mean, things are fine the way they are. I ... don't know. I mean, I can't ..."

Aadil stood up. "I know. But please don't say no. Don't dismiss it. I want you to think about it. And I also need to think about it. But I mean it. I would like to get to know you better ... as my wife. I think we could be happy together. I would be honoured." There, the words were out.

Ayesha sat on the sofa—confused—thousands of thoughts scrambling through her mind. Did he see something in her that she didn't? How could he want a future with her? Her? She felt worthless—she felt ecstatic and flattered—all at once.

He kissed her on the cheek and then left. She held his hand, feeling it slip away as he made his way to the door. She felt like crying. She felt guilty. She felt content. Content with him. What was that? Was she using him as a distraction to occupy her mind while she eased into her case, back into her old career.

She switched off the lights, got undressed and switched off the bedside lamp as she climbed into bed.

Outside on the street, a man in a car took a sip of his take-away coffee as the lights went out. It was going to be a long shift until dawn.

Chapter 5

They all sat outside the director's office. Xholisa Mahanjana, head of surveillance operations, had confirmed and initialled the report now being read by the director. They were nervous. The case had made the early morning news.

The main suspect in the brutal attack of a woman in the Hatfield area has been found murdered. He was being kept under surveillance by the elite SCU when he was murdered. Sources close to the Minister of Justice say that no further suspects have been identified. Asked for comment last night, the minister declined to make a statement until he had received a full report from the SCU head, Ben de Villiers. De Villiers was seen leaving the minister's residence late last night.

The footage showed the director leaving, curtly giving the press the standard 'no comment' response.

The door opened and the figure of Ben de Villiers appeared. "Good morning, everyone. I think we should begin."

They filed in. Ayesha was the last to stand and follow him in. Inside the office a screen had been set up with some chairs scattered in front of it. On a small table was the control station with a woman from the media unit fiddling with projector leads. They took their seats. On the director's desk an array of photographs had been laid out. Ayesha noticed that the painting of the president was on the floor, leaning against the wall.

De Villiers walked to the front of the room and told the female technician at the control desk to dim the lights. Immediately, a picture of Ellen Fischer appeared on the screen. It was the picture taken of her when she'd first arrived at hospital.

"Ladies and gentlemen, you know why you are here. I don't think it's any secret now that one of our high-profile cases is not going the way we'd planned. The media think we are a bunch of bumbling Keystone Cops. So, first things first. What the hell happened yesterday? How did our only suspect find himself in a toilet bowl with his head blown off? How on earth is it possible that all this took place under our very noses?"

Xholisa stood up, a tall man with a large belly At thirty-eight, he was young for a divisional head. He had transferred from the National Intelligence Agency when the SCU was born. There was nothing wrong with the way he did his job. In fact, up until yesterday, he'd delivered sterling results. But now, his usually jolly, unassuming disposition had given way to a face chained in stress and strain.

"As I mentioned in my report, we changed our shifts regularly and we managed to keep an eye on the suspect's movement and use of his cell phone. His house was successfully searched without his knowledge. If someone took him out, then it must have been planned long in advance."

De Villiers looked irritated. He wanted to bellow at Xholisa, ask him if he was doing his job, how the hell did the killer make it onto the used car lot and kill their only suspect? "I understand, Xholisa, but please explain to me how you missed the suspect? I mean, he was killed on the lot! The same lot that you were supposed to be watching. A recap please."

"Sir, we've been over the footage again and again. We didn't see anybody leaving the scene." Xholisa motioned to the technician. She dimmed the lights again.

Copies of the photos strewn across the director's desk flashed up on the screen. "If we can look at the photos together ..."

There were multiple shots of the now-dead suspect with a variety of people. "All the photos are of the suspect with people he met and talked to in person on the day in question. He made a number of sales."

He motioned for the technician to bring up the last photo on the screen. "This is the only person we have not been able to identify. He has his cap pulled low over his head and his jacket collar up. We didn't think much of it at the time. It was cold yesterday. We saw him accompany the suspect around the back. We lost sight of him and we didn't see him come out. We're still trying to sift through the footage to see if anyone matching his description left after the time of the murder. We're not sure because the victim was only found and identified two hours later. But this is our man, I'm sure of it."

De Villiers stood up. "Thank you, Xholisa." He turned to face Ayesha, then the surveillance team. "Well, if that's the story, then it's piss-poor. It's a shitty fucking excuse for not doing our jobs. We fucked up. Now, let me tell you where we are. Last night I met with the minister. As you know, this case was given to us because of its brutality and because it took place in an area a little too close to home for the powers-that-be. Our bosses have bosses. Get my drift? The idea was that we'd solve this faster than the local police. But that hasn't been the case and we look like incompetent fools. With immediate effect, this case is now a band-one priority, which means that no one, I repeat no one, outside of this room will have access to any information whatsoever on this case. I want to see the footage from when Verster met his last client. There's a pattern here, people, and that man we pulled out of the toilet was not working alone. He didn't shoot himself."

The director paused to wipe his brow, his eyes boring into the assembled operatives. "Xholisa, I want you and your team to check everything ... phone records, customers, number plates. Check everything ... again and again and again. The has to be something in there. Something you've missed. Identify all the people that our suspect met with. Someone knew we were getting close. Find him, people. Remember this is band one. It takes priority over everything. And Xholisa, keep me updated on an hourly basis if needs be, anytime—day or night." The director nodded. "Thank you, you can go." He waved them away. "Oh, the lead investigator, I'd like you to stay behind, please."

He didn't use her name. Everyone got up to leave. The technician left. De Villers switched the lights on. "Ayesha, something you want to tell me?"

Ayesha knew immediately it was a reference to the painting, the files that were behind them. How did he know?

"Okay, let me make it easy for you. You were in my office, you found the files and you read through them, you then put them back. Have I missed anything?"

"I know what it looks like, sir, but there was something bothering me about the files. I had to read them again. There were a lot of questions left unanswered. So I read them again. I know I should have asked you but I knew you'd tell me there was nothing. However, I think I've found something ... sir," she concluded, nervously.

"Well, next time you do that, you might be in for a little more than you bargained for." He glared at her, almost fondly she thought. "Well! Out with it. What did you find?"

"A name. One name that occurs in every file. Remember, you said there was a link? Well, I looked. We already know who they are and that their IDs are fake. We know that Ellen Fischer was born a man and that Greg Swart was born a woman. But I couldn't link them to Wouter Verster until I dug a little deeper. One name links them both ... Doctor André Blignaut."

Ben de Villiers went cold. Dr André Blignaut. He didn't need to check the name. The murder and assault now made a little more sense. He could have kicked himself. Why the hell had he not thought about that first? Dr André Blignaut. The man who'd headed up the top-secret programme in the SADF. The retired psychiatrist who only a few months ago had suffered the kidnapping and murder of his grandson. His daughter had been injured in the attack as well.

Director Ben de Villiers could see it all now.

"You seem to know the name. Do you know who he is?"

He ignored the question. His eyes grew steely. "Ayesha, have you told anyone about your findings?"

"No, I haven't. Do you want to hear about my interview with Ellen Fischer?"

"Not now. Come back around three. We need to talk. But first I have to make some calls. I have to check this tape."

Ayesha left him sitting in front of the screen with the remote in his hand.

He checked through the tape again. He fast-forwarded through it, making notes. The last customer that Wouter Verster served. He was shielding himself from the cameras. He knew he was being watched. He tried zooming in but lost picture quality. Then it struck him. He fast-forwarded some more. The customer and Wouter Verster talked for a long time before walking round to the back. They passed the side of the building. He hit the pause button and zoomed in.

He picked up the phone. "Xholisa, did you question the receptionist? Get onto her now and get back to me."

Chapter 6

Downtown Johannesburg at night was reserved for the brave and the reckless. The police and criminals operated together there; sometimes the lines blurred. Ben de Villiers had recognized the face reflected in the window of the used car office. It was blurry but he saw enough to know. He knew what he was in for if he tried to pick up Slang but this was a one-time-only chance. It wouldn't be a simple arrest; they were dealing with no ordinary murderer.

While rounding up his troops, the inevitable inter-departmental feeding frenzy bubbled to the surface. Directors from the South African Police Service media relations section were throwing around arguments on who should and shouldn't be giving interviews, who should take the credit once the media got wind of developments and how the arrests would be orchestrated. Ben hated these contests. Usually he was diplomatic about it and allowed them their slice of the action but this time he wasn't having any of it. Too often these junkyard dogs were prone to leaking information in the furore; personality clashes didn't help. If Slang escaped they would never find him again.

So he'd pulled rank. There would be no South African Police Service in on this. They could dispute it later. The SAPS official protested vehemently but Ben had made up his mind. He'd wasted enough time already. It was a pity he'd not taken better precautions in keeping news of the arrest off the wire. Now he could only hope they'd get to Slang before the information leaked, which it would—just a matter of time.

That evening twelve SCU cars, accompanied by a tactical APC—

armoured personnel carrier—with two dozen heavily armed officers, wound their way through downtown Johannesburg. Some of them knew the area well, having worked a New Year's Eve or two, like doing riot duty. The cars bore no readily identifiable markings but had blue flashing lights on the roofs just in case. The director travelled in the APC, manning the radio control station. They operated on a separate frequency to the regular police. He scanned the police frequencies. There was nothing on their operation. He had given specific orders that radio silence was to be maintained until they were at the target. The men had been briefed—expect resistance, expect no co-operation from anyone. It wouldn't be easy. They needed Hannes Wessels alive but it was important that no officer take any risk in the process. Kill if necessary.

The men were silent. In all likelihood there would be spotters who would see the cavalcade of black sedans entering Hillbrow and sound the alarm. Some of them operated their own police scanners, bought from bent cops, which necessitated complete radio silence. The director had instructed Ayesha to sit out the operation. Things would get hairy—he didn't want to risk his top investigator.

She had been dispatched to the safe-house where Ellen Fischer had been moved the day before without her knowledge. The director's discovery that Ayesha had uncovered the link to Dr André Blignaut had changed everything.

Johannesburg smelled different to other cities. It smelled of money, desperation, competition and very often the wrong side of humanity. The troops in the APC nervously clasped their weapons as they approached Hillbrow with its droves of prostitutes, illegal immigrants, drug-dealers, pimps, gangsters, dilapidated buildings, garbage and the dregs of humanity.

The vehicle slowed. Ben grabbed the radio handset. "Okay, listen in. Vehicles Four, Five, Nine, Ten and Twelve, behind the building. The rest, form a laager in the front. Keep your helmets on. Keep your weapons at the ready. Stay alert. Stand by for Blue Team. Out."

Blue Team was the call sign for the specialists in the APC. Four of them were communications operatives, the other twenty specialists in hostage situations. Ben wasn't sure what to expect going in; chances were good that there'd be a fire fight with Slang's gunmen. This was Hillbrow with every likelihood that the gunmen inside would be armed with deadlier automatics than the police outside. He turned to a burly trooper who looked like the Jolly Green Giant, except he wasn't green or jolly right now.

"Okay, captain, it's all yours now. I want him alive. You've read the file. We'll keep in radio contact."

The burly man turned to his team and nodded as they cocked their weapons and stood up clumsily, adjusting helmets, flak jackets, webbing, ready to disembark. Someone was shouting as the steel door at the back of the APC clanked open and they bustled out onto the street.

The building loomed ominously across the pavement. Outside, old Coca-Cola signs had been papered over with posters advertising everything from boxing matches to hip-hop concerts. The prostitutes had seen the cavalcade approaching, disappearing to wherever prostitutes disappear when the police are around. In fact, by the time Blue Team had exited the APC, the street was empty.

Ben clutched the microphone, standing in the hatch of the APC. It crackled. "Hannes Wessels. This is the Special Crimes Unit. We have a warrant for your arrest. Come out with your hands in the air."

The deathly hush on the street was suddenly torn apart by the blaring of police sirens, flashing lights, flickering searchlights and a helicopter circling above. Ben looked up, what he'd been dreading. Fuck! They'd been compromised by the police. This was not an arrest anymore, it was a siege. The men inside that rundown, dilapidated nightclub were certainly not going to come out now. The SCU operatives dropped down behind their cars, weapons at the ready, covering the the building.

A crackle over the radio. "Director de Villiers, we have an order from the Director-General of the Department of Safety and Security, that the South African Police Service is to effect an arrest on the suspect Hannes Wessels. You are ordered to withdraw immediately— repeat—withdraw immediately."

The SCU vehicles were formed up in a protective ring in front of the building, and around the whole block. There was no movement inside, no indication that the director's demand had been heard, that the police sirens or the circling helicopter had even been noticed.

But the gunmen had seen and heard everything. The tension was palpable. Without warning, a rifle shot was fired from inside the club. A single shot that signalled mayhem as the hidden gunmen opened up with everything they had—AK-47 assault rifles, machine pistols, revolvers. Officers returned fire as the street erupted in carnage. Several officers went down, moaning behind bullet-ridden vehicles, blood staining the asphalt, shards of glass, twisted metal, doorways riddled and pock-marked.

The shooting from the building was relentless. The gun battle raged into the night.

Chapter 7

News reports called it a classic Wild West shoot-out, a bloodbath. Media experts and government spokesmen vied for television airtime. News crews were able to capture the last moments of the gun battle between the police, SCU and Hannes Wessels' "small but deadly force of gangsters".

The fallout was massive. The SCU was under ministerial orders not to give any interviews whatsoever on the nature of the exercise or the suspects or the case ... anything. Unfortunately, this did not extend to the competing SAPS.

Ayesha watched the news coverage. She had been bitter about being left out but now she was grateful. She hadn't used her weapon in a long time; who knows what would have happened if she had been there? She'd been fortunate to have been with Ellen while her colleagues were bloodily trying to bring in their only suspect.

Ellen Fischer was unhappy about being cooped up in a government safe-house in spite of Ayesha's arguments about how necessary it was for her own safety. Ellen was in a wheelchair with Ayesha on the couch in the lounge watching television. Two officers were outside in a car.

The two women had spoken little. Eventually, Ellen broke the silence. "I didn't see a wedding ring."

"Excuse me?"

"I was looking to see if there was somewhere else you should be? If sitting here was the ideal place for you tonight?"

"It's my job." Ayesha didn't know what to make off Ellen. Since arriving at the safe-house, Ellen had deliberately kept silent. Ayesha had told her about André Blignaut and that she knew he was the link between her, Greg Swart, a victim in Port Elizabeth and on record as a link to the suspects. She told Ellen how they'd managed to identify one suspect's fingerprints and how Dr Blignaut's name had appeared on his file.

"You're committed to your job."

"Well, I want to make sure we get these people."

"Why?"

"What do you mean? I just told you, it's my job."

"You know, there's more to life than a job. Long after you're gone, the job will still be there."

And so they began chatting, slowly, hesitantly at first. About general stuff. Ayesha studied Ellen, gradually beginning to see the real person under the bruising. The voice had changed, become softer since she'd first questioned her. She wore no make-up. And Ayesha was amazed. She'd stopped herself from asking questions relating to the case as Ellen spoke freely, more freely than she'd spoken to anyone in a long time. She had been in love once. But life had not worked out. Ayesha should take time to embrace life. Real life. Not her job.

Ellen was a fighter, Ayesha thought to herself. A survivor. Lesser beings would have died, have given up a long, long time ago. But Ellen refused to succumb, refused to give up.

*****

Hannes Wessels was apprehended after a two-hour-long shoot-out. He'd been critically wounded before he eventually surrendered. He was wheeled out under Blue Team escort to the hospital. Doctors kept him under observation for several days before releasing him into state custody.

Ben de Villiers was in and out of meetings with senior government officials, the inevitable politicians hovering around the sensational story to highlight their own profiles. He decided to call a press conference to release some of the facts of the case and hopefully reign in some of the media harassing Ayesha and the members of his SCU team. That was his job, to protect his people. The media was duly summoned and informed that the Director of Operations, Special Crimes Unit would be issuing a statement concerning the arrest of Hannes Wessels. He would be answering questions.

Ayesha hung back while Ben de Villers and the directors-general of the various law enforcement ministries prepared for the briefing. The South African Police Service was conspicuous by its absence.

De Villers sat in the middle of a semi-circle arrangement of tables and chairs facing a battery of cameras, microphones, tape recorders, pens and notepads flashed by eager journalists waiting to be unleashed. He appeared uncomfortable sitting there with the top brass under the glare of TV lights.

"Ladies and gentlemen. Excuse me. Ladies and gentlemen, can we get started, please?"

A shuffle and bustle as latecomers and opportunists jostled for seats and position. Ben waited for them to settle down.

"Ladies and gentlemen, welcome, and thank you for coming here today. I will release a brief statement and then open the floor for limited questions. I remind you to please wait your turn, until you have been addressed and to please direct all questions through me."

Ayesha listened. He sounded different, the impatience growing within, irritated. It was obvious this wasn't his idea, that there were a million other things he'd rather be doing than feeding the media frenzy.

"Hannes Wessels was arrested in connection with the murder of a suspect in a very sensitive case. Due to his past history in the former South African Defence Force, it was decided to take appropriate precautions while implementing the arrest. Four officers from the

SAPS and SCU were regrettably killed in the operation, with several wounded, some critically. The names of the officers killed in the line of duty will be released once the next of kin have been informed. Thank you."

The statement shed no light on 'the why' and, most importantly, 'the who' that the press were anticipating. The disappointment was palpable. This smacked of yet another government cover-up.

The questions were as Ben had expected. Who was murdered? Who was assaulted? Was it linked to the apartheid regime? Was there an attempt to overthrow the government?

Director Ben de Villiers replied with the standard, "We are at a sensitive stage in our investigations, but more information will be made available in due course."

After the briefing Ben was positively livid. This was not his style. This was not how he operated. Since his appointment he had been a media target. While some people craved the media spotlight, he despised it.

In his office, Ayesha sat waiting for the go-ahead to begin the interrogation process on Hannes Wessels. He had been placed in protective custody for his own safety. An apartheid assassin would not be particularly welcome in a regular prison, high security or not.

"Ayesha, I want you to prepare this carefully for the prosecutors. I don't want them sending some fucking idiot over here fucking everything up. Then bring Ellen Fischer in. I want to make sure we have all our ducks in a row."

"Ellen's not going to give us anything. I don't think she wants any part of this."

"I thought you two had done some bonding? Use your influence. I want her side of the story first. Did she know Greg Swart? Does she know Blignaut? Does she know Slang? I had her moved after we made the arrest. If she's been watching the news, she'll talk to us."

"What do you mean?"

Ben wrote something on a piece of paper and handed it to Ayesha. "She's been moved again. Go fetch her. Make sure you aren't tailed. Don't tell anyone where you're going."

Ayesha stood up. "Have we heard from Wessels' lawyer yet?"

"You know what they say, no news is good news. Anyway, that isn't our problem yet. Get hold of the prosecutor's office and find out who they're sending over."

As Ayesha left the SCU underground parking lot a car pulled up behind her in the same lane. It kept a safe distance, far enough not to be noticed, close enough to keep her in sight.

She followed the expressway to an address out in the suburbs.

Chapter 8

Ayesha drove up slowly. She double-checked the address written on the scrap of paper, before parking in the street. She checked her face in the rear-view mirror and got out of the car, checking up and down the street for anything untoward. She straightened her jacket and walked up to the intercom. She pressed the button. After a few seconds a raspy voice responded.

"Hello?"

"Hi. This Ayesha Mansoor from the Special Crimes Unit."

"Okay."

The raspy voice hung up. Ayesha stepped back from the intercom, noticing the camera on the wall facing down the driveway. The walls were high enough, not conspicuously so, for passing traffic not to be able to see in. This was one of those safe-houses that not even the other SCU operatives were aware of.

The gate buzzed open. Ayesha was about to enter when a tall man and a nurse wheeling Ellen Fischer in a chair approached the gate. They had obviously been told to be ready. Ayesha waited as a sickly looking Ellen Fischer was wheeled up to the car. It appeared she'd regressed since their last encounter.

Ellen looked up at Ayesha. Her glance gave nothing away, her face void of the personality she'd demonstrated during their previous meeting, a frosty vacancy. The nurse wheeled her past Ayesha without so much as an acknowledgement. Ayesha grimaced.

"You know where to take her?" the tall man asked.

"Yes, I have orders to take her to headquarters."

"Good. I'll let them know you've left." With that he turned and strode back up the driveway.

Ayesha unlocked the car doors with her remote. The nurse helped Ellen into the back seat, fastening her seat belt, checking she was comfortable, before she climbed into the back seat on the other side.

Ayesha felt awkward. She wanted to strike up a conversation with her passengers, to ease the tension, to make small talk. She needed to get Ellen on sides again, get her to relax and open up. The director wasn't always too subtle and the last thing she needed was for de Villiers to climb in to Ellen like a bull at a gate. But she had no idea how she was going to break through Ellen's protective shell.

Ayesha hadn't noticed the car that had been following her since she'd left the office, which was still following her at a distance. As they approached the office building, she looked into the rear-view mirror to make sure no one was on her tail. A stopped vehicle was always a target. Her eyes met Ellen's.

"Ellen, we're going to take you up to one of the interview rooms. You will be questioned by the director, Ben de Villiers, and myself. After which, we'll move you to another location until you are well enough to go home."

Ellen stared blankly. The bruises were blue, pinkish, no longer purple. Her neck was still heavily bandaged. She was wearing make-up, masking the scars from the attack all those weeks before. It seemed like a lifetime ago.

"Is that okay?"

Ayesha looked back at Ellen for a reaction but Ellen turned away, looking out the window. Ayesha pulled up at the boom at the entrance of the underground parking. She rolled down her window and flashed her ID tag. The officer flagged her through as he lifted the boom.

She pulled into her bay as the nurse, in a businesslike manner, manoeuvred Ellen into the wheelchair and followed Ayesha to the elevators. The ride up was deafening for its awkward silence. As the elevator opened, Ayesha noticed the director walking into his office with a tallish man in a baggy suit. She held the lift door open for the nurse, directing her to wheel Ellen to the interview room down the passage.

She stopped dead. A hot flush came over her as she made eye contact with the power-suit-sporting, bun-wearing, bespectacled woman who'd just stood up from the bench across from the elevator. Both women stared at each other, their eyes locked, neither wanting to avert their gaze.

After a few seconds Ayesha relented, dropping her gaze, remembering the nurse and Ellen Fischer. She led them into the interview room and told them she'd be back shortly. Closing the door behind her, she went to her desk to gather her composure.

*****

Ben de Villiers was a workaholic at the best of times. It was no exaggeration to say he was married to his job. The disadvantage of course was that he took everything personally.

Which is exactly what Victor Basson was discovering.

"You must think you are very powerful dragging me up here in front of everyone."

"Well, when I called you the other day you didn't turn up. I have some questions for you. And you're going to answer them."

"Or else what? You'll tell your boss?"

Victor Basson was smugly arrogant. He knew enough to keep his job; he was loyal and morally flexible—a true company man.

Ben de Villiers was angry and it showed. The two had a shared history under the bad old days of apartheid South Africa. Ben's job in the elite had been to 'clean up' when things didn't work out, when things went sour. "You knew Slang was involved. Why didn't you just tell me? You could have saved us a lot of trouble, not to mention lives. Those dead cops have families, you know!"

"Ben, as much as I like you, there are some things that I cannot tell you. If you couldn't make use of those tapes and find the information you needed, then …"

"So, if this is so simple, why are you involved? Huh?"

"Well, the government has an interest in the case. At cabinet level. When this breaks the whole country is going to erupt. There's going to be national outcry and it's going to embarrass the government to its very foundations."

"Because of the programme?"

"Not only that, but because they were victims of apartheid and no one did a thing about it. In fact, people tried to suppress the whole thing, kill them even. A cover-up, a conspiracy."

De Villers shook his head. "Don't waste my time with your games. I'm not one of those youngsters you sent to die on the border. I want all the files. Every last one. The proper ones. Not that shit you gave me."

Victor Basson stood up. "And where were you, Ben, when I sent those youngsters to the bush, to fight our enemies, red and black? Where were you Ben? Who did Slang run Groenfontein for? Who did Slang answer to? Who did Slang report to in Pretoria? Is that why she left you? She found out?" Basson was making his way towards the door.

"Fuck you!"

Basson ignored the insult. "No one gets those files. What do you think we did with them when we saw everything changing? What we all did. Do you think we kept those records lying around? That we were that stupid?" He left the office, the door swinging ajar.

Ben de Villers sat quietly at his his desk, alone with his thoughts. The question hung there. He had also destroyed his own share of records, like everyone else. Some things were indeed better off buried forever, unstated. He reached over to the phone and dialled. "Bring the prisoner up. Four guards. Put him in room one. Now."

He dialled again. Ayesha answered..

"Is she here? Good. I want you to start questioning her on your own. Get the nurse out of there. I'll join you later when I'm done interrogating Wessels."

It was unusual for prisoners to be kept in the SCU holding cells, only in extreme circumstances and Hannes Wessels was one of those extreme circumstances.

As De Villiers was hanging up, Ayesha interrupted, blurting out a peculiar request. It couldn't wait. She needed to speak to him right now, as a matter of extreme urgency. It needed to be done now.

Chapter 9

Ayesha left the director's office. He had calmly listened to her rant. She'd accused him of sidelining her, of pushing her back into the field only for her to do the grunt work. The director had sat across from her, listening as she poured out her frustrations. When she'd run out of steam, of insults to throw at him, she asked him what he had to say about it all.

"When I told you take this case, I didn't imagine it would end up like this. This is not an ordinary case. These are not ordinary men; they don't think or operate on the same level as the rest of the scum we ordinarily deal with. When I asked you to handle the victim, it wasn't so I could steal your glory. It was because I know how to deal with these people. There are a lot of things involved here that could jeopardize your safety. I have had you followed for a few weeks now. Just because I suspected someone might take you out. That's the type of people we are dealing with. Now, if you want to take some time off I understand."

Ayesha was shocked. The explanation was suitably vague. But it made sense. She nodded.

"Good. But first I need you to interrogate Ellen Fischer. We're going to get to the bottom of this. Once and for all."

Ayesha smiled to herself. The director was different to other bosses. There was no baggage. It was all about work.

As she opened the door, she turned, "Oh, our suspect's lawyer is here. You'd better deal with her."

"Her?"

"Yes, her."

Chapter 10

Ayesha entered. The nurse sat on a chair at the back of the room reading an old magazine. She didn't look up. Ellen sat at the table looking miserable. Ayesha looked at her, a survivor, and here she was, recovering, contrary to all expectations. She should have been dead but she wasn't. Here she sat, battered and bruised, not looking her best, but here she was nevertheless. Ayesha smiled to herself.

She nodded to the nurse to leave the room.

"If you have the suspect, I don't think you need me."

"Ellen, I'm sorry for keeping you waiting, but unfortunately this place has been a total madhouse since we arrested Hannes Wessels."

Ayesha searched for a reaction on Ellen's face. There was a brief, very brief, moment of suprise, perhaps shock.

"Do you know him?" Ayesha took a seat, studying Ellen closely.

"Not that I recall. Who is he?"

"We'll get to him in a moment."

Ayesha had been briefed by the director. Paint her into a corner. She knows more than she's letting on. Use what you know. Drop one item at a time until she cracks.

"Ellen, is there anything you remember from your attack that can help us identify your assailants?"

"I've told you before. A hundred times. I don't remember. They knocked me out and that's all I remember."

"Okay." Ayesha opened a file and took out a black and white photo. "Do you know this man?"

Ellen took the picture. Her face drained. She went pale. It was the one who'd laughed and grabbed her breast to arouse himself. The one who'd used the box-cutter to slice open her stomach. She looked up to meet Ayesha's eyes, sensing Ayesha knew more than she was letting on. Something was wrong. She felt uncomfortable.

"Yes," she replied quietly.

"Where do you know him from?"

Ellen mumbled an unintelligible whisper.

"I'm sorry, you're going to have to speak up, please."

"He was the one who cut my stomach open!" she spat.

"So, you do remember your assailants? Do you remember who else was involved?"

"Who? No, I don't know who did this. Can I identify them? Yes!"

Ayesha took the photo. "Okay, let me tell you what we've got so far. Firstly, we've managed to trace the man in the picture after we found his fingerprints at the crime scene. We managed to identify him, tried to keep him under surveillance but someone killed him. We have arrested that someone—Hannes Wessels. He is in the building. In fact, I am going to interrogate him when I'm finished here and ascertain how he knows you. We did some checking into your background, Greg Swart's and that of your assailant, Wouter Verster." Ayesha was checking off her mental list. One item at a time, leading her witness down a corridor, closing each door along the way until she was in a corner with no escape.

"I hope you didn't rush me out of hospital for this? I thought you said I was in danger," Ellen's nervousness was more than obvious under the fragile veneer of self-assurance.

"I'm glad you asked that. We moved you from the hospital because you were in danger. I told you, we did some checking. Do you remember when I asked you if you knew a Doctor André Blignaut? You said no. We checked your military files. You were placed under his care during the early eighties at One Military Hospital. We also know that one of your assailants was ex-military who'd also been under Doctor Blignaut's care at one stage."

Ellen looked at Ayesha, She was slightly amused. "Care? Do you even know who you're talking about?"

Ayesha jotted something down on her notepad.

"No, I didn't know him," Ellen continued. "That was a psychiatric ward. There were thousands of us who needed his *care*." The word came out like venom.

Ayesha picked up on it. "Just a few more questions, Ellen, if you don't mind."

"Actually, I *do* mind. I've been told I'm in great danger and that I have to leave the hospital. Then you bring me here ... for this! If you don't mind, I don't feel well enough to carry on with your interrogation. Next time, I will bring my lawyer." Ellen stood up, the nurse suddenly appearing at the door.

"Please, Ellen, if we could just …"

"Please nothing! If you need me, speak to my lawyer." She hobbled across to the door, the nurse fussing around her, frowning at Ayesha. "Get someone to take me home now!" Ellen was screaming, sobbing.

"Very well."

As Ellen stepped through the doorway her heart skipped a beat, pounded in her brain. Fear gripped her every muscle. She froze. The man she was staring at in the passage was handcuffed and shackled in leg-irons, with four armed guards clustered around him. The leg-irons clattered jarringly as the guards shuffled him towards the next-door interview room. She recognized him immediately. He recognized her immediately. His surprise was quickly replaced with a wry smile.

"Hello, Allan."

Ellen fled from the room, driven by a sudden fear, a terror that she hadn't felt in many, many years. The nurse followed her, trying to stop her, placate her.

The guards dragged Hannes Wessels into the interview room. Waiting inside was Ameena Daya, the attorney appointed to represent him.

Ayesha considered chasing after Ellen, but then she couldn't go far, she couldn't escape. Perhaps the coincidental crossing of paths would be beneficial. If Ellen wouldn't co-operate, then maybe fear would change her mind.

She stepped into the corridor and asked an officer to locate Ellen Fischer and the nurse and escort them to her office. In the meantime she'd confirm with the director if he wanted to question Ellen or where she needed to be taken. If her hunch was correct, he'd instruct her to take Ellen back to her flat, tell her that there seemed to be little threat, that it was therefore unnecessary to keep her in a safe-house anymore. After a few hours without visible police protection, she might be more co-operative.

Ayesha went into the next-door interview room and her eyes met Ameena Daya, the woman her husband had left her for. She walked straight out again without saying a word.

The director looked up quizzically but said nothing. Hannes Wessels sat at the table, the handcuffs clipped onto a table leg, his leg-irons hooked around the chair leg.

"Mr Wessels, this is your court-appointed attorney. She is here for your benefit and she is sitting in on your questioning." The director clicked a button on the portable tape recorder.

Ameena Daya introduced herself to her client. She advised him to answer through her first and that if he felt he didn't want to pursue the matter he should inform her.

"Let me cut straight to the chase here, Hannes. I think enough water has passed under the bridge to dispense with the pleasantries."

Hannes Wessels looked directly at Director de Villiers. "Let me lay it out for you, boss. You haven't charged me because you know you have nothing on me." He stood up, chains clanking.

"Sit down!" the director shouted.

Slang looked at him, then to the door at the guards with their stun guns lowered at him. He sat down.

"We have charged you. This is your lawyer. Court appointed." He nodded to the mouse-like Ameena sitting at his side.

Slang glanced at her with little interest, then returned his gaze to the director. "What have you charged me with?"

"The list is long enough, but I'm sure you'll have plenty of time to read it."

Slang looked at the man sitting across the table. The man's hands were just as dirty as his and yet there he sat, opposite him, squeaky clean.

"Take me back to my cell! I want my own lawyer, not this thing!" He turned his back on her like a petulant child. "And I want my phone call."

Well, Ms Daya will be your attorney for your hearing tomorrow. After that, you can choose whomever you want. When you get to your cell, we'll make arrangements for you to make your call."

"I would just like to remind you of my client's right to …"

"Yes, don't worry, Ms Daya, your client's rights are safe with me."

The session had worked out better than expected. Ben de Villiers got up to leave. "I'll give you and your lawyer time on your own to discuss your strategy, or whatever it is you might want to talk about."

"Just take me to my cell. Now!"

Ben nodded to the men with the stun guns at the door. Two of the guards came in, unlocked the cuffs around the table leg, unwrapped the leg-irons, lifted Slang to his feet and escorted him out.

There was a payphone downstairs in the holding area. Each prisoner was granted twenty-five rands to make his call, normally enough to phone a family member or a lawyer, sometimes both. The director was curious—who would Slang phone? In the old days he would have been able to listen in. Not now. Human rights.

Slang waited for the guard to leave when he'd done with padlocking his leg-irons to the metal stool under the payphone. He was given twenty-five rands in five-rand coins. There were to be no incoming calls. The guard was a big black beast of a man named Thato who didn't appear to need much of an excuse to crack your skull if you stepped out of line. Slang dialled. Nothing. It rang and rang. The number eventually went to voicemail. Slang hung up, the first coin wasted. He cursed under his breath and tried another number. The phone rang.

An irritated voice answered. "Hello?"

"Dis ek." *It's me.*

"Wie is 'ek'?" *Who is 'me'?*

"Colonel, it's Slang."

"I don't know any Slang. You've got the wrong number. Goodbye."

"I also know where all the bodies are buried."

"Okay, wait, wait. I can't talk now, where can we meet?"

"Don't act stupid. You know where I am. You better get me out of here or else."

"Or else what? You have no proof. What can you do from there?"

"You think you can laugh at me? Do you think I was stupid enough to trust you? Get me out of this and they won't come knocking on your door. They're taking me for my bail hearing. My lawyer is some charra woman."

"I'll see what I can do."

"Don't see, just do it."

André Blignaut hung up and made his way to his study. He had half expected such a call after he'd seen the arrest on the news. He knew the swine would try to start dealing to save his own skin. God alone knew what evidence he had against him. He opened the safe and pulled out three brown A4 envelopes. He had been saving this for a rainy day. It was about to start pouring. It was time.

He picked up the phone. He asked a few questions and scribbled down a name and a cell phone number. Ameena Daya. He called the number.

"Good evening, ma'am, May I take a few minutes of your time, please?"

"I'm sorry, but I'm driving right now, so you'll have to call me back." She sounded bothered.

"Ma'am, it concerns your new client, Hannes Wessels. Can I meet you tomorrow?"

"I'm sorry, you're going to have to explain."

"Ma'am, please, I wouldn't call you if it was not critically important. I'll call you back in twenty minutes or so."

André Blignaut hung up. He had to make preparations. He could no longer stay here, in his beloved South Africa. It had come to that. This was the end of the road. It would be tough convincing his wife. But his daughter would be an ally, especially since her divorce from Cobus. She blamed him for their son's death. André hated to admit it but the kidnapping had been a blessing in disguise. At least his daughter was rid of that imbecile. She could always have more children, one day, when she met a decent man.

A few of his former colleagues worked in reputable academic and medical institutions overseas. Finding a new job would be simple enough. But he had to overcome the first hurdle—to break the news to the family. In the morning he would finalize the arrangements.

Chapter 11

Ayesha tried to phone Aadil. It rang but there was no answer. She hung up and went to the kitchen. She had the TV on. It was permanently on while she was home, even if she was not watching it. It killed the sense of being alone, even with the volume turned right down. She put the kettle on, her thoughts on Ellen Fischer. The woman was mad as all hell, which meant she was hiding something. Ayesha turned to the television. Hannes Wessels was still news. Police were tight-lipped about the murder victim, which Ayesha knew was only because the director had given nothing away. Her cell phone rang, interrupting her thoughts as it whirred angrily on the glass-topped coffee table. She didn't recognize the number.

"Hello?"

"Hello, Ayesha."

She recognized the voice immediately. "Ellen? Hi, how are you? Where are you?"

"I'm outside. I hope you don't mind. I asked the officer to bring me over. I need to speak to you. Do you mind?"

"Of course not, come right up."

A few minutes later there was a soft knock on the door. Almost faint. Hesitant. Ayesha opened up.

"Hi. Come in."

Ellen smiled awkwardly. Ayesha noticed for the first time how tall she was, even with hunched shoulders."

"Please, have a seat."

Ayesha felt nervous. She felt they'd made a connection but that had been ruined today.

"I wanted to talk to you," Ellen's voice was warmer than earlier, "about today. I wasn't very nice to you. I'm sorry."

"It's okay, I had a job to do and I wasn't …"

Ellen raised a hand. "Yes, you had a job to do. But I was rude. I am not normally rude. I'm not a bad person. And I wanted to say that I am sorry."

Ayesha was perplexed. "Please don't apologize. I understand. I mean, I am sorry too. I didn't know that man would be there. That wasn't our intention. I just wanted to question you before we interrogated him. You know?"

Ellen nodded.

"Would you like some tea? I was just making a cup."

Ellen nodded again. Tears were welling.

Ayesha knew what she must be feeling. This freak show. The fact that perfect strangers now knew the intimate details of your life. Secrets, dark pasts, that you had worked so hard to cover up. It must be tough. The trauma of being brutalized and then being forced into the spotlight. And this was only the beginning. The media would feed on this for months. They would dissect and analyze and Ellen Fischer would become a living martyr, a symbol, a reluctant icon of everything wrong with our past, her carefully constructed life laid bare for mass consumption.

Ayesha went to the kitchen to make the tea. Ellen sat on the couch, observing her. She was still young, a beautiful woman. Her tough exterior covered a wounded past. She could tell. Her job was her security. She looked at her setting out the cups, waiting for the kettle to boil. Under different circumstances they might have been friends. Under different circumstances …

It felt odd having to explain yourself to a person who knew so much about you but about whom you knew nothing. But they had connected. Things would change soon though and Ellen fervently hoped that Ayesha would be able to understand. She trusted her, that was it. The two women sat on the couch talking. For Ayesha it was something she hadn't done in a while. She talked about Aadil, about his proposal. She didn't know if she could make that commitment.

"No one knows what tomorrow will bring, Ayesha. The people we love won't be here forever. We should be grateful for the time we have. The last thing you want is for regret to creep in. There is no point in regret."

Ayesha listened intently. Ellen was obviously talking from experience. She didn't ask why or about whom. She felt strongly about Aadil but whether she was ready to get married, to move on, she wasn't sure yet.

Neither mentioned the case. It seemed unimportant. Eventually Ellen said she had to leave. She knew this would be the last time she'd see Ayesha like this. It didn't make sense but she'd needed to see her. She didn't want Ayesha's last image of her to be of that cold bitch in the interrogation room.

Ayesha walked Ellen to the car where the officer was waiting. In the lift, on the way back up to her flat, she mused on how Ellen had seemed different—almost relieved, at peace with something. Herself? She couldn't put her finger on it.

She tried calling Aadil. His phone was switched off. She nodded off to sleep on the couch, her energy sapped. Sleep came quickly. She woke early the following morning. The TV was still on—news anchors with vacuous smiles reporting the previous day's events. She got up and put the kettle on while she took a shower. Her face felt dry, her body stiff from the couch. The hot water felt good, cleansing.

She stepped out of the shower, wrapped herself in a towel, her hair still dripping as she heard a sharp knock at the door. At this hour? She frowned.

"Who is it?" she called out.

No answer.

She went to the bedroom and retrieved her service pistol from the side table, cocking it. The sun was beginning to rise. She dropped her towel and quickly threw on her Habaya, a long, flowing cape that covered her body without giving away her nakedness beneath. She moved cautiously towards the front door, weapon at the ready, ears straining. The chain was still on the latch. Her apartment block was secure, but Ellen Fischer's had also seemed safe. She looked at the light streaming in from underneath the door. The corridor light was still on. Something was blocking the light, a shadow.

"Who's there?" she called out sharply.

No answer.

"I can see you. I have a gun."

Still no answer.

She moved to the side of the door. Her breathing was heavy, she could feel the pounding of her heart, her body still damp from the shower. She slowly, quietly lifted the chain from the latch. There was the key and then the bolt. She gently turned the key, leaving the bolt till she'd gathered herself. She dropped down onto her haunches and checked her weapon. One last breath as she reached for the bolt. She flung open the door, almost falling through the doorway. There was nothing. No one. She was on her belly, her Habaya hitched up around her waist, her pistol at the ready.

As she gathered herself to stand up, she noticed the brown A4 enevelope. Written in black marker was the name Ellen Fischer. She scanned the corridor before going back inside, locking the door behind her. She felt slightly foolish—all that over an enevlope. But the directors words still echoed in her head—that they would try and get her. She boiled the kettle again and opened the envelope.

There were several pages, like some kind of report. She started reading.

Find Mark Simpson and Ricardo Texeira. They were Wouter Verster's partners. They were employed by Hannes Wessels. Check his phone records and bank details. Hannes Wessels paid them. If you ask his staff to identify the pictures, you might be surprised.

Attached to the first page were two military photographs, one labelled Mark Simpson and the other Ricardo Texeira. The following pages listed dates, venues, meetings, phone calls, phone numbers. Also attached was a copy of a receipt from a Port Elizabeth hotel.

That was it. Ayesha hurriedly dressed and raced over to the office.

Ameena Daya was also speeding halfway across Pretoria to get to SCU headquarters. Her envelope would in all likelihood get her client off completely. Ameena Daya got there first. It was just after eight in the morning. Ayesha arrived just as Ameena was leaving the director's office. Ameena stopped, looking as if she wanted to say something but changed her mind and briskly walked towards the lifts.

The director noticed Ayesha standing at his door, clutching a brown envelope. "Please don't tell me you also received an anonymous tip-off. Two in one morning would be too much."

"What do you mean?" Ayesha was confused.

The director looked at her quizzically. "Your friend over there has also just come in with an envelope. In fact, she called me this morning and asked me to get the bail hearing postponed, until I'd had a chance to look at some new evidence."

"What evidence?"

"I think you'd better come in and close the door, Ayesha."

Chapter 12

The news broke later that evening with such impact that regular programming was interrupted. Apartheid assassin Hannes 'Slang' Wessels had been released, having turned state witness. His testimony was enough to solve the case of the brutal murder of the grandson of prominent apartheid doctor, André Blignaut, the same doctor once accused of conducting medical experiments on homosexual conscripts and alleged deviants, as investigated by the Truth and Reconciliation Commission. The news report went on to say that the doctor, when contacted for comment, had stated his intention to emigrate purely to ensure the safety of his family. The arrested suspect was a woman called Ellen Fischer who had allegedly suffered at the hands of Dr Blignaut while serving in the SADF.

The director was not involved with the arrest of Ellen Fischer. It sickened him. It was political. Child murderer versus the child murderer's brutal assailant. When Ameena Daya had shown him the file, he simply could not believe it. He did not want to believe it. The deal was simple. Give her client immunity from prosecution on the charges he faced, including the murder of Wouter Verster and his involvement in the police shoot-out during his arrest and in return her client would help solve the brutal murder of a young child. When the director asked which missing child she was talking about, his heart skipped a beat as Dr Blignaut's name was mentioned.

The file was shown to the director so that he could confirm its *bona fides* before the contents were relayed to his superiors. The evidence caught him totally off guard. And his superiors did exactly as expected. South Africa's international image had taken a beating of late for its poor record of child abuse. This was a golden opportunity to make an example of a high-profile perpetrator. Hannes Wessels was granted immunity. Even with Ayesha's mounting evidence on the Ellen Fisher attack and the Greg Swart murder it was considered policy to deal with the child killer. Justice would be triumphant—public outcry was always more intense when the murder victim was a defenceless child.

Ayesha protested angrily, vehemently. She threatened to go to the Constitutional Court—to the press, but the director could do nothing. The deal was done. It had come from the top. People had grown weary of hearing about apartheid killers—old news. The government needed to get tough on crime against women and children.

Hannes Wessels was released. His statement to the police implicated Mark Simpson and Ricardo Texeira in the Ellen Fisher attack. He said it had been Wouter Verster's idea to blackmail Ellen Fischer and Simpson and Texeira got carried away one night when Ellen Fischer refused to pay up. At no time did he or anyone in the gang know anything of Fischer's involvement in the kidnapping or murder of the child. He admitted to killing Verster but in self-defence when Verster had pulled a gun on him, demanding his share of the blackmail money he was convinced Slang had been paid.

The evidence around Greg Swart's murder was circumstantial at best. The case stayed open and unsolved. He did not implicate Dr André Blignaut, other than to admit that he was a former SADF colleague.

Slang's club was closed down after the shoot-out. He was later found dead, shot once through the back of the head, execution style. The investigating officer put it down to a gang-land slaying. Drugs, no doubt.

Ellen Fischer was arrested and charged with the kidnapping and the murder of the baby, Cobus Jnr. Ellen said others were involved, she did not know where the remains were buried, she refused to name her accomplices. She refused legal representation and pleaded guilty, accepting responsibility for her part in the kidnapping and subsequent murder.

Ayesha wanted to see Ellen Fischer but her request was denied.

Mark Simpson and Ricardo Texeira were never found. Both are still wanted for questioning in connection with the attack on Ellen Fischer.

Ellen Fischer's trial was full of drama. She co-operated but made sure she didn't incriminate anyone other than herself. She refused to answer certain questions even when threatened with contempt of court. She told the court how she'd hired people to act for her. She told the court how she'd come to live like something less than human, incapable of intimate human contact. She told the court how she had been like this since she was eighteen. She told the court how she'd been through endless legal channels to get her day in court, to get justice, but she had got nothing, how her attempts to bring her perpetrators to justice before the Truth and Reconciliation Commission had failed. How the Department of Defence had stopped paying for her hormone therapy medication. It was not their problem, they'd said. She was not their victim, they'd said. Justice had been denied her, ignored. Over and over and over.

Throughout the trial, Ellen was the cold person Ayesha had seen in the back seat of her car that day. She was not the same person who had come to her flat to apologize. Ayesha sat at the back of the court and felt her heart would break. Ellen Fischer described how she had planned to kidnap the child as a way to scare Dr Blignaut. But anger and hatred had got the better of her. They'd decided to kill the baby. She was a victim of apartheid but no one cared. She had been robbed of her life, one man had robbed her of everything. She was remorseful about having taken the life of a child but she wanted the doctor to go to sleep every night and know that he was responsible.

She spoke deliberately, the malice of her words fuelling the growing animosity from the public gallery.

This was not living. This was not life. She envied her friend Greg Swart.

It was no surprise that the court accepted her guilty plea. She had taken the life of an innocent child to quench her thirst for revenge. There were thousands upon thousand of victims of apartheid but they didn't go around committing murder to get even. Revenge was not justice. Justice was the responsibility of the courts, not some twisted vigilante.

Everyone expected it. She was sentenced to eighteen years imprisonment. She didn't flinch as sentence was handed down. She did not hang her head. She did not cry or show any emotion.

Ayesha closed her eyes.

But there was more. A final twist of the knife. The judge made sure of that. Almost an insignificant addendum to the sentence. Ellen Fischer was to be removed from her single, awaiting-trial cell and taken to a maximum-security, all-male facility. Ellen protested angrily. But the judge called for order, making it clear that in this instance the law bound him as it stood.

"The South African Law of Persons does not yet recognize the transgender person. The law as it stands is very specific; you are the sex you are born with, irrespective of your claimed gender. Irrespective of the cosmetic changes you make."

It was a bomshell that no one expected. Ellen Fischer had been tried as Allan Fischer. The judge was unmoved. As Ellen was taken from the court to the holding cells below, she knew that it was now only a matter of time.

Ayesha cried.

Several days later, Ellen Fischer was found naked and unconscious in the shower. Within two nights of her incarceration she was brutally raped and sodomized. She died in hospital, never regaining consciousness. There were no witnesses and the investigation never proceeded beyond a preliminary. The murder wasn't reported in the press—prison killings generally weren't.

Dr André Blignaut immigrated to Canada just as the trial was beginning. He took up a position as an academic at a leading medical school. Although his name was linked to several cases of human rights abuse, he has never been charged due to a lack of evidence. He still maintains his innocence. There are no records to corroborate either side. Former colleagues refuse to acknowledge his or their roles in the programme to cure lesbians and homosexuals. When questioned by a newspaper reporter in Los Angeles on whether he'd left South Africa to avoid prosecution, Dr Blignaut claimed it was the rampant crime rate and the attack on his daughter and murder of his grandson that had driven him from the country of his birth. He still lives in Canada, vowing never to return to South Africa and jeopardize the safety of his family.

Ayesha Mansoor became Ayesha Munshi. She resigned the day Ellen Fischer was arrested. The lines had become too blurred. Her life was empty, her energy now meaningless. The couple were married in a simple, low-key ceremony. She'd lost her burning desire to save the world. She was building a new one for herself.

finis

Acknowledgments

This book would not have been possible without the contributions of many people. When acknowledging contributions there is always a chance that someone's name will be forgotten. Please forgive me if I've forgotten to list yours.

To Carla Tsampiras of Rhodes University's History Department for opening our minds and giving me the idea for this story.

To Professor Robert Kaplan of the Graduate Medical School, University of Wollongong, Australia, for providing me with valuable information that changed the direction of my work.

To Anthony Manion of GALA at Wits University for providing me with the vital research and interview reports from the victims of the Aversion Project.

To my family for always supporting me, especially through the darker times.

To my friends from Zambia—Poraro, Minnie, Riyaad and Atiyah—for letting me sleep on your couch and listening to my plot lines over and over again.

To my best friend, Zaheer 'Gongz' Bhayat, for making me laugh at myself and keeping me focused. Balconies will never be the same again.

To Shakira Hoosain for helpful advice and comments.

To Saaleha for telling me to go for it.

To Prixie and Waseem for reading countless chapters and offering helpful advice.

To Robbie Muzzell and Mike Hendrikse for your significant presence in my life and for giving me so much to look forward to.

My final thanks go to three groups of exceptionally significant people. Thanks to everyone who voted for this book during the Citizen Book Prize competition, to *The Citizen* newspaper for sponsoring the competition and to all the wonderful people at 30° South for publishing my work. My gratitude for this opportunity and my sincere thanks.

HHP